Previous novels by A. K. Adams

An Unknown Paradise

Searching for Juliette

Shouldn't Have Done That

They Fade and Die

The Locked Room

DOWN A LONG DARK ROAD

He wanted his wife followed
She had other plans

A. K. ADAMS

Published by New Generation Publishing in 2020

Copyright © A. K. Adams 2020

First Edition

The author asserts the moral right under the Copyright, Designs and Patents Act 1988 to be identified as the author of this work.

All Rights reserved. No part of this publication may be reproduced, stored in a retrieval system or transmitted, in any form or by any means without the prior consent of the author, nor be otherwise circulated in any form of binding or cover other than that in which it is published and without a similar condition being imposed on the subsequent purchaser.

ISBN: 978-1-80031-924-0

www.newgeneration-publishing.com

New Generation Publishing

For Andrew and Karl

When Saturday evening was half a Mars Bar each and some Rolo's.

And watching Columbo and Ironside on a black and white television.

I love you

Things had been a quiet for a few months for Tommy Archer. Well, apart from following Gavin Wood to check his movements on behalf of a jealous wife. Was he really going to the pub twenty miles away to meet with friends, she'd wondered? And an unsuccessful attempt to follow the juvenile son of a local estate agent who'd absconded from a detention centre and driven off in a stolen Nissan, and not forgetting the forty - year old malingerer who'd been off work for three months with a bad back, yet found time to referee football matches on a Sunday morning. Nothing much was happening, and Tommy began to wonder what life held in store for him.

Ten years in the North Yorkshire Police had been enjoyable, apart from twice failing his exams for promotion to Sergeant, but he needed a change. Too much form filling, and political correctness gone mad, had removed the cut and thrust of being a bobby. Life in the force was moving away from 'people contact' – which he liked – to administration . . . too much paperwork. He'd once been reprimanded by his Inspector for putting his index finger on someone's lapel when making a point about them telling lies. Heck! When he was a lad a cuff round the ear from the local constable was considered normal. And he prayed his father never found out!

Now almost 37 years old, Tommy had joined the police from the Royal Air Force where he'd worked on aircraft engines. An HND in engineering, courtesy of the RAF, had taken him down a long path of manual but complex technical activities. He was able to strip the engine of a Tornado Fighter jet, or look at twenty dials in the cockpit of a helicopter and tell you what was wrong within seconds. But after a decade of cogs and sprockets, nuts and bolts and the smell of grease, Tommy hankered after a new challenge. A good friend, Joe Blackwell, had suggested joining the police force. Joe had been in the Military Police and was now Head of Security with a small chain of hotels - the Northcliffe Group - covering North Yorkshire and Teesside. Joe's attention to detail in everything he did was an asset. Tommy made some enquiries, and after an interview and short written test, had become PC Thomas Archer. Number 2140.

But the time was now. It was all water under the bridge. So, on leaving the thin blue line, he became a Private Investigator. A Private Eye, a Private Detective, call it what you will. Tommy Archer was for hire. The Yellow Pages said so. And he had his own web site; gone the proper way about things.

He knew he needed a qualification, be registered, and understand the Criminal Procedure & Investigation Act of 1996 and the Data Protection Act of 1998 to keep within the law. Well, he was OK with the law part – but he had to get his QCF/EDI Qualified Professional Investigator Level 3 along with a BTEC Qualified Surveillance Level 3, too. A 5 - day full tutored programme in Leeds helped sort that out.

So, with PI Thomas Archer licensed and a member of the Association of British Investigators, he was up for hire. He'd even chosen a catchy name. THOMARCH Investigations, had the business cards printed. But for a while things were quiet. It seemed that few folks in North Yorkshire wanted family or friends spied on, followed, photos taken . . . that was until that morning when the rain was hitting the kitchen window hard as he read his first email of the day.

From: Paul.Dawson@gmx.com
To: ThomArchInvestigations@gmail.com
Date: 13 June 2016

Dear Mr. Archer,

I obtained your details from your web site. I have some concerns about my wife. Can we meet as soon as possible to discuss? I'm free on Wednesday afternoons. Please call me on my mobile 09770 450911 between noon and 1 pm today if possible.

Thank you,
Paul Dawson.

Tommy picked up his mug of coffee, scratched his trimmed black beard as the caffeine kick-started his brain on a wet Monday morning.

In the beginning . . .

Tommy Archer wasn't what you'd call one of life's losers, but bad luck hung around him like a shroud. Some people are like that – been cast a bad roll of the dice at birth. He didn't believe in horoscopes . . . born on the eighteenth of November, he was a Scorpio, but he never paid any heed to all that stuff. Of course, he'd glance at the Scorpio prediction in the daily newspaper but smiled inwardly when it told him *'you are going to come into money'* or *'soon you will meet the girl of your dreams.'* His mother, who'd passed away three years ago from cancer, was a great believer in luck. She always wore a charm bracelet, handed down from Tommy's grandma, said it brought her 'good fortune' as she called it. His mother used to fondle it for minutes before buying a lottery ticket because she said it would improve her chances of winning. Improve her chances? Tommy couldn't recall a single instance of a lottery win, apart from a scratch-card she'd once bought on a whim. £25 wasn't bad, though. And then when the big C got her, he used to wonder where 'Mr. Luck' had gone. Harry, Tommy's father, had sold his wife's jewellery after she'd passed away to one of those 'We buy any used gold and silver' shops in the High Street.

Tommy was divorced and living in a small stone cottage in Pomfreton, a pretty little market town in North Yorkshire. The cottage was tidy, a place for everything and everything in its place. If a picture wasn't level, he had to straighten it. The cutlery draw held the knives, forks and spoons in an orderly fashion. His first love was a girl he called Looby-Loo. Her father was in the army and they'd moved abroad somewhere when she was thirteen. After one or two girlfriends he'd married Ruth just after he'd joined the police in 2006 but it didn't work out. Strange in a way, they'd been in love, held hands wherever they went, but as time went by little things began to happen that signalled the end of the line. She'd go shopping with her friends every week-end, didn't like him going to watch his local football team, spent time on their smart-phones when they sat in a cafe . . . they just drifted apart like a couple on two rafts in the middle of the ocean. But the divorce was amicable. Well, as amicable as these things can be.

But Tommy was happy. Pomfreton had a decent watering hole – the Frog and Ferret – and Roger Grimes, the landlord, was a rotund, chirpy type with big red cheeks ideally suited for playing a trumpet. His black eyebrows almost met in the middle. Sally, his devoted wife, who wore a calliper after her early onset of polio, had failed to see a speeding bus when she'd crossed a road in Middlesbrough whilst out shopping. She died instantly according to the coroner. The bus driver was over the drink-drive limit and sentenced to five years. That was ten years ago, and Roger had brought up his son, Ian, with the help of his sister, Iris. Tommy popped in two or three times a week, and he was always greeted with 'A pint of the usual, Tommy?' by Roger as he entered the 18th century inn, needing to duck slightly to avoid the low solid wooden beam over the front door. The regulars were a friendly bunch, apart from a 'newcomer' to the town, Mark Finch, a cravat-wearing southerner, who'd bought the manor house on the edge of Pomfreton fifteen months ago with his wife, Louise, with whom he had a difficult relationship. Finch had friends in high places apparently, and when Tommy once asked Roger how Finch made a living, he said that Finch defined himself as a businessman. 'Now that can mean anything,' thought Tommy to himself. Finch had told the landlord he was ten years away from official retirement so Tommy had put his age at around 55.

Tommy's old friend, Joe Blackwell, looked in from time to time when he was passing, going from one hotel to another as Head of Security of the Northcliffe hotel chain. Joe's time in the Military Police had left its mark on his appearance – short haircut, upright gait, smartly dressed and shoes polished to a mirror finish. They'd catch up on any news and gossip, Joe even discreetly passing on

Tommy's details to anyone who might be in need of a little 'surveillance.' But Tommy was careful. As a Private Investigator he couldn't allow a pint of Roger's best bitter to do the talking. People paid him to do a job as their PI and to keep his mouth shut. And as much as he liked Joe, Tommy avoided tittle tattle on any jobs. Joe understood that, and respected Tommy for it. If word got out that Thomas Archer could not be trusted he might as well throw his button camera and microphone pen into the rubbish bin now.

It was Joe who told Tommy about Roger's son. Ian Grimes had committed suicide whilst still at secondary school.

***

Paul Dawson worked at Middlesbrough Library, situated in Central Square. He'd been there almost nine years. He had always been interested in books, ever since his first *Beano* annual for Christmas when he was five years old. Paul had been Library Monitor at school and took pride in ensuring that all the shelves had books properly stored and that the whole library contents were correctly catalogued. At his last count before he left, just after taking his A levels, the library had 3,458 individual items including a full set of the now extinct *Encyclopaedia Britannica*.

Paul considered himself a man of accuracy. Friends called him pedantic, but he preferred the word 'precision.' Everything had its place, and he had a place for everything. He hated sloppiness and inaccuracy. Facts were what life was about. 'If the facts are correct, the rest falls into place' was his motto. He was fascinated in particular by the life of Arnold Schoenberg, an American composer who was born on September 13, 1874. Being superstitious, Schoenberg always said he would die on his seventy sixth birthday because 7 plus 6 makes 13. Schoenberg died in Los Angeles on Friday, July 13, 1951 at 13 minutes to midnight in his seventy-sixth year.

One day at the library a young lady came in who caught his eye. Paul wasn't what you'd call a 'lady's man,' he was content doing his job as Senior Librarian and getting his monthly salary to pay the bills. He had a few acquaintances, those to whom he'd send a Christmas card, even a birthday card, but not a real 'let's have a heart-to-heart over a beer' type of friend. He'd been busy going through a new delivery of books dropped off the day before, but it was the smell of her perfume that hit him before he even saw her. Down on one knee behind the main desk he looked up as his nose told him that someone different had entered. She looked slightly confused, turning her head quickly from side to side, like a fledgling waiting to be fed.

"Can I help you?" Paul had asked, rising from his prayer posture. "You seem lost?" She turned, surprised to see him suddenly appear like a puppet as if in a magic show.

"Er, yes, I'm looking for the mathematics section." She blushed, her lovely cheeks gaining an extra tint of rouge. Paul walked around the desk, keeping his distance.

"This way, follow me. It's along here." The woman walked a few paces behind Paul. She couldn't help but notice the newness of the soles of his leather shoes as he lifted his feet after each step. "Are you a member of the library?" They'd reached Mathematics and stopped. Looking at a slip of paper in her hand she showed it to Paul. *The Intricacy of Unusual Numbers* by John Baez.

"Afraid not. Do I have to join just to browse?" She spoke so softly, like whipped cream, but with authority. Paul was tempted to let her spend some time going through whatever she wanted to pore over, but he had to be resolute. He glanced at her left hand and noticed she wasn't wearing a wedding ring.

"No, it's not library policy. But it's free to join, of course. We'd need some personal details." The bit about 'library policy' defrayed the slight barrier that was about to appear. "Look, why don't you take a look at the books we have while I get the form ready for you to complete as you leave." She smiled with her eyes and nodded. Paul left her to it and felt his neck turning pink as his pulse quickened slightly. He pulled up the form on a computer alongside the main desk so that he was ready to complete matters as the woman left. He fiddled with an invoice from the UPS driver, adjusted his cuff-links several times, put a mint into his mouth and generally wasted time until he registered the new library member. That would make eleven this week – good going he mused – considering nearly everybody used their own means of reading books and accessing data these days.

Glancing across to the aisle, he saw that she was sitting at a round table with a book, head down, and writing something in a notebook. Her platinum blonde hair was partly tied back, but two long strands hung down loosely, framing her face. She looked up at him and smiled but he quickly turned away. Paul cursed himself for staring. He checked the invoice again, pretending to be engrossed in the contents as he played with a ballpoint pen. He noticed the digital clock on the wall behind the desk. 16.55 and 45 seconds. Not long to closing time. He didn't want to rush the woman, but he did want to get her registered today, after all, she might not come back. His heart missed a beat as she walked towards him, her steel blue eyes focused on his, her long coat and silk scarf hiding whatever she wore underneath, but it showed off the knee high, brown leather boots that she wore like a Prussian soldier. Paul braced himself.

"Right, did you find what you were looking for? I assume so. Shall we get your membership application done, then I can issue you with a membership card?" The woman stopped and leant over Paul's computer. Her white teeth gleamed as she spoke, her earrings dangled.

"Yes and no. I did find what I was looking for . . . and no, I do not want a membership card. Thank you. You've been very considerate. Good bye." Paul was speechless. She left the library in strides as if marching in a rally.

'Blast,' he thought. 'And I was all prepared to enter her name, address, phone number and email address.' The fragrance of her perfume was left hanging in her wake as the heavy glass library door closed. The library clock showed 17.00 and 10 seconds.

***

"Good morning, Tom, it's Gordon here, Gordon Ashby. Now listen, my son is still on the run and I don't want you to stop looking. I'd rather you found him before the police do and it would give me a chance to talk to him. The silly sod, it makes my blood boil to think he'd had a damn good education, too!" Gordon Ashby, of Ashby Estate Agents in Yarm, was phoning before Tommy had even had a shower. Tommy had been assigned to trace Dick Ashby three weeks ago after he'd run away from Hartshot Detention Centre located in the Dales. Taking a Nissan from a fuel station forecourt, keys left in the ignition courtesy of the absent - minded driver, the vehicle had been later found partly wrapped around an oak tree on the main road to Whitby. Police still hadn't managed to trace Dick Ashby despite an infinite number of enquiries throughout Teesside and surrounding areas.

"Morning, Gordon. No problem. I know I spent some time on this case, but I'll review the notes I took when we met and check out any other avenues that are worth following." Hell, Tommy had exhausted his PI activities a while back, but he was telling Gordon Ashby what he wanted to hear. "I know he has friends in Middlesbrough so I'll take another sniff around some of the places where he was known." Dick Ashby had been caught drug dealing in North Ormesby and given an eighteen months sentence at Hartshot, and in spite of three good A levels at Yarm School, had got mixed up in the Teesside underworld. "Listen, leave it with me, Gordon, and I'll get onto it today. As usual, you can trust me to keep a log of activity and I'll keep you informed." With that the phone call ended. This case wasn't going to get Tommy over-excited, but it would help pay the mortgage. At his charge of £50 per hour and 45p per mile, plus incidentals, it would all add up. Ashby Estate Agents had been the source of Tommy's cottage in Pomfreton, so he felt a moral obligation to help Gordon find his missing son.

Tom showered, had his black coffee with one sweetener, and a bowl of cereal. He picked up the folder containing details of Dick Ashby. A filing cabinet held over thirty folders, some marked 'Finished' when the case was closed and final payment made. There were others that were still active. He took out the photo of Dick that Gordon had given him, slipping it to one side. Scanning the information, Tom noticed an entry regarding the David Logan Leisure Centre in Thornaby, tucked away alongside the River Tees. He hadn't been there yet. Tommy entered the information into his phone. He'd call in very soon.

Tomorrow he was meeting with Paul Dawson. Tommy had called around 12.30 pm as agreed and arranged to see Dawson in Dressers Tea Room at the Dorman Museum in Linthorpe Road on Wednesday at exactly 3.00 pm. The basic gist of Dawson's request was that he wanted to know why his wife was going out once or twice a week to see a friend or friends for a girlie chat and catch up, but when she got home appeared reluctant to want to talk about it. He'd considered doing the investigative work himself but knew she'd go ballistic if she found out. Dawson had trawled the internet beginning with www.wad.net, the World Association of Detectives, then www.abi.co.uk, the Association of British Investigators, finally narrowing his search down to agencies in the north east of England and finding Thomas Archer's web site. Tom carried two mobile phones, one for personal use, the other PI work only. And of course, two separate email addresses.

Balancing several cases at once wasn't an issue. Although he wasn't overworked right now, a year ago he was handling five situations at the same time. He enjoyed surveillance. Being able to follow somebody all day without them knowing – hopefully – gave him a kind of adrenalin rush. At first, he was amazed at what people got up to . . . in shops, supermarkets, cafes, and time spent in toilets! Driving behind the target was always a challenge. He could never predict a quick left or right turn in traffic, and U-turns became quite normal. Following a vehicle in a town was easy compared to the country. Once he had to trail a yellow Hyundai along a country lane lined with a tall hedge – stay too far back and he'd lose it, get too close and the driver would get suspicious. All in the day's work of a PI, Tommy often told himself.

Tommy closed the folder on Dick Ashby and headed across to the A19 and drove north. The sun was trying its hardest to shine but on industrial Teesside you could never be certain you'd see that golden orb in the sky. With traffic being fairly light he was soon parking at the David Logan Leisure Centre. Signs offered fourteen days gym membership for £28 and the promise of a fit and healthy body. Tommy recalled the Latin motto *Mens sana in corpore sano* and wondered for a second whether he had a healthy mind in a healthy body? Was he fit enough these days? Twenty years ago, he could run the 100 yards in eleven seconds but now . . . maybe not. He locked his smoke grey, 09 plate VW Golf GTI, a car Tommy had chosen for its blandness. Nothing flashy, not eye catching, no GTI badge on the boot, but it was the proverbial 'dirt off a shovel' when it was necessary to floor the accelerator. He stepped up to the reception desk.

"Good morning. Is it possible to see the manager?" Tommy was dressed casually as usual. No tie, loose jacket. Not threatening. Both hands free – so he didn't come across as a rep wanting to sell anything. The dark - haired girl, with a badge that read CLARE, asked Tommy for his name. In these circumstances he had to decide whether it was the 'card or no card' tactic. He opted for the business card approach and handed her one. She made a phone call, gave the manager the details, and hung up.

"He'll be with you shortly. Take a seat," Clare

suggested as she turned to deal with somebody enquiring about membership. Tommy sat down on a three - seat settee and picked up a copy of *Bodybuilder Today*. He aimlessly flicked through it and recalled a Ken Dodd saying – 'all that meat and no gravy.' Male, female, and some body builders whose sexuality was dubious. Men had big chests, women had small breasts, the in-betweeners were a mixture, and Tommy's conclusion was there was no way he ever wanted to pump iron.

"Mr. Archer?" said a tall, bronzed figure. "I'm Chris Butler the manager. Do you want to come this way?"

***

To say that Paul Dawson was disappointed not to have registered the 'Maths Enquirer' as a new library member was an understatement. A week had passed since she'd been in leaving her vapour trail of Gucci or YSL or whatever it was. Call it providence or serendipity, but one day after work when he was meandering the aisles of his local supermarket, he saw her. She was bending over a slide-open freezer cabinet, those long pieces of blonde hair hanging down. He could walk on by, pretend she wasn't there, or . . . stop and say 'hello.'

"Hi, looking for anything in particular?" Paul said in a half jocular manner, being careful not to catch her with his half-full basket. She stood up, perhaps an inch or so taller than Paul. He looked into those blue eyes – cold and piercing but friendly.

"Hello! You're the librarian!" She paused for a second. "No, just something to have in when I can't be bothered to cook." Paul thought he heard the hint of a foreign accent as she spoke. The way she said 'bothered to cook' certainly wasn't from North Yorkshire. She smiled, her white teeth showing. "And you?"

"Yes, a few items so that I don't starve." They both laughed. He liked the way her head went back as she did so. Was this a chance to find out more about her? He glanced at his watch. "Look, there's a cafe here, do you fancy a coffee – on me, of course." He asked the question firmly. He wanted a positive reply. Her smile disappeared and his heart sank. She moved a fraction closer.

"I'd like that very much," she chuckled as Paul gripped his shopping basket tighter. He'd expected a rejection. They moved to the end of the aisle, turned right and headed for the Willow Tree cafe in the far corner of the store. Paul suggested she take a seat, gave her his not-too-heavy basket which she placed inside her shopping trolley and joined the short queue. Within a few minutes he'd placed the two cafe lattes on the table as he sat opposite her.

"Thank you," she said. "I know you are Paul. I saw your badge when I came into the library. I'm Maria. How do you do?" She held out her slender hand and he shook it. How civilised, thought Paul. Maria was confident, self-assured and polite. He liked that. Maybe she was dominant, too? They sipped their lattes and chatted for half an hour about everything and nothing. Likes and interests, music and hobbies. Anyone observing them would think this couple had known each other for ages; they seemed to get on so well. Maria looked at her watch, a diamond encrusted Rolex.

"I really must go, Paul. I'm meeting somebody in an hour. Here's my card. Give me a call sometime." And with that, Maria stood, went over to her trolley, gave Paul his basket, and headed for the check-out. She didn't look back. He sat there for a few more minutes reflecting on what had happened since he'd spotted her as he played with the card in his hand. There were so many things that he could have asked her but didn't. He reined himself in. It was the first time they'd had a chance to talk. Best not to go OTT, he decided.

He now knew her name, Maria Makarova, where she lived and had her mobile phone number. There was no mention of husband or boyfriend, but he couldn't sit in the Willow Tree all day. As he was about to leave, he glanced down at the two coffee mugs. He was tempted to take hers with him. The trace of the red, lip-shaped imprint on the rim held his fascination. His hand reached out for it but a rough voice behind him shook him out of his fantasy.

"Finished 'ere? I got work to do. Thank you. Have a nice day." The diminutive figure of the cafe waitress with the smell of chip fat on her clothes eased past him to collect the two mugs.

'Sod it,' said Paul to himself. And he hadn't even asked her why she wanted to look at *The Intricacy of Unusual Numbers* by John Baez.

***

Reciting a silly nursery rhyme always brought a smile.

This little piggy went to market, this little piggy stayed at home.

This little piggy had roast beef and this little piggy had none . . . and this little went all the way hoooooome!

It was time to do some planning.

***

Chris Butler's office was sparsely furnished. A wooden desk was straddled by a chair each side and a bookcase held about ten books. Two trophies stood on the windowsill, and a framed college PE certificate with the name *Christopher Butler* in italics, hung on the wall behind him. Butler offered Tommy a drink but he refused. Butler leant forwards, fingers intertwined, and looked at Tommy as if to say 'go ahead.'

"Thanks for your time, Chris. I've been asked by a client to find somebody. Any conversation between us is, of course, confidential – on both sides, yeah?" Butler smiled and nodded. "I understand that somebody called Dick Ashby has used your Leisure Centre – either as a guest of someone, or as a temporary or full member. He's gone missing and his father has asked me to find him. Do you think you could help out here?" Tommy smiled and crossed both of his index and middle fingers below the desk. The centre manager looked at his laptop and tapped a few keys. Tommy swallowed hard.

"Hmmm, well, I can't give too much away, but I *can* tell you that someone named Dick Ashby was signed in on two occasions. Once by a member named Dave Teague, then a month later by a girl called Gillian Finch. Teague brought Ashby here as a temporary member eighteen months ago, and Finch twelve months back." Tommy leant forward and smiled. He lowered his voice.

"Any chance of a contact number, Chris?" Chris Butler hesitated, then stared at Tommy. "Please, it's important." The manager angled his desk top computer slightly. As he eased back on his office chair, he told Tommy he'd give him ten seconds to get what information he needed. In the time he was given, Tommy jotted down two mobile phone numbers and the first line of two addresses with post code.

"You didn't get that from me, right?" Butler was firm, but felt that he could trust the PI. "When Ashby did come here, I particularly noticed he became friendly with a guy named Carl. He still works here. I can give you a few minutes with him." Tommy nodded, his day getter better by the minute. "Wait here, back in a second." Shortly afterwards, Butler was back.

"This is Carl Williams." Tommy stood up and shook hands, Carl's grip tight. "Carl's our body-building expert; he manages the programmes on increasing body mass, toning up muscles, as well as being responsible for all of the equipment." Snow white teeth gleamed from a tanned face, his T shirt a good fit across his broad chest.

"Let's grab a coffee in the staff lounge, Tommy. This way." Tommy thanked Chris for his help, but didn't overdo it – he couldn't be certain what Butler had told Williams about why he was there. Tommy walked a pace behind the muscular frame and was offered a chair near the water dispenser in the room whose door was marked Staff Only. "Coffee, Tommy?" He nodded and asked for it black. The machine gurgled as it pressurised hot water through a coffee capsule. Tommy tapped a sweetener into it and stirred it with a small white plastic spoon. "So, what is it you want to know about Dick Ashby?" Tommy took a sip from the cardboard cup and sat upright.

"This is between us, Carl. My work as a PI means I have to be discreet. You OK with that?" Carl nodded. "I'm trying to find out more about Dick Ashby. Chris tells me you seemed to get on well with him when he was here." Tommy casually removed his notepad from his jacket pocket. "What sort of a guy he is, and what do you know about him?"

When Tommy Archer left the Leisure Centre half an hour later her had some very useful data - a good slant on Dick Ashby, and information on Dave Teague and Gillian Finch. Sitting in his VW Golf, Tommy looked at his notes again. Two part - addresses, two mobile numbers. He'd listen to his microphone pen recording later. It had been so easy to switch it on when he'd entered Chris Butler's office and turn it off as he exited the Centre.

***

Dressers Tea Room was everything Tommy expected. Trip Advisor had given it a well above average rating and the meeting venue with Paul Dawson had been at Paul's suggestion. Tommy's watch showed 2.52 pm. He always liked to be early for a first - time meeting, and, on entering the tea room, made his way to a corner table led by a waitress wearing a white blouse, black skirt, black shoes, and a tiny lace hat with a black band like a starched tiara. A white, spotless apron completed her uniform. Tommy briefly explained that he was waiting for a friend.

"I'll bring you two menus, sir," she offered and strode back to the counter like a cat-walk model. Tommy glanced around. Several small duos and trios sat huddled at separate tables, most adorned with china teapots or tall coffee pots, plates of cakes, sandwiches and scones expertly balanced on tiered, china plates. The waitress gently placed the menus on the green and white tablecloth. Tommy scanned 'Drinks, Snacks, Light Bites and the Cake' listing. He felt saliva building up in his mouth as the graphic descriptions amused him. Putting the menu down, he suddenly heard a voice behind him.

"Mr. Archer?" A man that Tommy put at six feet two inches and weighing about thirteen stone stood next to him. It was Paul Dawson. The time was exactly 3.00 pm. Tommy rose a little awkwardly as Paul Dawson filled his immediate space.

"You must be Paul?" After shaking hands, they both sat down and Paul unbuttoned his jacket. Those initial moments, when strangers first meet, seem to be like trying to pluck a chicken wearing a pair of boxing gloves; awkward to say the least. Both spoke simultaneously, and then laughed. Paul got the first words in.

"Tommy, thank you for coming today. There's quite a lot to talk about so shall we order and get started?" Paul smiled, his thin gold bracelet with an initialled charm catching the light. A large cafetiere with a jug of cream, sugar bowl, and two small complimentary biscuits were placed between them. Tommy flicked his sweetener in as Paul poured a generous portion of cream into his and tonged in three brown sugar cubes. Paul began his account, explaining how he'd first met his wife, Maria, three years ago at the Central library where he still worked. She hadn't joined the library but he'd seen her in a supermarket shortly afterwards, had coffee and they'd dated for a couple of months after that. Tommy scribbled notes. Paul described Maria, emphasising her beauty and her outgoing character which he liked. She had an interest in maths, and nine months after she'd first entered the library, they went on holiday together. Moscow. Staying at the Holiday Inn Sokolniki for a week, Maria had told Paul that it was a place she'd always wanted to visit. Red Square, the Tsar's grand palaces, the culture – Cossack folklore, the thrill of visiting a city with such history! And they split the total cost – went Dutch on everything. Paul stated that it appeared Maria didn't want to be in his debt; be a financial burden to him, and he was fine with that. Six weeks after they'd returned, she suggested they get married. Paul stressed to Tommy that this was most unexpected but he agreed. She was beautiful and he felt privileged to be in her company. The wedding was a quiet affair, one of Paul's friends was present and someone Maria called Chloe, but no parents. She sold her apartment on Teesside and moved in with Paul, who had a two bedroomed, detached bungalow on a corner site in a cul-de-sac in Eston.

"What does Maria do, Paul?" Tommy held his ball point pen, although his microphone pen was active. Paul put his cup down.

"She works for a travel agent in town. GoWorldTravel. Reports in to the Managing Director. She looks after the office administration and deals with the more important enquiries." Tommy made a note as Paul carried on. He went on to focus on his concern that he'd briefly explained to Tommy over the phone. "Some weeks Maria goes out on her own, sometimes a friend calls for her. She leaves the bungalow anywhere around six thirty to half past seven, then gets home at about ten o'clock, occasionally later. When I ask about her social evening, she doesn't want to talk about it. Clams up, changes the subject, just says 'fine' and moves on. She takes a shower, often has an early night." Paul paused to sip his coffee. Tactfully, Tommy asked about their sex life. It was good. Paul then continued, telling Tommy that Maria had been going out to 'see friends' for the past six months and had recently opened her own 'above-average' interest bank account and changed her laptop password. When challenged, she gave Paul what were plausible answers. A sum of money that an uncle had left her in his will was wallowing in a nil return account, and she often forgot her computer password so she changed it. Paul hadn't asked his wife what it was – he knew better than that. And when he'd mentioned her uncle, she swept the query away like brushing dust under the

Turkish rug in the lounge.

Tommy wrote notes and asked questions. There were some things that didn't quite sit right with Maria. He asked Paul if anything really unusual had happened since they'd met, anything at all that gave him cause for concern? Paul's reply was simple.

"When we were on holiday in Moscow she disappeared twice."

"'Disappeared?' What do you mean?" Tommy poured more coffee for both of them.

"On the second night, after dinner in the hotel, we went for a stroll. We stopped to look in a window filled with jewellery but when I turned around, she wasn't there. I looked all over for her and after an hour went back to the hotel. She turned up half an hour after that, saying she'd gone down a side street and got lost." Paul couldn't disprove it, and the more he asked leading questions the more she clammed up. "And the night before we came back the same thing happened. She used an upstairs toilet in a restaurant, went walkabouts, and came back about forty minutes later saying she'd had a dizzy spell."

"And you took all this at face value?" Paul nodded, feeling himself reddening slightly as if being chastised by a schoolmaster. Seconds passed. "On a scale of one to ten, how well do you believe you know Maria? Where one is not at all and ten is really well."

"Do you want me to be honest?" Tommy smiled and his eyes made it clear. "Three, maybe four," was the response. Tommy whistled quietly.

"So, you want me to find out where she's going . . . and if possible, who she's seeing and report back?" Paul's face brightened a little. "I'll need some details on Maria. A recent photo, make of her car and number plate, your home address, names of any friends or acquaintances you know of. Might be useful if you set up a post office box number where I can send any material – reports and photos. Be safer than emails."

Paul paid the bill and, at Tommy's suggestion, they left Dressers Tea Room five minutes apart.

***

Dave Teague, who lived in Ayresome Street, Middlesbrough, was going to be contacted first. Teague had been a member at the David Logan centre for three years, using the gym facilities frequently. Tommy had asked Carl Williams about him, too. Williams didn't know Teague that well, estimated his age at between 25 and 30, but he'd always struck the body building expert as 'odd.' The exact word he'd used. Some days his eyes looked as if they couldn't focus properly. He said very little and when he did talk seemed guarded in any response to a question. Teague had once knocked a cup of coffee over in the snack bar and instead of letting any staff know, or getting a cloth to wipe it up, he just walked away from the table. Williams challenged Teague a few days later, politely suggesting that next time he did that he ought to do something about it.

Williams had also noticed that when Teague and Ashby were together, they sat close. He didn't think they were gay; it was as if they didn't want anybody else to hear a single word they were saying. If they noticed anyone nearby, they'd clam up. Williams knew that Dick Ashby, now aged 23, had been incarcerated in Hartshot Detention Centre for an eighteen months sentence. News reports had been in the local newspaper as well as local television news. Tommy knew that he'd have to approach Dave Teague with care if he was going to get anything out of him at all. But before Tommy made contact with Teague, he looked at the information on Gillian Finch. The address that Tommy had written down from Butler's computer – The Old Manor House, Pomfreton, confirmed that she was the daughter of Mark Finch. Now Tommy wasn't going to jump to any conclusions, but Gillian Finch must know Dick Ashby to sign him in as a temporary member. But did Teague and Gillian Finch know each other? Maybe, but not necessarily. Carl Williams had put Finch's age at around 24 or 25. Nobody at the gym, or Tommy, had any idea where either Teague or Finch worked . . . if they worked at all.

"Hi, is that Dave Teague?" Tommy was on his mobile, 141 in front of Teague's phone number.

"Yes, who's this?" Teague's phone screen showed *Unavailable*.

"Oh, hi! My name is Tom. I'm a friend of Dick Ashby – we go back a long way. In fact, we both went to Yarm School." Tommy tried to sound as genuine as possible. "Chances are he won't remember me but I've just moved back into the area and wanted to catch up – we used to get up to all sorts of mischief when we went to a youth club in Stockton!" Tommy had obtained the school details from Gordon Ashby and prayed that his story sounded genuine.

"So how did you get my number?" Teague was guarded.

"I met up with a guy at the David Logan centre in Thornaby for coffee, an old work colleague. We were chatting and I overheard somebody mention Dick Ashby. Of course, the name rang a bell so I asked if he knew anything about him. He didn't say much but he mentioned your name, scrolled through his phone contacts . . . and voila!"

"Who was that, then?" Tommy gave an involuntary shrug.

"Dunno, didn't ask his name. Tallish, dark hair, brown eyes, jeans, plain T-shirt." Tommy knew that fitted a fair proportion of the visitors to the Leisure Centre. "Look, we could meet for a beer or something, or lunch. My treat." Silence on the other end for a few seconds.

"OK. I work at *Film & Video* in Victoria Road. Do you know *The Black Lion*? I can see you there at one o'clock tomorrow. It's just around the corner from here." Tommy confirmed the arrangement - he'd had a decent sandwich there recently. That was considerate, too, Dave Teague actually letting Tommy know where he worked. Tommy wished all of his contacts were that forthcoming.

Looking again at Gillian Finch's details, Tommy had to handle any contact with her carefully. Last thing he wanted was to pop into the Frog and Ferret for a sharp half after he'd met with her, and then find Mark Finch in there with his daughter. Or worse still, be assaulted by Finch or a hired thug on some dark, desolate pathway in Pomfreton after closing time. No, he'd leave Gillian for now, meet Dave Teague and ease Gillian's name into the conversation. Regulars in the Frog would know something about the Finch family, and Tommy felt he could trust the landlord, Roger Grimes. Keeping ears open while pretending to read the newspaper in the bar could pay dividends, too. Tommy had learnt to scan the pages and see nothing on them, the buzz of words from those around him filling his head and linking up as if in a crossword puzzle.

Tommy's mobile beeped. It was a message from Paul Dawson.

Please see photo and details of Maria attached in the email. PO box number set up. It's 2108. She's going out next Tuesday evening. Leaving home about 6.30 pm.

***

Tommy had taken three more investigations in the last few days. Talk about London bus syndrome! Quiet for ages then several enquiries come along at once. He was able to handle about half a dozen competently, depending on time allocation. The longest PI case he'd had was six months, when he'd followed the Romanian husband of a slightly disabled British woman. They lived on Teesside but the well-built guy kept disappearing abroad and it was a long drawn out situation but the end result was that he'd married her for convenience and was still seeing his family. Of course, Tommy didn't follow him once he'd checked in at Newcastle Airport, but he'd obtained flight details and his wife got a friend to hack into his emails when he did the booking for the flights. Tommy's observations were mainly concerned with the Romanian's shady dealings in Middlesbrough. He was a painter and decorator by trade but had been hired by one of the Boro underground to 'break fingers' when people didn't honour the payment of their loans. Thankfully for Tommy he only heard knuckles being snapped on two occasions. But two was enough. Eventually she reported him to the police and even Interpol became involved. There was sufficient evidence to send him down for a long time.

Looking at folders on his desk, Tommy picked up the one marked MD/13/06/16. Maria Dawson – 13 June 2016. Initials and date of first contact. Taking a sip of his coffee he opened the dark red cover. He sifted through what he knew about Maria Dawson as provided by her husband, Paul.

Date of birth: 21 August 1980.
Place of birth: St. Petersburg
Father's occupation: Military Officer.
Mother: Housewife.

Moved to England when she was six years old. Schooled in London and Cheltenham & Stockton-on-Tees. Gained a BA in Politics from Durham University, then a postgraduate teaching certificate. Taught politics at Durham School for twelve years, becoming department head. Wanted a career change, so took a secretarial course on Teesside then began working for a travel agent MD in Middlesbrough.

Current position – Senior Administrative Executive.
One sister two years her senior. No other siblings.
Current address: 89, St. Roseberry Close, Eston,
Cleveland TS15 8PT.
Hobbies: Keeping fit; doing the Times crossword; buying clothes; dolls. Salary: c £34K
Car: Red Mazda MX5 sports coupe.

Tommy stared at the two photos of Maria he'd printed off his computer. Not the clearest, but they'd do for now. One head and shoulders, the other head to toe – probably taken at a wedding or similar. Full length coat, hat, high heels, small handbag. And smiling nicely. He looked at the first one for some minutes. For a fleeting moment, Tommy thought he'd seen her before, there was a skip of a heartbeat. His mind re-wound, trying to think where it could have been.

He told himself that she had those features that seemed common to a number of attractive women. The eyes, aquiline nose, high cheek bones, hair that fell in waves. If she had buying clothes as a hobby, she probably had a good hairdresser, too. But it was nearly Monday, and Tommy's first observations of Maria Dawson would soon begin. A red Mazda sports car – what a boon! Easy to follow. But he wanted to do a recce of Eston first. Know where to park his VW, 'get the lie of the land.' Keep his distance, of course, have a newspaper or magazine to hand; something to part shield his face if necessary. His Nikon camera with the telephoto lens and the high power, Pentax binoculars, would be in the passenger footwell. The VW fuel tank would be full, or almost. Didn't want to have to pull into a garage for diesel when following somebody! No, Tommy would be ready to see where Mrs. Dawson was going and who she was meeting.

Such events still gave Tommy an adrenalin rush. A new challenge, new faces, curiosity satisfied, and the thrill of finding out what made somebody do what he was being paid to discover. And as soon as Tuesday came around Tommy would have an early tea, maybe scrambled eggs with black pepper on toast, and head towards Eston.

***

Paul Dawson saw his neighbour's car on the drive as soon as he'd pulled up and switched off the engine. It looked brand new, gleaming, and the tyre walls were shiny black.

His neighbour went in, virtually swaggering, as he zapped the car casually to lock it. He walked like John Wayne. Dawson felt envious. His eight - year old Renault Megane was tired. There were a number of features that it didn't have . . . auto windscreen wipers, reverse sensors, sat-nav. He had enough in his own bank account to trade the Renault in against something better. Why shouldn't he treat himself? He worked hard enough. 'No, sod it,' he thought. 'I want one like that!'

A week later Paul was easing onto his tarmac driveway in a yellow Ford Focus. A month old, with a few extras and only 100 miles on the clock, he was a happy bunny.

***

The Black Lion was busy. Tommy wanted to be visible to Dave Teague and had told Teague he'd be wearing a pillar box red tie. It was 12.50 pm and Tommy stood at the bar with a glass of lime and lemonade – always a safe bet when you had car keys in your jacket pocket. Not wanting to appear too obvious, Tommy kept glancing at the crossword in *The Northern Echo* folded in front of him, the crossword half complete. He'd just solved 3 across (Clue: Risk a speculation about northern composer. Answer: Wagner) when he was approached.

"Tom?" asked the man. "Are you Tom?" Tommy nodded, picked up his newspaper and drink and pointed toward a vacant table in the window. "I've got half an hour."

"Hi, and you're Dave. Thanks for coming." Tommy had avoided a handshake, always a minor diplomatic challenge at such a time. Teague was six feet tall and his upper body filled his mock leather bomber jacket. He had a slight resemblance to a younger Arnie Schwarznegger. "OK here?" asked Tommy looking at the round table with a brass 21 tag on the smooth surface. "What can I get you, Dave?" Teague ordered a ham and cheese toastie and a half a lager without looking at the menu. Tommy put his own drink down and threw the *Echo* onto a chair. "I'll be back in a minute." Tommy went to the bar and placed his order. He fancied a pork pie topped with cranberry sauce.

"So, you're an old pal of Dick Ashby? He's never mentioned you." Teague seemed slightly anxious. He didn't really know what Tommy wanted, but he was buying lunch so there was something he needed.

"Yes, that's right. Last saw Richard, or Dick as he's now known, back in about 2012. We lost contact a while back. We played pool at a club on Teesside – he was quite good. Think his old man was an estate agent or something like that." Tommy was balancing vagueness against credibility. "I couldn't believe it when I heard someone mention his name at the gym. I'd certainly like to catch up with him! But . . ." Tommy added quickly, ". . . I want it to be a surprise!" The waitress put the sandwich and pie on the table along with half a lager and another lime and lemonade. "So, what's he up to these days?" Tommy continued without taking his eyes off Teague.

"Well, I don't know if you saw the papers recently but Dick was in a detention centre and he escaped. One of these young offender places – some barbed wire on the fences but not quite Fort Knox. He'd stolen a car and crashed it on the Whitby road. Probably high as a kite. He's still on the run." Tommy was part way through his tasty pie, cut into quarters, and took a sip of his drink. He pretended not to know any of Teague's information and was careful in not pushing him too hard. There were twenty minutes left before Teague was due to leave.

"So how did you and Dick meet?" Teague told Tommy that they'd met in a bar in Middlesbrough one Friday night about two years ago and seemed to hit it off. 8.00 pm on Fridays became a regular feature, a night for forgetting the week's problems, 'getting ratted' as Teague put it, and trying a bit of hash or cocaine. After telling Dick Ashby about the David Logan Leisure Centre, Ashby fancied having a go. Teague had signed his friend in for a couple of sessions, just as Carl Williams at the centre had said, but

Ashby had hesitated in joining as a full member. Tommy wiped his mouth on a thin paper napkin. He needed more and took a gamble. Discreetly he removed a crisp £50 from his wallet and placed it under the coaster in front of Teague.

"So, where's Dick now, Dave? Any ideas? I really would like to catch up with him after all this time." Tommy smiled as Teague looked uncomfortable for a second. Glancing down at the crimson note, Dave Teague slid it from under the cardboard and flicked it into his shirt top pocket like a magician about to exchange it for a playing card. Glancing at his watch, Tommy knew he wanted a name or two, some crumb of information to go on. Teague's Adams apple moved up and down.

"You didn't hear this from me, but there are a couple of guys who get down to a club, the Blue Umbrella, two or three times a week. Steve Attridge and Nicky Barlay. They're both good friends of Dick. I think Attridge is a plumber, or 'hydrostatic operative' as he likes to call himself and Barlay runs his own taxi business. He could be staying with either of them. That's a rumour I've heard, anyway." Teague filled Tommy in with a few more details and the two men, apparently, were both in the Teesside telephone directory. "Listen, I've said enough already." Teague stood up and held out his hand. Tommy shook it in response to Teague's gesture and felt his knuckles crack as Dave Teague's grip tightened briefly. "By the way, Tommy, what's your surname?"

"Smith," Tommy replied as Dave Teague zipped up his jacket over his barrel chest. "Oh, do you know Gillian Finch?" Tommy added quickly.

"Sure. She gets into Logan's now and then. We've spoken a few times. "Don't know much about her but she works at Teesport. Administration for one of the shipping companies. A PA for some manager, something like that." Teague looked at his watch, more to make the point of going than needing to know the time.

"Take care, Tom," offered Teague as he walked out of

the pub and headed back to his office, smiling as he thought of the note in his pocket. That will help pay for a few beers on Friday night.

If Tommy had a crystal ball, he would have known that Dave Teague from *Film & Video* wasn't long out of HMP Northumberland near Morpeth. He'd been sent there for eighteen months regarding a serious case of GBH in The Blue Umbrella.

***

The drive from Pomfreton to Eston took thirty - two minutes. The traffic was light and there weren't any tractors and trailers on the roads, or any careful caravan towers. Tommy hated 'caravan man' – why mess about pulling your second home around when you could get a B & B for under £30? He parked up far enough away from the Dawson address so as not to be obviously visible from the property, but close enough to see when the red Mazda left the property. It was 7.13 pm and his watch kept good time. The Omega Seamaster automatic he'd bought off the Gumtree web site for a grand had been a good investment. The woman he purchased it from wanted to get rid of it – her husband had died the previous year and it only served to remind her of him. It was easily worth twice what he paid.

Tommy stifled a slight belch. His scrambled eggs on toast for tea had been tasty but perhaps he should avoid putting a teaspoon of vinegar in next time. Slipping a spearmint into his mouth, Tommy focused on the house; a buzzard waiting for its prey. His strategy at times like this was to look at the screen of his smartphone and pretend he was searching for some data whilst casually glancing round every few seconds. The last thing he wanted was PC Plod tapping on his window as a result of an over-zealous Neighbourhood Watch Samaritan phoning the police.

Having thought that, however, Tommy was on friendly terms with Detective Chief Inspector Jim Adamson of

Cleveland Police and a mention of his name might be his 'get out of jail card' if that happened. Adamson had been a useful ally some time back when Tommy was working on a case for ICI in Billingham regarding an engineer who was on long term sick leave allegedly because of a bad back. The DCI had not revealed any confidential information but had given Tommy a couple of leads that came in very handy. Turned out the malingerer was enjoying an active life that included two rounds of golf each week at Blackburn Grange, Darlington as well as Saturday morning football! But Tommy never abused contacts such as Adamson and only used them sparingly. He hadn't been in touch with Adamson for a while, but having the direct line number for the DCI was a bonus. Maybe he'd call him soon, even if it was just to say hello and enquire after his wife, Helen, who'd been diagnosed with a mild form of MS six months ago.

The red Mazda slowly backed out of the driveway in St. Roseberry Close. Tommy started the Golf engine and eased it into first gear. At the end of the Close, the Mazda turned right and headed towards the coast on the A174. Tommy stayed within two hundred yards or so of the sports car, not getting too close, nor too far behind to lose its trail. Maria Dawson was a careful driver, never accelerating hard nor taking chances at junctions or roundabouts. Just the job. Tommy hated following people like Lewis Hamilton's mum and dad or Jensen Button's grannie. Passing through Kirkleatham, Maria drove toward Marske-on-Sea and slowed to pull into the car park of the Seaview Hotel. Tommy stopped at the side of the road, engine idling, while he watched Maria get out and lock her car. He grabbed his Nikon and took three quick shots as she strode elegantly across the smooth tarmac surface, skipped up the five front steps and entered the hotel courtesy of the automatic glass doors.

Tommy decided to leave the Golf where he'd stopped. It wasn't restricted parking, and there were a few spaces left. Going into the hotel car park was too risky. Avoiding eye contact or closeness with anyone he followed was always preferred. It had to be. He gave Maria a few minutes and then Tommy went in. The bar was always high on the list for a clandestine meeting, followed by the restaurant, then a bedroom. He hoped it was the first one – much easier to mingle amongst the clientele, get a drink, take a seat. Restaurants in hotels were more difficult, but not impossible – Tommy could always force an omelette or a jacket potato down. But when it came to bedrooms, it was the waiting game. He'd once spent all night parked up outside of a motel on the A66 only to fall asleep and miss the guy he was trailing. Bad news.

The Seaview Hotel looked tired. Probably built a hundred and fifty years ago, it was in need of a face-lift. It had been refurbished recently, but it had that look of a hotel favoured by the Victorians. A pale lemon facade, the letter 't' in the name Hotel was slightly askew, and the hanging baskets were in need of a good watering. But the car park was nearly full so the manager must be doing something right. Tommy hadn't been here before so he quickly googled the place as he stood nonchalantly near a display of leaflets and brochures for local attractions. It had a restaurant with an average score of 9.2! So, the food ought to be pretty good, decided Tommy.

There was a hum of babbling voices coming from the Captain Cook bar to the left of reception. Tommy went in and headed toward the counter, a line of spirit optics against the wall. He ordered a lime and lemonade, parked his backside on a bar stool, and flicked through a leaflet he'd just picked up. He wasn't going to the RSPB site at nearby Saltholme, but it was an ideal foil. Sipping his iced drink, he casually scanned the room as he gathered facts about bird life on Teesside's newest bird sanctuary.

Maria Dawson was sitting alone at a table near a window in the far corner of the bar. She looked at her watch several times every few seconds, twiddling it left to right on her wrist as if to make the seconds pass quicker. Tommy guessed her meeting was arranged for eight o'clock. The long drink in a highball glass with an ice cube and wedge of lemon was her only company, but her face changed as she stood to greet the man who approached her. Tommy estimated the guy to be between thirty and forty. Even from the back view, Tommy had an eye for estimating age. It was the way people walked, what they wore, their hair style and how they held themselves. He'd even studied photos of the archetypal European and was 95% certain of their country of origin. The man sat with his back to Tommy some twelve paces away.

Despite a quick peck on each cheek from the visitor, Maria's body language suggested she didn't know the guy that well. 'Maybe a first meeting,' thought Tommy. Sipping his lime and lemonade Tommy half - glimpsed the leaflet but also watched the man carefully. He was asking Maria if she wanted another drink but she shook her head and pointed at her glass. Rising from the table, Maria and the guy walked away from Tommy towards the restaurant. The name *BOUNTY* was inscribed on a pseudo scroll over the door. As they entered, a waiter greeted them and ushered the pair to a table. Being a passable lip reader, and good at interpreting body language, Tommy's gut instinct was that a table had been reserved, but who had booked it, he wondered? In two seconds, the couple had disappeared from view. Tommy had to try one of his old tricks.

"Good evening, sir, a table for one?" asked Georgio in a strained Italian accent. "We're rather busy right now. Have you booked?"

"Yes, phoned two days ago. Table for one at 8.15 pm." Georgio ran his finger down the booking list spread out like a bible on a lectern. He shook his head slowly.

"Don't seem to have you down, sir." He hesitated. "Are you sure you reserved a table?" By now there was another couple stood behind Tommy.

"Not again! This happened last month! Morgan. Colonel Stephen Morgan. Of course. I booked a damned table!" Tommy flicked the bottom of his military style tie at the waiter as if to make a point. Georgio was suitably embarrassed. Then another couple joined the queue for a table in the *BOUNTY*. Georgio couldn't let his customers know there was an issue here. His finger pointed at the list again. Then he beamed.

"Ah, here we are, sir. My apologies. Didn't spot it first time. Follow me." Tommy followed the waiter and was seated one table away from Maria Dawson and her guest. Or was Maria the guest? Either way, Tommy was able to face the guy when he casually glanced up from the menu. A rugged face, small brown eyes, black hair and a crew cut, he pigeon-holed him as East European and around thirty years of age. Tommy's microphone pen was good for up to twenty five feet and the button camera, with its Pentax lens, could handle the distance nicely.

Tommy simply had to take his time eating, listen carefully, take a few photos. Jottings in his pocket diary proved an ideal distraction, the pen picking up their voices nearby. He'd be able to listen to the recording later and filter out most of the other surrounding, unwanted chatter.

And there was one more thing. He hoped he had enough cash to pay for his meal. 'Colonel Morgan' wasn't carrying his credit card with him that night.

***

Gillian Finch, five feet three and with auburn hair and always smartly dressed, had been brought up to have what some would call 'a charmed life.' Words like *silver spoon* and *mouth* came to mind when some of the locals got to know more about her. She used the village shop, a hundred yards from the Frog and Ferret, and Gillian was a customer there. Not necessarily a daily or even weekly caller, but a customer nevertheless. The problem was that after attending the same public school as Princess Anne she expected quick service. Gillian Finch didn't do queues. At Benenden School the scholars were moulded into young ladies. By the time they left the sixth form not only did they have excellent grades in subjects studied, but they'd been tutored in important matters like deportment, social skills and how to lay the cutlery, and stemmed glasses, for a five - course meal. Most could also tell the difference between a Merlot and a Shiraz without drinking it, although midnight feasts in the dormitories inevitably meant that several bottles were consumed on a regular basis.

Her father, Mark Finch, was a failed medical student who'd opted out of his course at St. Georges Medical School in London in his third year. His father had left him a fair sum of cash in his will when Mark was 23and he'd apparently made his money in property when the UK house building index was at its height. Buying up a few acres of land, using jobbing contractors to put up a handful of detached houses on it and selling them himself had made him a nice tidy profit. He'd done that on a number of occasions and his Swiss bank balance was distinctly healthy as was his UK account at Lloyds Bank. His wife, Louise, had no interest in his dealings. She had, of course, always wished that her husband had been a surgeon instead of throwing a good career in medicine away. As long as she could use her platinum credit card as she wanted, she was happy. Her shoe collection wasn't far short of that of Imelda Marcos, and she liked fast cars. A blade silver convertible Mercedes Benz 500 SEL currently had pride of place on her side of the double garage at The Old Manor, kept clean by Jenkins the 'gardener come odd job' man.

But although Gillian hadn't wanted for anything, she also had a burning desire to be more self - sufficient; be independent, stand on her own two feet. The thing that really pissed her off, though, was that her father had cancelled her family credit card on her twenty fifth birthday. Now, at 26, she was driving a Suzuki Swift that she'd traded in for the BMW 320i bought for her twenty first birthday.

"She's a spoilt brat, that one," some of the locals would say behind her back after she'd left the village shop. "She even asked if we could deliver to her home!" murmured the owner, Mrs. Higgins, on one occasion. "What does she think we are? Bloody Sainsbury's or what?"

If there was a plus side on the financial aspect of Gillian's life it was that she still lived at home free of charge. Despite that, she was beginning to think about renting her own place. Neither her father nor her mother had ever suggested that she paid her way. Food, drink, her laundry and a very comfortable existence in the manor house could have cost her a tidy sum, so the 'spoilt brat' had something to be grateful for even if she had to park her Suzuki un-garaged on the edge of the curved gravel drive. It got dirty, with bird muck on the door mirrors from time to time, but Jenkins would clean her car and Gillian slipped him a tenner whenever he did so.

In a quest to keep her body in good shape, and for social reasons, she had joined the David Logan centre where she'd met some interesting people. Somewhat below her status she felt, but it was good fun nevertheless. A few weeks after becoming a member she first tried 'recreational' drugs. *Hashish* and *crack cocaine* mostly. Gently inhaling on a spliff with a few grams of cannabis seemed to make the troubles of the world just drift away. Dave Teague became friendly with her and they'd attended a couple of parties. Teague tried it on when Gillian was 'away with the fairies' and feeling happy and elated, but she'd left him in no doubt that she was not attracted to him. A swing of her handbag into his groin when leaving the party, and looks that could kill, meant Teague didn't need to waste his time trying to seduce Gillian Finch, even if he thought he was God's gift to women.

Gillian Finch had a position at Teesport, a busy dock one mile from the mouth of the Tees. The port handled over five thousand vessels a year – everything from ferries to heavy freight containers. It suited her skills – social and intellectual, and after all she had been well educated. She was PA to the Director of Marine Operations for HBF Shipping. Not too demanding, as long as she kept her boss,

Mr. Sewell, happy. Gillian had been working there for eighteen months and had made a few friends, one of whom was called Steve Attridge. And Attridge, a contract plumber at Teesport, was a close pal of Dick Ashby. But Dick Ashby was still missing.

***

When Tommy had finished his meal, and sipped the last of his drink, he asked for the bill. It was clear that Maria Dawson and her East European dinner partner were closing their discussion – a small dessert followed by an espresso for each of them signalled the end of the meal. Tommy had recorded most of their discussion and taken a dozen shots from his mini camera. A glance into his calfskin wallet revealed two £20 notes, enough to cover his small but tasty sirloin steak, with a small pile of railway sleeper chips and refried beans. Not a blow-out, but adequate enough after his earlier scrambled eggs. He'd taken his time eating; no need to rush. He was sparrow-hawking his prey.

And all the time he watched the couple, he felt again that he'd seen Mrs. Dawson somewhere before. He replayed visits to his regular haunts . . . the supermarket, W. H. Smith, the local Shell fuel station, the Post Office . . . but no, he couldn't place her. Never mind, it wasn't important right there and then. It would come to him – probably at the most unlikely moment – like cleaning his teeth or boiling the kettle.

Dawson and Mr. X, as Tommy dubbed him, left the table. Tommy noticed that he paid the bill with a credit card. Heading for the bar, Mr X ordered drinks whilst Maria Dawson went to the Ladies. Tommy had to be wary here. Sitting close by in the restaurant was one thing, being too close in the bar was another. He had an option now – wait for them outside in his car, or try to blend in with the dozen or so drinkers that gently buzzed with conversation in the Captain Cook bar. He had enough to go on – to give

Paul Dawson a report, but he needed to see how the evening ended. How well did these two know each other? Tommy was getting mixed messages about their friendship.

Tommy went for the safe option. He ambled out to his Golf, unlocked it and eased into the driver's seat. This was the bit that he didn't enjoy. Waiting – just damn well waiting. Unable to read the newspaper or a paperback in case he missed something, he simply had to keep his eyes on the front door of the hotel, his camera on the passenger seat. But Tommy had the ability to flip between reading a page and pinpointing his target. On his lap he had The Phone Book for Teesside, kept under his front seat. Tommy's eyes scanned the listings under A, his finger hovering over the names beginning AT then down to ATT. There it was Attridge, S. 37, Leeds Road, Middlesbrough. He did the same for Nicky Barlay. Bingo! 49, The Crescent, South Bank. Only one entry each for those two names. During his phone book scanning he'd looked at the front of The Seaview six times. Nothing of any interest, three couples had left the hotel, two individuals had entered. The sky was now becoming darker, street lamps twinkling like Christmas tree fairy lights as a gentle fret began to swirl in from the North Sea. Tommy switched on a LED mini-torch he kept in the car.

He had just entered both telephone numbers into his smart-phone when he flicked to the pink coloured pages of the classified directory. T brought up Taxis. There were 21 listed. The second one was Barlay Taxis. A small block advert showed his office landline number and the offer of 'a reliable service at competitive prices.' There was a mobile number, too. How useful, thought Tommy. After the number was added to his phone Contacts list, Tommy turned off the light.

It was 9.55 pm when Tommy spotted Maria and her dinner partner, the hotel car park well illuminated by the high perimeter lamp posts. They walked down the hotel steps together, Mr. X carrying a medium sized, dark suitcase that he placed into the boot of the MX5. A pair of night vision binoculars helped Tommy see a tag on the suitcase handle. He wondered what was on it? After another cheek-to-cheek brush, Maria got into her Mazda sports car, reversed out of the space and drove towards the OUT sign of the car park without looking back.

The East European watched her until she'd disappeared from view.

***

The cellar was dank. An old 25W bulb tried its best to illuminate the enclosed space, and his thumping headache didn't help. The metal door in the middle of one wall was moist, light reflecting off the cold surface. There was a rickety wooden bed against one wall with a portable toilet in one corner. An excuse for a table sat in the centre of the room, a three-legged stool his only seat. How long could anyone live in a place like this?

Cold. Hungry. Stale body odour. A dark place.

He was tired. With tiredness grew the sense of confusion about time. How long had he been here? Feeling his left wrist, he realised his wristwatch wasn't there. Had it been removed? Had he lost it? What day was it?

Sitting on the edge of the bed, he ran his fingers through his matted hair. Trying hard to recall how he'd got here, he felt knitted strands of brown hair coagulated together, maybe with dried blood. He remembered the car – it was travelling too fast. The double bend sign had been blown down in the hurricane across the moors so there hadn't been any warning.

A pile of old sacks and disused domestic machinery, including a Singer sewing machine and two ancient vacuum cleaners, were strewn along the skirting board opposite the bed. Once or twice the tiny glow of two red eyes indicated his only friend was a rat, scuttling along between the detritus. What the hell did it feed on?

Was this how prisoners in solitary confinement felt? He

recalled the film *Papillon,* where the character, played by Steve McQueen, escapes several times from a penal colony in French Guyana and every time he's recaptured, he's put into a cell on his own, fed on bread and water. But he never gives up on the hope that one day he'll escape.

But how could he get out of this God forsaken place? The small flap at the bottom of the metal door was opened three times on a regular basis coinciding with meal times. Breakfast, lunch and evening meal – that's what it was. He could often hear footsteps on the stone steps that led down to the metal door. But sometimes he'd wake to see a cardboard plate already there, and a bottle of spring water that had rolled under his bed. The flap was unbolted from the outside and a cardboard plate of food and bottle of water was quickly pushed through the foot square gap. A plastic knife, fork and spoon in a sealed cellophane sleeve came with each delivery, but weren't always needed.

After each meal he threw the white cutlery into a galvanised bucket at the end of the bed. Three forks a day. The total number of forks divided by three. Getting off the bed he dipped into the bucket, feeling only for the pronged cutlery. He began to count . . . twelve forks. He'd been in the cellar for four days. It seemed so much longer.

And the first meal of the day was always porridge, the ready-made kind where you poured hot water into the plastic tub and stirred. This morning he'd pulled a paintbrush bristle from between his teeth after his first mouthful. Was his captor decorating? Perhaps painting the kitchen? Except that it wasn't a paintbrush bristle.

It was a rat's whisker.

***

"A favour? What kind of favour?" Joe Blackwell was taking an early call from Tommy on his hands-free phone. Tommy explained that he'd been working on a case at The Seaview Hotel the night before. Details were kept brief, but Tommy hoped Joe would help. "You want me to divulge hotel confidences by giving you information on a guy who looked like an East European?" Tommy swallowed and gave Joe the first name, the one that Maria had used. A few seconds passed. "Well, I'm not making any promises but it so happens that I do know the manager there. A woman called Libby Barr. Leave it with me, Tom. No promises, mind!" Tommy thanked Joe and ended the call.

If Tommy could get the guy's surname it would help complete his first report to Paul Dawson about Maria. He had three good photos and a 200 words transcript of their conversation at dinner. And although Tommy was not one for wanting to get overly involved in any of his cases, some of the discussion over their haute cuisine was interesting. She called her dinner guest Ivo. Hell, how many Ivo's were staying at The Seaview Hotel last night?

Tommy always gave the facts. It was up to his clients if they wanted to interpret his report. Of course, he would always answer any queries, but he made a point of stating clearly what he'd seen and heard. In this case, at least so far, Tommy couldn't be certain how far Paul Dawson might want to take this matter. Tommy was well aware that if Paul confronted his wife after one report if would be the end of the Dawson case. So sometimes he would add a rider to the effect that further surveillance would (in all probability) result in more evidence, whatever that form of evidence may take. He had developed the reporting skills to help a client to 'extend' their need for ThomArch Investigations.

The dark coloured suitcase was mentioned in Tommy's report. He had no idea what was in it. Suffice to say, Ivo had lifted the luggage into the Mazda boot with two hands suggesting it was fairly heavy. Ivo hadn't entered the restaurant with the case, so it was a fair assumption that he was a resident at the hotel, at least for one night. Tommy could have taken a chance and phoned the hotel himself, make something up about a 'friend' who was staying there, but he didn't have enough to go on. And hotels these days were getting much stricter with confidentiality. There was a time when Tommy had waltzed into The Swallow Hotel in Stockton and asked about a woman's husband that he'd been trailing. The young, naïve receptionist gave him name, address and the fact that he'd paid his bill in cash!

Tommy had almost finished writing his first report for Paul Dawson, and three clear photographs were in an envelope - one of Maria entering the hotel and two of the happy couple at the dining table. Wondering how long Joe would be in returning with the information on Ivo, Tommy picked up his Garmin satnav and entered two addresses. 37, Leeds Road and 49, The Crescent. Messrs. Attridge and Barlay. He was planning a visit, and sometimes it helped if he knew the kind of place some people lived. Big house, small house, detached, semi-detached, terraced. Nice garden, untidy garden. Gates, no gates. Parking on the drive, parking on the street. The kind of area pointed to the type of person who lived there. But Tommy didn't jump to conclusions. 'Books' and 'covers' he often reminded himself.

If Dave Teague's comments were correct, and Steve Attridge and Nicky Barlay were buddies with Dick Ashby, then Ashby could be sleeping in a spare bedroom, or on a sofa. Some surveillance was very likely if Ashby hadn't turned up in the next 24 hours. Tommy didn't know if these two guys were married or single – another reason to spend some time in Leeds Road and The Crescent. Tommy had just made himself a mug of coffee when Joe Blackwell's number showed on his mobile screen.

"Hi Joe. What news?" Tommy looked out of the window as he leant over the kitchen worktop.

"The things I do for you! Listen. There was nobody called Ivo staying at The Seaview last night. In fact, nobody with a foreign sounding name at all." 'Sod it,' thought Tommy. "However, a room has been booked for next Tuesday night in the name of Nejc Kodric. That's N-E-J-C space K-O-D-R-I-C. Arrival time estimated as five pm. A Lithuanian from Vilnius. Thought you'd find that interesting." Tommy thanked Joe and ended the call.

Nobody named Ivo staying at the hotel? Bang went Tommy's theory. So how did Ivo get to his meeting with Maria? Car, taxi, a lift from a friend? And a guy called Kodric? Tommy's phone rang. It was Joe again.

"Tommy. Libby Barr has just called me. After my enquiry she happened to take a look at the rear car park CCTV footage from yesterday." Rear car park? Tommy didn't know there was another car park. "A Skoda with foreign number plates pulled into the car park, normally used by staff only, at 6.53 pm. A guy can be seen getting out and lifting a suitcase from the boot, apparently." As this sunk in, Joe continued. "Thing is, the car is still there this morning. The CCTV at the front of the hotel, however, was out of order."

***

Paul Dawson had received his PO Box number six days after his on-line application. The collection point in the Cleveland Centre was ideal. He'd visit it whenever Tommy texted him to let him know there was a package waiting for him. Renting the box number for six months, he was uncertain as to how long Tommy's PI activity would last but he could renew it if needed. Paul was expectant, and his heart would palpitate occasionally during his library duties, wondering what Tommy had discovered. Twice this week Paul had made a fundamental mistake in his job. Misclassifying a new batch of books of which there were only six, and sending a cancellation order to the book wholesalers, Gardners, when it ought to have been a confirmation. He knew he had to concentrate more, but his mind drifted.

The conversation between Paul and his wife had grown ugly when she'd arrived home on the Tuesday night around a quarter to midnight. She hadn't been anywhere near drunk, didn't smell of cigarette smoke and answered his questions – to a degree. Getting undressed as she spoke,

Maria casually told her husband that she'd met with two friends, Becky and Rachel, at a hotel on Marske seafront for a light meal and drinks. She paid for her own food with cash but Maria said that Becky took the receipt. Maria claimed that she'd lost track of time and was careful driving home, so drove slowly. Roadworks on the road from Marske to Eston and a broken - down lorry had also delayed her return trip. They argued, but when Paul realised that he was getting nowhere he gave in.

Two weeks previously Maria had put fresh sheets on a single bed in another bedroom and that Tuesday night was when she told Paul she was going to sleep on her own, claiming to have an awful headache and his occasional snoring kept her awake. Being tired, she needed her sleep so that was the start of separate bedrooms. Not every night, but two or three times a week. Paul meekly accepted it.

A text from Tommy signalled that a package was available to collect at his PO box. Inside the brown A4 envelope were a stapled, two pages report and three large matte photos. As usual, Paul parked his yellow Ford Focus around the back of the library building in his allocated space. He'd allowed himself extra time that morning and sat in the car reading the account of what Tommy had seen on Maria's visit to The Seaview after he'd looked at the photos. He scrutinised the images. Who was this man? Why did she meet with him at a mediocre hotel in a place like Marske? And what was in the suitcase. W*here* was the suitcase? Still in the MX-5 boot? Paul would have to have it out with Maria as soon as she got in from the travel agent. Challenge her. Ask her to open the car boot.

***

Tommy watched the front of 37, Leeds Road as he sat across the road on the cold, narrow stainless - steel bus shelter seat. Four different buses passed at the stop at regular intervals but he kept scanning his newspaper. He wasn't going anywhere. It was almost 5.30 pm as a white van with *Steve Attridge Your Friendly Plumber* on the side pulled onto the short driveway, number plate SA 1234. A mobile phone number was shown below his details and underneath it read *Hydrostatic Operative Par Excellence* in smaller, green letters. What the hell is a 'hydrostatic operative' wondered Tommy. Was it the same as a plumber, or just a fancy title to get the public's attention?

Just as Attridge opened the van door an articulated lorry slowly drove past. Tommy had put his paper down ready to take a photo of Attridge but by the time the rear of the vehicle had cleared the front of the house Attridge had disappeared inside. There were no obvious signs of a wife or partner, no extra car on the drive, but Tommy would make a phone call later, ask for Mrs. Attridge and pretend to be from a supermarket. He'd tell her that she'd won a prize in a monthly draw. But if Attridge was single, Tommy would make some excuse and ring off. Conversely, if Mrs. Attridge did exist he'd feed her some line about calling at the supermarket desk to claim a voucher for £50 once she'd answered some questions about herself. Did she have any children? What hobbies did she and her husband enjoy? Their favourite family holiday destinations . . .

It all helped Tommy to build up a profile of those in which he was interested. Harmless enough, he felt. As Tommy waited for another half an hour – without any sign of comings or goings – the male occupant of 37, Leeds Road was cleaning and sharpening his tools. One of his favourite items were his tungsten-carbide cutters that could slice through a tough copper pipe like a cut throat razor through fudge. When he used his cutters, they gave him a feeling of satisfaction. Real satisfaction.

When Tommy's backside was almost numb, he eased off the smooth bench, stretched, and casually walked around the corner to his Golf. Placing his Nikon camera into the passenger foot-well, he entered an address, 49, The Crescent, South Bank, into his sat-nav. It was time to go pay Nicky Barlay a visit. This would be a ditto surveillance exercise. And if Dave Teague was right, could one of these two be sheltering Dick Ashby? Tommy would get as much basic information as he could before his visit to The Blue Umbrella.

He knew that Gordon Ashby would be asking questions again very soon and ThomArch Investigations had to provide some answers.

***

The Teesside Gazette headline was attention grabbing.

MAN'S BODY FOUND IN CAR BOOT

The body of a man has been found inside the boot of a Skoda Fabia parked in the staff car park at the rear of the Seaview Hotel in Marske-on-Sea after the hotel manager reported a slight odour coming from the vehicle. Police, having had to force entry into the boot, have identified him as Ivo Stavinsky, an Estonian from Tallinn. Mr. Stavinsky was not staying at the hotel, but police say a CCTV camera at reception shows him entering the hotel last Tuesday evening at 8.04 pm.

He was carrying a small, dark coloured suitcase when he entered the hotel and Middlesbrough Operational Crime Team would ask any member of the public who think they may have seen this man, or have any information on the suitcase, to contact them on 101 quoting event number 487332.

What the police didn't tell the Gazette reporter was that Stavinsky's left ear was missing, cleanly sliced off with a sharp instrument. Neither did they state that his car keys had not been found. Stavinsky's wallet was missing but his passport was found inside the unlocked glove compartment of the Skoda. Contact with ports around the UK quickly showed that Stavinsky had driven off a DFDS ferry at Newcastle coming from Amsterdam the day before he'd been seen on CCTV at the hotel. His black car was clearly seen on the footage of vehicles driving from the roll on – roll off and heading westward, probably for the A19 southbound. That could easily be confirmed from traffic cameras on this major road.

Police sniffer dogs had been inside the Skoda, but there were no signs of any drugs. In fact, the car was remarkably clean. No items in the door pockets, no sat-nav, no tools – not even a torch. The boot, apart from the ear-less Estonian, only contained a red, warning triangle and a set of light bulbs, plus a high visibility slip-on jacket.

DCI Jim Adamson was involved with the case, and, as usual, was determined to solve it. Jim Adamson sat in his office and looked at the credit card details taken from the hand-held, hotel restaurant payment machine.

BANK OF ESTONIA
THE SEAVIEW HOTEL –
BOUNTY RESTAURANT
FOOD   £35.58
DEBIT CARD NO. **** **** **** 1211

But for some reason Georgio the head waiter, who'd been helpful with the questions from the DCI, couldn't quite recall what Mr. Stavinsky's partner looked like. He'd told Adamson that he was flustered that evening; something to do with over-booking tables and an irate customer – some military chap.

What neither Tommy nor Adamson knew was that Stavinsky had put his suitcase on top of the cistern in one of four toilet cubicles in the hotel, then turned the ENGAGED dial from the outside using a coin. A handy place to leave it while he met with Maria Dawson.

***

Maria Dawson had been involved in numerical matters

since she was a little girl. Her ability to complete a Rubic's cube from a haphazard configuration took an average of forty seconds. Dr John Carlos Baez, a Professor of Mathematics in California was her favourite author. Maria's interest about quantum gravity mechanisms and general relativity was almost a driving force for her brain. Wasn't this how she had met her husband after all, seeking a book on mathematics in the Middlesbrough library?

One of her many web visits had been to www.numerology.com. The site had issues relating to the letters of a name. Apparently, every letter has a meaning - the first letter of your name is the 'Cornerstone' letter and relates to your approach to life, it's ups and downs. The last letter is the 'Capstone' letter – it demonstrates your ability to see things through to the end. Maria had established some facts about her own name. It turned out she was a workaholic, a high energy workhorse that doesn't need much sleep, her own person, ambitious and freethinking. She was pleased with that.

One of Maria's favourite numbers was 7. She realised that there were so many things related to this number. When she was seven years old, she'd made a list. Seven days in a week, seven colours of the rainbow, hills of Rome, the seas of our planet, the continents and deadly sins. James Bond was 007, a popular drink was 7Up, you got seven years bad luck for breaking a mirror, the spots on the opposite faces of a dice added up to 7 and there are seven letters in Roman numerals. Maria wasn't sure if she believed in seventh heaven, or Shakespeare's seven ages of man, had never seen the film *Seven Brides for Seven Brothers,* but she knew that the Russian country access code for international dialling was 7.

Before she was ten years of age Maria had been fascinated by Greek architecture following a week's holiday to Athens with her parents. There seemed to be a constant relationship between the height and width of pillars that supported buildings such as the Parthenon. When she asked her maths teacher about it, Maria got little response. Persevering, she got a book from the school library and discovered the 'Golden Ratio.' It entranced her. She began to look at things like picture frames and doorways in a different light. It wasn't just something with a width and height, but a *specific* width and height. And as a ratio the figure is always 1.618. Mathematicians call it Phi. And when it came to Pi, the ratio between the radius and the circumference of a circle, Maria could quote it to eleven decimal places.

There was no doubt about it, Maria Dawson loved numbers.

***

The pathologist's report on Ivo Stavinsky revealed that he'd been asphyxiated. The thin, purple line around his neck had been made with a 5mm cord. Several white fibres remained embedded in the epidermis when the pathologist began his examination. On the inner right forearm, the numbers 01123 had been carved with a sharp instrument.

***

Tommy's vigil in South Bank had proven fruitless. He'd parked the Golf within fifty yards of 49, The Crescent, but had not seen anybody enter or leave the property. Why wasn't he surprised? Nicky Barlay owned and ran a taxi firm. Taxi drivers were busy people, but with a dip in business for many of them, they had to put the hours in to make a profit. Tommy wasn't sure how many taxis Barlay owned, but he could soon find out. A phone call made to Barlay from 'the local council Hackney Carriage licensing' department would give him the answer.

A good source for a steady income was contract work. School runs, airport collections, care home pick - ups . . . they all added up. And one thing Nicky Barlay liked was meeting people. He often told himself that when he retired, he'd put all of his experiences down on paper, convinced he could easily fill 300 pages of a paperback book.

There were some lovely people, like old Mrs. Wiggington. She visited her husband, Ralph, at the Hillside Nursing Home every day for a year. Poor old devil, he had Parkinson's and dementia and she couldn't care for him at home. Mrs. Wigginton would tell Barlay all about each visit on the way home. She was very hard of hearing so it was usually a one - way conversation. When Barlay asked her a question she'd give him the reply to something else.

"Well, he seemed a little better today. Perked up a bit, some colour in his cheeks. Couldn't remember what he had for breakfast . . . was worried about his tomatoes in the greenhouse. He hasn't grown any for years."

"So, what else did he say to you? Anything interesting? Is the food OK?"

"About half past ten, I think."

And that was how the twenty minutes trip back to her semi-detached bungalow went. Barlay didn't mind. She was one of those old ladies who had aged gracefully and kept herself smart. He'd once asked her what she did for a living and she surprised him by saying she'd been a model. After that she'd joined British Airways as a stewardess on long haul flights to the Far East and Australia, then, to cap it all, she married the captain of one of the regular scheduled runs from Heathrow to Sydney. Her husband was a fine upstanding, handsome man who'd won an Olympic silver medal in sailing. Nicky Barlay realised that her husband, Captain Ralph Wigginton, was now decaying in a private nursing home. Next stop would be a flight higher than the 35,000 feet he was used to.

Barlay hated collecting children, but it helped pay the mortgage. Pick - ups from big country houses with long drives and fields all around were scenic, but he often had to restrain himself when some snotty-nosed kid from a posh background argued the toss about the importance of going to a university like Oxford or Cambridge, or why the Conservatives were the only political party capable of running the country. He amused himself by conjuring up an image of the kid being thrashed by Barlay using a good, strong birch and seeing red welts across his buttocks. But when mummy or daddy were paying him good money to take the brat to the local academy who was he to worry? Then there was the work at Teesport.

Freddie Sewell, the Director of Marine Operations at Teesport was a likeable character and Gillian Finch was content working for him. She'd kept his appointments, organised things, and kept his diary on a tight schedule. Gillian always had biscuits for him with his tea at 11.00 am and 3.00 pm prompt. Fresh, crisp Rington's ones, from an airtight tin. But a year before Gillian Finch had started to work for Sewell, Nicky Barlay got the contract for collecting overseas visitors from either Newcastle International or Durham Tees Valley airport. It wasn't regular work. The average month would involve two or three round trips, sometimes two a week, but perhaps only once a fortnight. Although Barlay owned three taxis, he always made certain that he did the airport runs. He enjoyed the semi-business banter, kept at a discreet level of course, and over the course of the last two and a half years he'd got to know a few clients quite well.

The men in dark suits didn't usually stay overnight – an early pick up and late departure meant that their business was often concluded in the working day. However, some of Barlay's clients booked into a hotel more often than not, from which they'd be collected the following morning for a 'red eye' flight to their destination. Newcastle or Durham Tees Valley (DTV) to Amsterdam was a popular route. From Amsterdam you could fly to anywhere in the world. Foreign customers were keen to negotiate a good deal for shipping goods into the UK and Teesport suited them perfectly. The more business Sewell generated, the higher his annual bonus. His hobby was his two classic cars - a Facel Vega HK500 in pearl silver with wire wheels, the other a 1954 2.4 litre Jaguar in British Racing Green.

***

After the recent torrential thunderstorm, the cellar was more damp than usual, the walls had an almost silvery lustre. The smell coming from the portable toilet hit his nose each time the lid was lifted, which wasn't often. When he hugged himself for warmth, he could feel his ribs more than the day before. Hell. Someone must be looking for him! People don't just vanish, do they? Or, when he thought about it, they did. Maddie McCann, Suzie Lamplugh, the girl from York whose name he couldn't recall. Claudia somebody. All missing. But soon somebody would come. There'd be a knock on the door as the lock was turned and the bolts slid open. Daylight might flood the room, a hot drink in a mug would be handed to him, and a proper meal like a McDonald's double cheeseburger with French fries set before him.

He heard a sound, the familiar unlocking of a door, probably at the top of the stone steps. There was that clink again, maybe a loose, steel heel tip on a boot or shoe? Perhaps a key ring? By the time he'd got off the musty bed, the cardboard plate, plastic cutlery and bottled water had been thrust through the flap and quickly closed again.

How was anyone supposed exist on a thin pizza and spring water?

***

Paul had heard the travel news and various roadworks, including the one on the road to Marske, were causing mayhem. They'd be there for at least another three weeks. A large lorry that had its engine fire put out last Tuesday evening was also still a problem but police were making arrangements for a heavy crane to lift it clear of the main road. What was of more concern was the reports filtering into the press and TV news of the body found in the car boot at the same hotel where Maria said she'd 'met her two girlfriends.'

She'd told Paul about the roadworks and a broken - down vehicle . . . had he doubted her reasons for getting home late? Clearly, he now knew of her meeting with a man called Ivo from Tommy's report. Paul recalled he had met the two girls, Becky and Rachel, at a friend's wedding about six months previously. They seemed nice from what he could remember about them. He wondered if Maria had gone on to meet her girlfriends later if Tommy Archer didn't follow her? But the contents of the envelope from Tommy Archer had stared him in the face – report and photos. Paul couldn't doubt what he'd read and seen. He had a dilemma - one he'd wrestled with since that first report. When Maria had returned home that night and she gave off a hint of arrogance, Paul was close to harming her; maybe a hand on her throat until she told him where she'd been? He wasn't a violent man by nature but occasionally he'd be edging close to the end of the 'seething scale.' For the past couple of days, he'd weighed up the pros and cons of having it out with his wife. But he'd be laying his cards on the table if he confronted her with Tommy's report – he would lose his current advantage - that of knowing what she had been up to.

No, after some reflection, Paul was going to let things ride for now. But there was a matter of significant importance. The murder at The Seaview Hotel of the man that his wife had gone to meet – have dinner with. The man called Ivo who gave her a suitcase.

Maria knew this man, Paul decided, and he was surprised that nobody had identified Maria from last Tuesday evening in the Bounty restaurant. No detectives had been ringing their front door bell. No phone calls asking to speak to Mrs. Maria Dawson. Was it because she'd tied her hair up into a ponytail? She sometimes wore it like that, but he could not recall if she had it in that style when she'd left home. One of the photos that Tommy had taken showed his wife wearing tortoiseshell framed spectacles. Maria seldom wore them; they were for reading small print. Had she just been reading something that Ivo had shown her?

When Paul had asked Maria for a comment on the murder enquiry all she would say was how awful it was and, 'no, she could not recall seeing the guy in the hotel that evening.' It was evident to Paul that she really didn't want to discuss the matter. And where was the damned suitcase? Paul backed down from a confrontation. He had told Maria that he wanted to check the spare tyre in the boot of the Mazda in case it needed air in it. When he first mentioned it, she said it was OK, having had it checked at the local Shell station only last week. He wasn't born yesterday! Checked my foot! *He would look*, take the suitcase out of the boot, open it in front of his wife and challenge her to explain herself.

On the evening after Paul had read Tommy's report, and when he knew Maria was asleep in the other bedroom, he crept downstairs and went into the garage as quietly as he could. He unlocked the boot. It was empty except for the spare wheel and a jack.

***

DCI Jim Adamson and his team had questioned several diners and hotel guests. He got conflicting reports of what they had seen last Tuesday at the hotel. He was used to this. Comments varied on the victim's dining partner. Height ranged between 4' 10" to 5' 8", hair colour from strawberry blonde to platinum, eye colour was a waste of time - he felt most guessed, and the clothing description was like listening to somebody reading the index of a John Lewis catalogue. The Seaview receptionist was being trained, but not, apparently, to observe.

The police still hadn't found the car keys or wallet, but Adamson's attention turned to the numbers cut into Stavinsky's arm. 01123. Was it a dialling code? Not in the UK it wasn't. No telephone codes began 0112 or 01223. The nearest code was Leeds – 0113. One household company sold a Premium Classic interior acrylic latex semi-gloss paint, product code 01123. A mineral website called *Minerain* was selling chunks of baryte crystals weighing about half a kilogram in honey yellow known as Baryte M 01123. LT 01123 was the post code for the town centre in Vilnius, Lithuania. 01123 came up as editions of a couple of obscure journals and a few other apparently unrelated items.

Adamson wasn't going to be beaten. That number was relevant, but for now he didn't know why. For the time being unless Ivo Stavinsky was an Estonian decorator who subscribed to some odd journal, had a property in Vilnius and collected mineral stones for a hobby, Jim Adamson was stumped. And as Adamson, sitting at his desk, looked at the teeth marks on the end of his 2H Cumberland pencil, Tommy Archer's phone was ringing. Tommy saw Joe Blackwell's name on the screen.

"Hi Joe!" said Tommy, hoping for some interesting news.

"Tommy, Libby Barr has just called me. Remember I told you that a man called Nejc Kodric had booked into the Seaview for this coming Tuesday night, 12 July. Well, he's cancelled the room. I'd asked one of our hotel chain managers to let me know of any reservations made by anyone with a foreign sounding name. Now, the interesting thing is that the same guy is booked into one of the other Northcliffe hotels - The Queen's Head in Yarm." Tommy listened intently.

"Bloody heck! Do you think we should let the police know?" Tommy asked.

"No! Why? Just because somebody who sounds like an expensive footballer has booked into one of my hotels doesn't mean we need to tell the fuzz!" On reflection, Tommy quickly agreed. "What's that going to do for our reputation?"

"Yes, you're right. OK, well thanks for letting me know. You're a pal. Cheers, Joe." Tommy sipped his black coffee as he glanced at the kitchen clock. He thought about this Ned guy, he'd call him that from now on, and wondered if he had anything to do with Stavinsky? It was unlikely. The north east was full of east Europeans who worked and lived in the area. You only had to spend ten minutes in a local budget supermarket to know that a good few customers came from across the English Channel and he didn't mean French or German. No, he wasn't going to make assumptions.

Tommy closed the folder on Dick Ashby that he'd been scrutinising again, knowing he needed to get some more answers for his father, Gordon. His brief surveillance of Steve Attridge and Nick Barlay hadn't resulted in much. Tommy had discovered that the taxi firm owned three cabs, a fact volunteered by a rival taxi driver in Middlesbrough. All Mercedes Benz, all black and all fitted with a removable roof sign, one that could be securely clipped on but taken off in under twenty seconds. One driver had stated that Barlay lived alone – his wife having gone off with the window cleaner, Harry Nevin. She was living with him in Redcar. Thankfully, Barlay and his wife didn't have any children.

There were times during Tommy's work when he was never sure about fact from rumour. But his PI nose was pretty good at filtering those things out and he could tell from the way that somebody gave him snippets of information whether it was God's own truth or pure fantasy. Tommy had phoned the landline number in the Barlay directory advert to discover that it belonged to an office where a girl named Mavis handled enquiries. The office was a downstairs poky room on the corner of Tees Street and River Lane in Grangetown. However, it was equipped with all the radio communications kit necessary for Mavis to take incoming calls and make requests to Barlay and the two other taxi drivers to take 'John Doe' from A to B. There was a kettle, a compact fridge, and a biscuit tin that was never empty. One problem with Mavis was that she wasn't losing any weight and her new resolution to shed a stone or two just wasn't working. Still, her piggy eyes were OK – no glasses needed, and her hearing wasn't affected by the fat around her thick neck and her chubby earlobes. Her other problem was that she liked to chatter. When Tommy first called the office number he asked if he was speaking to Mary. Of course, Mavis being Mavis replied 'no' and told him her name outright. Not 'Who's calling . . . who wants to know . . . how can I help?'

If Tommy was careful, and used some of his charm, he could find out a few things from Mavis.

***

If there was one thing that Mark Finch enjoyed it was a good bottle of red wine. He'd once been on a 'learn about wine' week-end, courtesy of *The Daily Telegraph*, that had lightened his wallet by £400 or thereabouts. Getting to know about grape varieties, soil types, benefits of southern slopes and methods of cultivation, not to mention actual wine tasting, Finch thought he was the county's foremost expert. He could discuss the optimal growing conditions, tell a Californian red from a South African red, and bore most regulars silly down at the Frog and Ferret.

Finch had been convinced by an article in *The Times* that investment in fine wines was an increasingly viable method of adding to a personal income portfolio. Bordeaux were a particularly good buy. As he'd just made a handsome profit on one of his housing deal's he decided to take the plunge and invest in a few bottles of a decent red. A week later one of London's biggest wine dealers, Corney & Barrow, delivered fifty cases of Sassicia Teuta San Guido and two burly men wearing brown leather aprons had carried the wine down the stone steps into the largest of the three cellars at The Old Manor House in Pomfreton. The middle - sized cellar was used for storage whilst the smallest one had little in it. The bottles were carefully unpacked and laid out, all 600 of them placed into wooden racks like new born babies into an incubator. At £535 per case, Finch convinced himself he had a good deal with the Italian red.

Now the bottles had a layer of dust on them, a few cobwebs wafting as he walked past, and every day his 'treasure' was growing in value. Finch was sometimes tempted to open a bottle or two, but at £8 a glass he knew he was better off buying his quaffing supplies from The Grape House, a reliable vintner in Billingham. But one problem Mark Finch had was that he bragged too much, especially after a few drinks down at the local. Roger the landlord didn't mind, Finch kept the till ringing over the course of an average week, but one evening Gordon Ashby was having a quiet half of cider on the way home after a particularly hectic day in the estate agents in Yarm when Finch dropped in. Tossing his Lexus leather car key fob onto the bar, Finch ordered a Jura whisky, no ice, with Harrogate Spring Water in equal measure.

"Busy day, Gordon?" asked Finch with no sincerity in his voice. Ashby nodded and posted a reply that gave nothing away. Roger passed Finch his glass and Finch took in the bouquet before sipping the amber liquid. Gordon Ashby, albeit with a sense of humour, was unfolding *The Times* and wasn't in the mood for the kind of idle chatter on which Finch seemed to thrive. "Yes, it's been all go for me, too." Ashby didn't take the bait; his pen suggested he was going to do the crossword, or perhaps the sudoku.

Their relationship went sour one evening a few weeks back when Gordon Ashby asked Finch if he was up for a challenge. He'd quietly said to Finch, who was sitting on a bar stool next to him, that he was impressed with his expertise in wine. He wondered if he wanted a small wager on being able to identify three red wines? Finch agreed on the £20 bet, but instantly wondered if he'd done the right thing. Ashby had purchased a bottle each of a Chilean Merlot, a French Bordeaux and an Italian Sangiovese and had asked Roger to be his accomplice in the challenge. The idea was simple. Roger would pour a glass of each red wine hidden from view and present all three to Finch at the bar, each set upon a drink's mat with A, B and C clearly marked on them – and this *before* Finch had taken his Jura.

Ashby wrote the names of all three wines against the three letters on the back of one of his business cards and laid it on the bar, wines listed face down. He smiled as he did so. On opening his wallet, he also placed a crisp £20 note on top of the card, Finch placing one on top to match. He had nosed the aroma of each wine, swirled it around the glass, taken a delicate sip and swallowed slowly. Minutes passed and the owner of The Old Manor House had to make a decision . . . a dozen or so customers went quiet that evening, only the tick of the old wall clock salvaged from Pomfreton station breaking the silence. Roger acted as referee and waited . . . they had all waited. Finch pontificated, then had pointed to each half empty glass and gave his decision. He was wrong! His three answers were *all wrong*! Finch had left the bar with the sniggers of some regulars ringing in his ears, his Jura and water left untouched. His £20 bet lost.

And that was how the uneasy relationship between them really began. After that episode Mark Finch decided he wasn't going to let this lie. He would get his revenge on the smart-ass estate agent who had dared to set him the challenge.

Right now, Finch was down in one of his three cellars looking at the line of three hundred bottles that lay on either side, wondering how much his investment had increased in value since he was last down here where the temperature was a fairly constant 7C to 9C. Perfect for his Sassicia wine. And this cellar was the best one. The adjacent cellar was fairly dry with a musty odour. The third one had a narrow downpipe in the corner that needed mending; it was always a little damp in there. The walls often glistened. Still, it was only a cellar.

***

"Hi Tommy, it's Paul. Maria has mentioned that she's going out tomorrow evening with her boss, Alan Clarke. I

know it's short notice, but can you see where she's going? I don't believe her for one second. Same procedure as before. She says she'll be leaving home around six thirty. Thanks. Oh, by the way, please let me know that you've got this message."

Tommy had picked up the voicemail message from his mobile after he'd got out of the shower on a bright Monday morning. Why wasn't Tommy surprised? Going out with her manager? It sounded plausible but unusual, but Paul had never met Alan Clarke. Local news reports had given details on Stavinsky, his description and movements from the Port of Tyne in Newcastle by car, the missing suitcase and still no sign of his wallet or car keys. Nobody had come forward with any significant information, either by telephoning the Middlesbrough Operational Crime Team (MOCT) or direct contact with the police.

Tommy's assumption was that tomorrow evening he'd park up near 89, St. Roseberry Close in good time to tail the Mazda. Tommy texted Paul to let him know he'd received his message and he would proceed as previously. He asked himself why Maria would tell her husband she was meeting Alan Clarke if it wasn't true? Or would she be seeing Becky and Rachel, or either one of them? Paul and Maria had visited Becky on a handful of occasions, but he knew very little about her. He couldn't recall her surname but thought she was a manicurist or hairdresser. He didn't know where Becky or Rachel worked; it had never come up in conversation. Probably on Teesside somewhere. But he had no definite contact information. In any event, if Maria was using them as an excuse, he'd bet a month's income on Maria having primed them anyway.

Perhaps she was seeing another 'friend' that she hadn't seen for ages and wanted a 'girlie' catch up. Or would she be meeting with Ned in Yarm? Tommy slapped himself hard on the neck. He did that from time to time to bring himself back down to earth. 'Slow down!' he told himself. The truth was Tommy *did not know* where Maria was going so why not just follow her and see what happens?

This Ned guy could be staying at The Queen's Head on perfectly legitimate business. In fact, statistically speaking, there was a chance that maybe 10% of all Teesside hotel bookings for any night of the week were made by non-UK residents. Big deal – we live in a cosmopolitan world where blacks and whites, Christians and Muslims, gays and straights and all the rest of them live together in reasonable harmony. And they move around the world, or the world moves around them. So, what was the big deal on a Lithuanian staying in the area for one night?

Later that Monday, Paul had phoned Tommy to let him know that Maria had confirmed that she was meeting with her manager. Apparently, he'd booked a table at a decent restaurant called The Cleveland Bay Horse in Kirklevington for 7.30 pm, and the reason for inviting Maria was that he was entertaining a guy who he had met in Vilnius. Not only that, but he was a travel agent, too. He knew Maria was born in the old Russian capital so it could make sense that her boss wanted her along to oil the wheels of conversation, and maybe as eye candy; her imposing tall figure, steel blue eyes and blonde hair attracted many men.

"I don't really know much about Alan, apart from the fact that he's widely travelled and a bachelor. He's meeting with a travel agent from Lithuania and he wants me along to make the meeting more 'comfortable,' whatever that means." Maria had made her point and Paul didn't debate it; perhaps more of 'he couldn't be bothered to argue.' So, on Tuesday evening, with Tommy parked at the end of the Close, Maria Dawson reversed off her driveway. Adopting his normal strategy, Tommy tailed the red coupe at a safe distance. He hadn't washed the Golf for some time so it blended in with most other vehicles, just an average, dull, medium sized car trundling around Teesside minding its own business. The likelihood of Maria Dawson knowing he was there was zilch. If she looked in her rear - view mirror, chances are it was to check her hair or lipstick.

Tommy was anticipating that he wasn't eating in any

restaurant tonight. This was going to be one of his surveillance jobs that might last two or three hours. Two bananas and a chunky cereal bar in his glove locker would have to do. The Mazda brake lights lit up as Maria slowed and pulled between two, sentry-like, copper beech trees into the wide gravelled car park of The Cleveland Bay Horse. So far, her story was true. Tommy stayed about fifty yards away but could make out two men sitting in an Audi A4. As soon as Maria swung her long legs out of her sports coupe door one of the passengers of the Audi walked across to greet her. A handshake ensued, followed by an introduction to the other man who'd now joined them. Tommy had taken six photos of the two males individually, and the group of three. The number plate of the Audi was also snapped – NT 65 PDY. It was almost half past seven.

After locking the car, they entered the front door past the pots of large, red geraniums and disappeared from view. Despite having decided not to adopt his Bounty restaurant tactic again, Tommy had made his mind up that he'd go in and take a look around, have a soft drink at the bar, and if anybody asked any questions, he was simply checking the place out for a birthday party he was organising. Ask for a brochure, get a business card, appear interested – it usually worked. The Cleveland Bay Horse dining area was separate from the bar with a double glass door. Tommy could see to the table where the trio were sitting, and he got a couple of quickly taken shots using his button camera. He couldn't let Maria see him – with a sharp mind like hers Tommy assumed she was reasonably vigilant, especially as he'd sat near her and Stavinsky at The Seaview.

The photos of her manager and his old friend were going to be clear, and Maria who sat between them looked like the proverbial rose between two thorns. Alan Clarke was smartly dressed, a tad over six feet tall with a mop of thick, blond hair, and wearing spectacles. After Tommy used the Gents, he had bought an orange squash and returned to his car. A stomach growl was soon quenched as he bit off small pieces of his peeled banana. He waited. He had to know what time they came out of the restaurant and his plan was to follow the Audi. No point in trailing the Mazda, Tommy was going to assume Maria went home. No, he'd follow the Audi and find out where it was headed.

Shortly after ten pm the three left the restaurant. Tommy fired up his engine but left the lights off. Waiting, he saw the Audi leave the car park first, followed closely by Maria; the two vehicles in convoy. Expecting Maria to peel off onto the main road back to Eston, Tommy was surprised when she continued to trail the Audi. The cars were half a mile from Yarm when Tommy's Golf lurched to one side, a loud bang coming from the front nearside wheel. 'Sod it!' he shouted as he came to a juddery halt at the side of the dimly lit road. He got out. Looking ahead he saw the Mazda tail lights disappear as he kicked the flat, crumpled tyre with his toe. It was 10.28 pm.

As he waited for the AA to arrive, breakdown included with his insurance cover, Tommy rubbed his eyes with the heels of his hands and wondered how he was going to include this in his report for Paul Dawson? As he opened them, he saw a speeding Mazda MX5 drive past him in the opposite direction. Unsure of the colour of the car in the darkness, and with a dirty rear number plate, he was fairly certain that it was Maria.

Tommy glanced at his Omega. The luminous hands showed 10.49 pm.

***

Maria Dawson had a hobby but not many people could tell her the name of her hobby. She was a collector of dolls. And if anyone asked her if she had a hobby, she was always proud to say she was a plangonologist. Of course, almost every time, she had to explain.

Her father had bought her a doll for Christmas in 1985 when Maria was five. It was a Heubach doll from

Germany made in the late eighteenth century. She adored that doll. Made of bisque porcelain, the face of the little girl was perfect in every way - eyes, nose, mouth . . . just perfect. She named her Josephine. And for most Christmases after that Maria was given a doll. Her collection totalled 21, but many were kept out of sight, each carefully wrapped, in a heavy trunk that was in the loft. Maria wasn't certain, but she estimated her collection was worth around £100,000. Paul was oblivious to this. All he knew was that his wife had a few pot dollies in a box somewhere above the lounge ceiling and he didn't give a fig. He sometimes wondered at her sanity when she mentioned them by name. 'So, what,' he would think, 'it's like giving the furniture names – Thomas the table, Sidney the sideboard, Charles the chair, Stanley the stool, Walter the wardrobe.' Crazy! But there it was.

More recently, Maria had brought home a Russian doll. Seven pieces carved in wood, each one painted, the outer doll was always a woman, she'd told Paul. The woman was dressed in a sarafan – a long and shapeless Russian peasant jumper dress. And when she felt that her husband was interested, she elaborated further. Russian dolls were also known as Matryoshka dolls, the name matryoshka meaning 'little matron' in the Russian language. But they were also called Babushka or Stacking dolls, the name babushka referred to a grandmother or old woman. And since she thought Paul's face suggested he wanted to know more, Maria went on to tell him that the first Russian dolls were manufactured in 1890, the inner ones being male *or* female, and the smallest, inner one was always a baby. But when Maria carried on and began to discuss the history of matryoshka figures, and the size of the largest one at 53.9 cm made in 2003 that consisted of fifty - one pieces with the smallest at 0.3 cm his eyes began to glaze over as he stifled a yawn. At the time there were highlights of an England v Australia test match due on Channel 5 in ten minutes and he didn't want to miss them.

He remembered that she accused him of not being

interested, he countered her disappointment by saying he was, and, in the words of a tennis umpire, ended up at deuce. They never talked about dolls again. But Maria Dawson had rekindled her interest in doll collecting. On television one Sunday evening a few weeks ago, an Antiques Roadshow expert had valued a 1930's Russian doll collection of six pieces at between £10,000 and £15,000. Maria had made her mind up. She was going to start collecting dolls again, and if her husband wasn't interested, he could go take a long walk off the end of Saltburn pier. And before she went to bed that night, in the spare bedroom, Maria caressed a red painted Russian doll that she had recently acquired. She wasn't going to give it a name. Not when she had another 39 sitting under the bed. That would be silly.

***

He couldn't remember the guy's face that well, it was dark after all, but about a year ago he'd had a call from Mavis in the taxi office to pick up a man in Middlesbrough town centre to take him to the David Logan Leisure Centre in Thornaby. Giving the address as McIver Street, Barlay had driven there as quickly as the wet roads would allow. With wipers slapping the windscreen in double time he'd driven along the street twice before seeing a guy sheltering from the rain under a bus shelter. Barlay had eased the window down an inch.

"You call the office? David Logan centre?" he shouted through the gap.

"Where the hell have you been?" snapped the man. "I phoned twenty minutes ago!" Yanking open the back door with enough strength to rip it off the hinges, the wet man had got in, slamming the door shut. Barlay stayed calm, not up for an argument in his taxi that was quickly becoming a Turkish bath. The aircon in the Merc was turned up.

"The David Logan centre, I believe?"

"That's what I told the bloody woman!" Barlay remained calm as he eased the auto gearbox into Drive. He wanted this journey to be over as soon as possible. But as he drove toward Thornaby he thought about how he'd like to take this guy and put his hands around his neck and squeeze so hard that his eyes popped out as if on stalks; squeezed until the little swine apologised for his rant, pressing his thumbs onto his Adam's apple until it came out the other side. "How long is this going to take? I'm missing my body building class, for Christ's sake!"

"Two minutes we'll be there." Barlay impressed himself with his self-discipline. The taxi-meter showed £6.50 as the car pulled up in front of the brightly lit leisure centre.

"There's three quid," shouted the passenger as he jumped out, "you were bloody late!" Three coins were tossed through Barlays open window landing somewhere in the driver's footwell of the taxi. Nicky Barlay didn't enjoy confrontation unless it was necessary, but this guy really had pissed him off. No, he would leave it and tell Mavis he would never pick him up again. He was barred from now on.

And that's how Barlay came to have a nice, gold plated business card holder. When he cleaned the Merc out the following morning there it was, on the back seat. Inside were a Post Office credit card, a Nectar loyalty card and a membership card for the David Logan Leisure Centre, as well as a dozen business cards:

> David Teague
> HighVisibility
> CCTV & Visual Monitoring Specialist
> email: daveteaguecctv@icloud.com
> web site: www.highvisibility.co.uk
> Mobile: 073441 992705

Barlay was certain that his passenger didn't know who he was. How would you recognise someone looking at the back of their head on a wet night in a dimly lit taxi? And sorry, but when the customer phoned the next day to ask Mavis about the golden card holder it was nowhere to be found. Now wasn't that a shame? And Mavis couldn't recall which driver had picked up the customer that evening. She could tell a lie when necessary.

***

Tommy was driving to the local supermarket when he heard the BBC Tees news on his car radio. A body had been found in a hotel room in Yarm. His ears pricked up.

'Police are not disclosing any details of the dead man found this morning at a local hotel. All they can say at this stage is that their enquiries are ongoing. If any member of the public saw anything suspicious in the immediate area of The Queen's Head Hotel near Yarm between ten pm last night, the twelfth of July, and six am this morning the police ask that they call the Middlesbrough Operational Crime Team on 101 quoting event number 488129.'

Who was the dead man? Parking at the supermarket, Tommy realised there were two people who would know - DCI Jim Adamson and Joe Blackwell. Adamson would be on the case right now, and The Queen's Head was one of Joe's Northcliffe group hotels.

Tommy couldn't help but wonder if it was Ncd - Nejc Kodric. Tommy got out his mobile phone and then put it away. What was he doing? Resting his head back he weighed up the situation. He'd written his report for Paul Dawson and included several photos - photos of the group together in the car park and in the restaurant, the Audi A4 with number plate shown, and a couple of close shots of the two men – Alan Clarke and his friend. If the 'friend' of Clarke was the dead man in the hotel, Adamson would be asking questions not only of Maria, but also of Tommy and consequently Paul if he knew that Tommy had been trailing them. Tommy had followed the two cars towards Yarm and it was a fair assumption that they may have been heading to The Queen's Head. But he wasn't certain. Nor was he now totally convinced that the sports car that passed him at 10.49 pm was the Mazda MX-5 belonging to Maria. It was a popular make, after all. But he hadn't asked Paul what time Maria had arrived home last night; Tommy estimated Yarm to Eston as 20 to 23 minutes. Maria ought to have been back between 11.10 and 11.15 pm.

Tommy could phone Joe, sound concerned. That would be OK since Joe had told Tommy about the Kodric hotel booking so there was prior knowledge there. Tell Joe he'd just heard it on the radio news and was 'interested.' Joe wasn't aware of Tommy's specific projects as a PI so he wouldn't ask questions, wouldn't probe. Tommy speed dialled Joe.

"Hello, Tommy. I can't speak now I'm in the middle of something. Call you back. Bye." Tommy picked up a canvas bag and went into the supermarket with a short shopping list in his hand. He wandered down the aisles, putting milk and a few tins of beans into the basket. Coffee and a couple of packets of biscuits, plus a sliced loaf and half a dozen eggs were all ticked off as he walked to an empty check-out.

"Good morning, how are you? Do you need any help with your packing?" The girl behind the desk smiled at him. Tommy shook his head as he stuffed the canvas bag with his purchases and wondered why the check-out staff gave him all this 'how are you today' rubbish. As if they really cared. He paid with a swipe of his credit card. Before he'd got to the big glass sliding doors his mobile started buzzing. Tommy exited the supermarket and tucked himself around the corner in a quiet spot.

"Hi Joe."

"Tommy, I'm guessing that you phoned about the death at the hotel? I couldn't talk before. The police were here."

"I heard the news on the car radio. Was it Nejc Kodric?" Joe hesitated.

"Yes, a nasty business, too. DCI Adamson told me that Kodric was found by the room service maid who had taken a pre-ordered breakfast to his room at 7.30 am. Apparently, he had a five - dot domino pushed into his left eye orbit and a marble octagon the size of a golf ball stuffed down his throat. Exact cause of death is yet to be determined, but he'll have had a grisly time of it. He had a rucksack with him when he checked in but that's disappeared. The room shows little signs of a struggle and the door wasn't forced so . . ."

"Joe, that sounds terrible. I hope it doesn't give the hotel a bad name. Do you know what Kodric looked like?" Was he the man with Clarke and Maria last night, Tommy wondered?

"I asked the hotel receptionist who checked him in. She told me he was short, about five feet, three inches tall with a beard. Why do you ask?" Tommy explained that as a PI, anything like this was always of interest, could give him some insight into a future case he might be handling. Tommy had lied to Joe and it didn't make him feel good, but he couldn't divulge the real reason. He ended the call Joe. Back in his VW Golf Tommy tossed his shopping onto the passenger seat and reached into the rear footwell for his Nikon. He switched it on and reviewed the photos he'd taken the evening before. It had to be him, Kodric, stood next to the tall, blond, bespectacled Alan Clarke as Maria meets them in the car park at The Cleveland Bay Horse - much shorter than her boss, and with a beard like a skein of midnight black knitting wool.

Was Tommy getting himself in too deep? Was it time to get off this case? Before he started the engine, he phoned Paul Dawson, told him the report would be sent today, and asked him one question. 'What time did Maria get home last night?'

"She didn't come home," replied Paul.

***

Steve Attridge, the hydrostatic operative, was working on a project at HBF Shipping. His father, Les, had been on friendly terms with Freddie Sewell before he passed away.

They played golf together at Corndale Golf Club but Paul Attridge dropped down dead at the third hole one Saturday morning. He was only 62. Friends said it was the way he would have wanted to go, but no consolation for those he left behind others thought.

Steve Attridge had been asked by Sewell to check over some major pipework in the warehousing facility, the odd leak having been reported a few months back. Attridge had been in the business for twelve years and managed to get the right pieces of paper to confirm he knew what he was doing. An inspection by the Health and Safety executive was due in two months and Sewell was aware that everything had to be in apple pie order. Not only that, but Sewell was sometimes asked by visitors if they could take a look around HBF Shipping, see the warehousing, the cranes and external storage units. So, it had to be right, and Sewell had also given Attridge scope to check any other aspects of the water supply and to take appropriate action as he felt necessary.

So Attridge got on and did what he did best, supported by coffee that Gillian Finch brought to him two or three times a day. Three mains water pipes needed new flanges, two T-pieces were getting rusty, a leak equalling about a drop per second in four pipes, and a mains water supply valve was stuck in the 'Open' position. Gillian Finch would take time out to talk to Attridge when she handed him the mug. Sewell didn't mind, as long as she wasn't too long. He hated answering his own telephone without Gillian being there as a filter. Attridge was charming. Gillian didn't see a 'Plumber' label when she handed him the coffee. At six feet tall with hazel eyes and a smile that would melt most women, his Guinness-like voice would hypnotise her as she looked at him, studying his rugged features and visualising Attridge in a western film – the hero, the guy who rescued cowgirls in distress.

"Here's your coffee, Steve. I've made it as I know you like it . . . with a touch of cream and brown sugar. My, you seem to be getting on well, all those pipe bits and nuts and bolts, wow, you are good at what you do, aren't you?" Finch went over the top with her praise and in his heart the hydrostatic operative could have puked. However, his am-dram skills never let him down and he'd smile and shrug off her comments, usually leaving it at 'well, I do my best and I can't do more than that.' Picking up a sharp, curved cutting tool he continued to slice a rubber gasket that would fit onto one of the T-pieces – his signal to Gillian that he wanted to complete the job.

And because Attridge was carrying out contract plumbing work on the site, he was able to come and go as he pleased. The two regular security guards on the main gate both knew Steve and on seeing his white van with its distinctive registration, SA 1234, the barrier would be lifted within seconds. Some of his equipment was kept on site in a remote corner where a solid brick building was situated. Being the only one who had a key to the building it was, in a way, his hide-a-way. There was a small stash of tinned and dried food, several packs of 12 shrink-wrapped bottles of water, a microwave cooker, and coffee-making facilities with a mini fridge. Paul Attridge had been a good friend of Freddie Sewell and the MD of HBF Shipping wanted to be sure his son was well cared for.

But Steve Attridge had a dark side to him. It wasn't only the autographed Black Sabbath tee shirt pinned to the wall, or the poster of Alice Cooper in his prime, or the photo of Johnny Rotten giving a V sign. It was the built-in, killer instinct that had been with him since he couldn't remember. Two cats belonging to his neighbours had been strangled when he'd caught them mewing too loudly, and three wood pigeons that coo-coo-ed for too long had been killed with a powerful catapult. These acts had made him feel good, feel alive.

Now, at the end of his day's work, before he went home, he needed to go down into the basement, down the concrete steps of the brick building to sort something out. He also reminded himself that he must take his boots to the cobbler; get the heels mended. And Attridge would have to do it himself as he was single. No wife at home. He wasn't interested in girls.

And if truth be known, Gillian wasn't interested in men.

***

"What the hell does the five - dot domino mean? A three and a two. And the eight - sided block stuck down his throat?" DCI Adamson was chewing his pencil again as he spoke to his Detective Sergeant, DS Kev Straker. "We still haven't found the significance of the numbers cut into Stavinsky's arm. What were they again . . . oh, yes. 01123. Now this." The post mortem report that Straker had just brought in showed that Kodric died of asphyxiation. No wonder, Adamson mused, with that lump of marble stuck down his gullet. "And the domino? Mock ivory apparently. Have we got an indoor games killer on our hands?" Straker laughed but stopped when he caught the glare of the DCI. "And the octagon? Why an octagon? Let's find out where this guy comes from, any news on his travel movements to the hotel, and if there's a link with Stavinsky. Straker nodded and left the office with a meaningful stride.

The wallet and car keys of Ivo Stavinsky were still missing, and Adamson was still waiting to hear if anything personal belonging to Kodric couldn't be accounted for. Stavinsky's Skoda that had been left at The Seaview Hotel had been taken to the Middlesbrough police pound where it would remain until the DPP cleared it for scrapping.

The Queen's Head receptionist who checked Kodric into the hotel was absolutely certain that he had a light blue rucksack with him when he completed the registration form. She noticed he was left - handed. Kodric was asked to pay for his room on check-in and used a Maestro card issued in Lithuania. She recalled him tugging the rucksack off his right shoulder and placing it on the floor next to his left foot. A different girl was at reception when Kodric left the hotel at about ten past seven, dropping his room key into the slot on the desk and, with the CCTV out of action, it was uncertain if Kodric was carrying the rucksack then. A guest at the hotel remembered seeing a blue coloured car collecting a man at the front door, and, other than the fact that the hotel guest had a beard, couldn't provide much more information.

When Joe Blackwell had heard some of the other facts about Nedj Kodric he called Tommy to let him know. Nothing was really confidential so far, and Joe didn't mind keeping Tommy in the picture, but now Tommy Archer was slowly moving into a moral dilemma vortex. He was in possession of some facts that the police didn't know – even regarding the death at The Seaview. As a 'distant' friend of Adamson, if the DCI got to know the current situation – ThomArch following a woman whose husband believed she was possibly being unfaithful and part of these two scenarios – he'd be in real trouble! Tempted as he was to speak to Jim Adamson, Tommy decided he wouldn't. The DCI might just ask him a question about anything he knew, snippets heard on the streets, any pub gossip about the deaths . . . and Tommy wasn't the best liar in the world, although he practised on a smaller scale from time to time. He'd keep an ear out for news on BBC Tees radio and local television. Details would be released to the general public, as much as the police thought necessary to keep them informed, as well as specific items which may act as a catalyst to prompt somebody to recall something – anything unusual, out of the ordinary.

But that was Tommy's problem. He knew things; was aware that Kodric had met with Alan Clarke and Maria Dawson. And as Maria was part of that meeting last night, what did she think, wondered Tommy? Maybe it was time to meet with Paul again, get his viewpoint on where all this was going.

The Northern Echo front page report appeared the day after Kodric's body was found in the hotel room on the Wednesday morning. His passport details had been taken by the receptionist showing he was a Lithuanian national. Police were still trying to trace his movements prior to his arrival at The Queen's Head but without any success. They had interviewed Libby Barr at The Seaview when they discovered that he was due to stay there, and Kodric had given the same address when he made the booking – an apartment in Vilnius. But the *Echo* report did state that there was no trace of a wallet, nor any sign of a credit or banker's card in Kodric's room, and no mobile phone.

The day after the front - page report, a taxi driver identified the photo of the dead man taken from his passport. He'd picked Kodric up at the railway station in Darlington at around 5.45 pm and taken him direct to the Yarm hotel. The taxi driver confirmed that his passenger was carrying a light blue rucksack, which seemed to be heavy from the way it was carried.

It was time for Tommy to meet up with Paul Dawson again and get his view on the situation. Assuming Paul and Maria were on speaking terms.

***

"Tommy, when the hell are you going to give me some information on my son?" Gordon Ashby wasn't in the mood for excuses. "I'm paying you good money to find him and quick! I know he stole that car and pranged the bloody thing, but since then nothing. Do you have an update for me?" Tommy gulped at the aggressive tone of Ashby's voice.

"I'm still working on it, Gordon." He tried to sound reassuring. "I've got a couple of contacts and I'm doing some surveillance activity on another two. These things don't happen overnight."

"Well, if you can't give me anything definite within a week, I'm going to find another private investigator. I'm not made of bloody money!" The phone line went dead. Gordon Ashby was not a happy man. Tommy, if he being honest with himself, knew he had neglected aspects of his search for Dick Ashby. There were two other cases he was also working on – a sixth form teenager who was bunking off school and a guy with two jobs. It all made for an interesting and varied life for ThomArch. Most days were busy, even if it meant sitting in his VW Golf and watching people, camera at the ready.

Although Tommy knew each case he worked on ought to be given equal priority, in his heart he couldn't do that. He was most interested in the cases that gave him the biggest thrill. And right now, Maria Dawson was doing that for him. It was becoming a roller-coaster ride, watching television news, listening to the radio reports and reading newspaper accounts of developments in the two recent deaths of Stavinsky and Kodric both being treated as murder cases. Why? Because he was a part of it all! But sometimes it seemed he was distanced from it, as if in a dream. And when he read the newspapers, he knew he could add so much more detail to what appeared in print. But then Tommy was very aware of the filtering of news. Adamson only told the press what he wanted them to print; drip - fed them small pieces of information as and when he decided, waiting for feedback from Joe Public, and following up leads, piecing together snippets of information like trying to finish a jigsaw puzzle.

And the more he looked at the photos of Maria he'd taken, the more Tommy continued to have the niggling thought that he'd seen her somewhere before. Two or three times he'd closed his eyes in a quiet moment and focused his mind, taking familiar journeys through shops and public places he'd been. The receptionist at the dentist's, the newsagents, the corner shop in a nearby town that sold his favourite sweets, the garden centre where he sometimes bought a few potted plants, the woman who delivered his free weekly newspaper, the supermarket checkout staff . . .

Then it hit him. It was the eyes – those steel blue eyes.

***

Mark Finch's wife, Louise, really didn't care where her husband went or what he got up to. His property and construction business hadn't impacted on her very much – he wandered about with folders and large sheets of paper depicting plans for more large detached houses on plots of land around Teesside. As far as she knew, he was currently busy with sixteen four-bedroomed properties near Wynyard just off the A19. He was never off his phone and he seemed able to send texts as quickly as the spotty faced kids she had seen exercising their thumbs when she had been out and about doing her shopping for clothes and shoes in Middlesbrough. Louise's smart phone was kept purely for contacting her friends, arranging to meet for coffee or lunch, or catching up with those who attended the Yorkshire Countrywomen's Association monthly get-togethers. She'd been to a YCA meeting last week and was nearly bored senseless. The guest speaker was a guy who spoke about creative writing – how he'd got into it, the importance of creating characters, the plot and sub plot, how to get published . . . and ended up with that old cliché 'we all have a book inside of us.' If it wasn't for getting the latest gossip from her 'ladies who lunch' pals, some of it very juicy, Louise would be seriously considering watching Big Brother or Judge Rinder on the 55" Toshiba television when she got home.

And although Louise loved her daughter, she and Gillian rarely had a heart-to-heart. Gillian seemed to enjoy working for Freddie Sewell at HBF Shipping, but when she got home, she spent time in her bedroom, door usually closed. Ever since she'd left public school Gillian had been a private person, keeping her thoughts to herself but never afraid to voice an opinion if asked. Once at a dinner party that Louise had organised at Pomfreton Manor, not long after they'd moved in, Gillian had been introduced to a previous Lord Lieutenant of the County, Brigadier Hendricks-Smyth. He'd asked her what she thought of the state of royal family matters and if Charles would ever become King. The blue touch paper had been lit. She gave Hendricks-Smyth both barrels and launched into her 'if he hadn't been unfaithful to Diana with that 'tart' she'd still be alive now' tirade. It didn't really matter as it turned out. Some of the party guests agreed with Gillian, and although the Brigadier never spoke to a Finch again, the family made other friends that evening.

***

The cellar walls seemed to be closing in on him. A narrow slit of light shone through the tiny gap at the bottom of the door. It was better than complete darkness. He wondered how blind people coped, losing their sight and wandering about groping from chair to table, door to sink. Did they still have the television on for the sound? A sit-com would be a waste of time – all that false, canned laughter as somebody slipped on a greasy floor. No dialogue, just fooling about.

He began to wonder how long he could go on. Mentally he'd been strong at the beginning, a day or two in the dank environment and then he'd be let out by his captor, or rescued by someone who knew where he was. But now quite a few days had passed. He guessed at seven or eight, but could be wrong. The cough that had developed became a rattle and hurt his throat. Remembering stories he'd read of castaways on some desert island, when they were found, their estimation of time was all to pot. Some had said a month when it turned out to be a year.

But now his mind was wandering. Did it have anything to do with poor nutrition? His blood stream had to be nearly empty of vital vitamins and minerals, the reserves of glycogen in his liver diminishing daily. What nourishment did porridge and a pizza provide? Pizza! How the hell did Italians live to be a hundred years of age? Dough, some cheese, tomato paste, a few olives and other odds and ends sliced and placed delicately on top . . . that wasn't proper food. For now, though, it was all he was getting in the evening, slid with the bottled water through the door flap. The tasteless porridge in the morning served only to fill his belly for a short while. In the dimness he felt his fingers and then his legs. He was losing weight. Bones were easier to feel. Scratching his head, a few lumps of hair came away leaving small bald patches and he wondered if he'd soon look like a monk.

Why was he here, in this hell hole, a musty, concrete walled room with a deep bucket for a toilet getting smellier daily. He had to be positive, think positively, adopt a positive mental attitude. Nobody was going to get the better of him.

He lay on his bed and pulled the thin blanket up to his chin. Would it help if he yelled out? Bang on the door with the heel of his hands? As he thought about his situation, he heard a sound. Not loud, more of a thud – like a car door perhaps? And then a short musical tone, a melody, a few tinkles of piano keys . . . a mobile phone ringing? And then silence, apart from the onset of a few barks of his chesty cough, but there was one thing he didn't realise. That he was being watched.

***

Mavis mumbled something about a guy who'd been asking questions over the phone – wanted to know about a Dick Ashby, telling Mavis that Nicky was a friend of his. But Nicky Barlay didn't hear the last sentence from Mavis as he jumped out of the taxi to tell two kids to get the hell off the front wing of his Mercedes, their tatty school bags scratching the polished paintwork. When he picked up his smart-phone again Mavis had rung off. Barlay wasn't bothered. He had things to attend to at home, at 49, The Crescent, South Bank.

The builders had been to carry out an initial survey for converting his bare basement into a granny flat. They didn't need access for their work, but took some external measurements and brick moisture readings. The slope on which his house had been built meant that there was space for additional accommodation under the main living area. Although Nicky Barlay lived alone, he'd often considered the possibility of changing the bare, grey, concrete walls of that under-build into a charming bedsit - single bed, small dining table and two chairs, kitchen work-top with appliances, double settee, 22" television, loo and shower. Light oak fittings, a Dulux pastel shade on the walls. Friends could use it; he could even let it out – a student at Teesside Uni perhaps? Generate some income. But there was one thing that the builders were slightly concerned about. Barlay would need a new damp-proof course right across the rear of the building.

***

May 1992

"Stop whispering at the back you two! Concentrate, please!" Tom was trying to ask Looby-Loo if he could share her packed lunch. He'd brought a cheese sandwich to school, along with an apple and a cereal bar. Tom liked to be with Looby-Loo during school hours, and walk her home when he could. Her dad was quite strict, and Tom knew that if he stepped out of line, he'd be in for it. But her mum was nice, and used to make tasty sandwiches for her. Tom hoped that he could swap a cheese one for one of hers. Perhaps today she had tuna mayonnaise or roast beef with a hint of horseradish sauce? Mr. Luttrell, the form master, didn't stand any nonsense, though, and whispering was not tolerated.

Tom shut up immediately as giggles wafted around the classroom. His ears reddened for a few minutes as he returned to his exercise book, part way through writing about Fagin and his influence on the children under his care in Oliver Twist. Glancing down he could not help but notice Looby-Loo's legs, firm below her navy - blue pleated skirt; how smooth they were, a delicate shade of pink. Tom was finding it difficult to concentrate. Her blonde hair was hanging down loosely, almost dishevelled, and it smelt of roses. Either way, attempting to discuss Fagin and his manipulative methods with handkerchiefs and pocket-watches was a challenge.

"Five minutes left!" shouted Luttrell. Tom looked across at Jimmy Adams' book. He was on his second page. Hell! Tom had only managed half a page of scrawl. His eyes turned to look at Looby-Loo's ivory white, knee-length socks . . . "OK, Johnson, collect the books, please," bellowed the form-master. Tom put his chewed ball-point pen in the long recess at the front of his wooden desk as the pimply faced Johnson picked up the exercise books and cradled them in the crook of his left arm before placing them on the master's desk. Being the last lesson of the morning, Luttrell saw them out of the classroom. Tom walked briskly, shimmying left and right before catching up with Looby-Loo. He asked her how she'd done with the Fagin project and she smiled. That meant she'd enjoyed it and would probably get a gold star. Tom anticipated a rollicking.

And so, their relationship developed. Tom and Looby-Loo got to know each other, grew to like each other, swapped sandwiches, told stories, and sometimes kissed. The thrill of a stolen kiss was priceless to Tom, bettered only by an accidental touching of their bare knees. They were only twelve years of age and she would soon be leaving school. Her father, a Captain in the Royal Army Intelligence Corps, had been posted to Germany. He would miss her but when they parted for the last time, he'd said to her 'Remember. Wherever you are, when you look up at the moon, I'll be looking up at the same moon as you. That way we can stay together until we meet again.'

And apart from the blonde Looby-Loo hair and nice legs, he also remembered her eyes. Those steel blue eyes. Tommy Archer could never have predicted in a million years that one day he'd be asked to follow and report on his childhood sweetheart.

***

Tommy had suggested a meeting during Paul's lunch break, and proposed a small, quiet cafe called Sugar & Spice not far from the library where Paul worked. It wasn't quite the charming tea room where they'd met before, but it was adequate. Two mugs of coffee and two bacon sandwiches were ordered by Tommy as they sat down at a Formica topped table.

"I like your jacket Tommy. Expensive?" Tommy glanced down at the tin - grey leather, brushing it with his hand as though caressing an expensive pet.

"Depends what expensive means? £250 at the Man About Town store on Linthorpe Road," replied Tommy. Paul stared at the collar, then at the cuffs. "So how are you and Maria getting on these days?" Tommy realised it was a weak question, but he wanted to move on. He now held Paul's gaze.

"It's bloody difficult. She's virtually clammed up. I can't get much sense out of her. I don't see her reading the newspaper much, and when the local TV news comes on, she ignores it – just doesn't want to know what's happening."

"Have you broached the subject of the two murders – Stavinsky and Kodric? Has she admitted to seeing these guys?" Tommy took a long sip from his mug.

"No. Obviously I know she was with them from your reports, but when I've made a passing comment after reading *The Northern Echo* and throwing it in front of her at breakfast, she mumbled something like ' these things happen . . . we live in an awful world.'

"But she told you she was going out for dinner with Clarke, and when I phoned you, you said she hadn't come home that night. What happened?"

"Claimed she'd had a glass of wine too many. Said she'd phoned her friend Becky who I now know lives in Norton, asked her to pick her up, and then stayed with her for the night. Borrowed a pair of her knickers, used a spare toothbrush. When I said I'd tried to call her several times, all she did was shrug her shoulders and say the battery was flat on her mobile phone. Maybe it was."

"Have you seen that suitcase, the one Stavinsky handed over to Maria. She put it into her car boot? I haven't read or heard that the police have found it yet."

"No. I looked into the Mazda car boot but it wasn't there. She must have hidden it." Paul took another bite of his sandwich. Tommy did the same and then spoke.

"How would you feel about telling Maria you know all about her clandestine meetings because you have the evidence. Even suggest she's directly involved in something." Tommy stayed focused on Paul's expression.

"Hell, no! Not yet, anyway. It would scupper our plans . . . well, my plans. No. It's our secret for the time being. I've hired you as my PI and that's our arrangement." Paul put his half - eaten sandwich down.

"Is there any more you can do?" asked Tommy riskily. "Go through her things, check her phone for text messages, her emails. Take her out for dinner, buy her some roses, get around her – she might let something slip? Her birthday is coming up soon, too! 21 August as I recall." He was leaning forward towards Paul, like a chess player might after a checkmate appeal.

"Waste of time . . . and money. I don't know . . . she seems set in her ways, almost as if she's pushing me away. Her laptop computer is password protected and she never goes anywhere without her phone. We now sleep in separate rooms, sometimes eat breakfast together and have little conversation in the evening. She's been in the attic recently, unpacking some of her dolls. Said she may sell some of them at auction. Bloody dolls! Hell, she's nearly 36, not bloody six." Paul finished his lunch, a length of crust left on the plate and he wiped his mouth with a serviette. Tommy adopted a more serious line of approach as he spoke in hushed tones. He tapped the Formica with his index finger.

"OK. But listen, there have been two murders in this

area and your wife, Maria, has been involved in both. Thank God the cops don't yet know. It's only you and I. We have photographic evidence of her meetings with Stavinsky and Kodric, now both dead. Not only murdered, but by some grisly methods! A cord around Stavinsky's neck and his ear cut off, numbers into his arm. Then Kodric, a domino forced into his eye, and a piece of marble stuffed down his throat! And," Tommy hesitated . . . "according to the police, their wallets are missing." Paul swallowed hard.

"Do you think the police are any nearer finding the murderer?" asked Paul.

"Singular? Do you think there's only one killer? What makes you think that?" Paul moved slightly on the padded bench. Smiling, he replied.

"Well, it's the sort of thing you see on these TV thrillers, isn't it? Some creepy man or woman moving around, covering a wide area, stalking people, you know – a psychopath on the loose?"

"Do you think Maria *might* be the murderer?" asked Tommy bluntly. Paul put both hands on his head and flattened his hair. Then he quickly sat upright

"No, not at all! She couldn't have done." The two sat in silence for a short while, coffee mugs empty, a forlorn crust on Paul's plate. A couple of customers glanced at Paul as he gazed out of the window, passing traffic clogging up the road. Tommy never took his eyes off him. "Could she?"

"Well, you did say that she was interested in mathematics," Tommy added. "It's almost death by numbers." They fell silent again. Paul had to get back to the library. Shaking Tommy's hand, he quickly left the cafe telling Tommy he'd be in touch again soon. Tommy ordered another coffee. As he sat there, he wondered if his Looby-Loo could really be a murderer? Had she changed from that sweet, innocent, fair haired little girl into a killer? Before Tommy took a gulp of his coffee, he checked that he'd switched off his microphone pen, laid on the Formica table next to a note pad. It had been there since their conversation began.

***

DCI Jim Adamson was getting frustrated to say the least. He was involved with several cases, but the murders of Stavinsky and Kodric were a challenge. He'd been in the force for thirty years and in his own opinion was a good detective. His Superintendent, Harry Charlton, occasionally thought otherwise. Charlton liked cases solved, clues assembled, perpetrator found, proven guilty and sentenced, the jigsaw completed.

"So, where have we got to, Jim?" Charlton put his coffee on a tatty I LOVE SCARBOROUGH coaster on Adamson's desk. The DCI's fingers rapidly brought up details on his desktop computer.

"The Skoda showed no more clues, no prints other than his, nothing to suggest someone else had been inside the car, and it has now been crushed. No sign of the suitcase that Stavinsky was seen carrying on the CCTV when he parked at The Seaview Hotel and nothing on the 01123 numbers on his arm. It isn't an STD code but we're still checking it out. No wallet or car keys found yet. No phone, if he had one. We've got an address for him near Dubrovnik. He was out of work but his occupation is a lorry driver. The Estonia police already have a file on the guy – involved in some kind of smuggling. His passport has been stamped seven times for trips over the Russian border. Father died a year ago, married, lives with his mother who's apparently got dementia, and she's of little use to the local police. Wife's in Denmark on a course. Neighbours there say he kept himself to himself. He stayed in a Motel24 place, one of a chain, in Bremen, Germany on his trip to the UK.

As far as Kodric is concerned his blue rucksack hasn't been discovered, nor his wallet or phone. The receptionist did notice he had a smartphone as he took a call before he left reception. We traced the letting agency of the apartment in Alnwick Road, Gateshead, who stated that the furnished apartment had been rented for a week but Kodric had only been in Gateshead for five days. He'd paid the letting agency when he'd made the booking on line. Same credit card. A guy in the apartment below said he heard comings and goings from time to time and he mentioned hearing foreign voices – and that coming from a Geordie!" Adamson grinned briefly as Charlton drank his coffee, face stern. "He was picked up at about 5.45 pm at Darlington station by a Pete Craggs, an ABC taxi driver, on the day he was murdered. We've found a large, green holdall in their Left Luggage section that belongs to Kodric. It contains clothes, a couple of pairs of shoes, a few other personal items including a bracelet charm – a gold elephant – on a short length of glitter string that also has a tag with a mobile phone number." Adamson looked at Charlton. "He must like elephants? As for the mobile phone number, we're still checking that. Oh, and there was an open rail ticket from Darlington to Kings Cross tucked in a side pocket."

"Get some more information on this guy, Jim. Something about him doesn't sound right. Why would he rent an apartment for a week when he could stay in a hotel?" Adamson looked at his computer screen again with a slight shrug.

"I've got Kev Straker following up several avenues. He's a good detective and I expect more leads any time soon." Adamson crossed his fingers over the keyboard, hoping his Detective Sergeant would deliver. We're giving the press as much information as is necessary, but have left out some of the gory details about dominoes and marble octagons. MOCT have told me that they've received around twenty calls, and all leads are, of course, being followed up." Charlton picked up his empty cup and turned to leave.

"OK, Jim, keep up the good work, and by the way, I hate Scarborough." Charlton stared at the coaster he'd just picked up. As soon as Charlton had left Adamson threw the coaster into the waste basket; it was past its use by date, coffee stained and slightly buckled.

And as the Superintendent closed the office door, somebody on Teesside was holding a Bank of Estonia credit card. The 16 digits across the middle was delicately touched, a finger moving over the numbers from left to right as if reading braille, light reflecting off the small, square, gold chip embedded in the plastic. The Skoda car key was almost a work of art – such a fine piece of metallic craftsmanship. All those little teeth – just like a steel piranha fish. Nice.

A gratifying smile passed across their lips. It had been another busy day and it was now time to get on. There were things to do.

***

Sitting in his kitchen with a cup of coffee, Tommy asked himself a basic question. 'Do I approach Maria and tell her I'm following her?' The pros and cons were weighed up in his head, first thinking one thing, then the opposite. He didn't have her mobile number but Tommy could phone her at the travel agents. That way it would be fairly safe – speak to her directly, suggest meeting up and then, over a coffee, hit her with the news that her husband had retained him to follow her because he wanted to know what she was up to. Tommy would have to tell Maria how he'd followed her to the two hotels, what he'd seen and heard, the photographic evidence. And if she did recognise the boy from Mr. Luttrell's class, looking older and with a beard, wouldn't she get a surprise?

Or he could adopt an innocent approach to begin, see if she did know who she was talking to. If not, he could use the 'haven't we met somewhere before?' tactic and watch her face as she recalled those halcyon school days, stolen kisses, white socks and knees that touched.

But what if she didn't remember him? No, that was silly. Maria *would* know the boy that tried to copy her homework and often wanted to swap sandwiches. Either way, he would be baring his soul to her – giving her the information on how he'd spied on her, sent reports to Paul. And then she would be aware that her husband knew everything . . . well, almost everything. The meetings with the two men, the suitcase in her car boot and its current whereabouts, the strange deaths of both guys – still unsolved . . . and that would be the end of ThomArch Investigations working for Mr. Paul Dawson. Perhaps the end of Tommy's PI business altogether, he mused as he sipped his coffee.

On the other hand, why tell Maria? He was getting paid good money for his PI activities. Any day now he might get another call from Paul, with a date and time when his wife would be leaving St. Roseberry Close, Eston. He'd tail the red Mazda, park up, maintain vigilance, take photos, get as close as possible, maybe within microphone distance . . . then write the report, send that and the photographic evidence to the P. O. Box number for the attention of Paul Dawson. But Tommy simply could not predict the outcome of telling Maria what he was up to. He had a moral dilemma. If she was involved in something criminal – and she had to be – she'd probably know a couple of heavies who would come calling to break his legs, or worse, heavy chains around his ankles and dropped head first off the Transporter bridge. An innocent woman doesn't meet two East Europeans as Maria did, who end up murdered, and not be into something that was, to put it mildly, damn well callous and ruthless.

No. Best leave it. Tommy also considered the next time he'd be tailing Maria. There'd been two meetings, two deaths. What were the chances that the third time he followed her, there'd be another murder? Should he come clean with DCI Adamson? Contact Jim and tell him everything he knew with an anonymous, muffled voice phone call. He'd seen old black and white films where a handkerchief was stretched over the mouthpiece of the telephone to alter the caller's voice. Or you could now get a synthesiser to create the same Dalek - like effect. Why not add 141 in front of the number for the police HQ in Ladgate Lane where Adamson worked so that the caller's number wouldn't show?

And when Tommy had suggested Paul could secretly check out Maria's emails and text messages, he hadn't seemed keen to do so. It was as if he was scared of her, afraid of the repercussions of being discovered. Tommy began to wonder if there was something that Paul wasn't telling him. He'd had cases similar to this before, possible infidelity where a partner was concerned, and the outcome of it all ending up with the car parked in a wood having its suspension tested, inside of the windows showing condensation from the physical effort inside. That was simple compared to what was happening now.

No. Tommy decided that he would tell nobody and keep quiet. Knowledge is power, and right there and then he'd made his mind up. He'd stay in control. Breathing out deeply after his mental gymnastics he put the empty mug into the washing up bowl, ran some water into it and picked up his jacket, phone and car keys. Before he'd unlocked the VW Golf his phone rang. It was Gordon Ashby.

Tommy hit the red button. He wasn't in the mood to talk about his missing son right there and then, but he was still on the case. He was on his way to meet Mavis at the taxi office in Grangetown and prayed she was on her own.

***

Nick Barlay was sitting in his taxi thinking about his wife. They divorce papers hadn't been signed yet, and he wondered how she was getting on with Harry Nevin. Were they happy together? Did she nag Nevin like she nagged him? Did she still buy expensive handbags? These questions were going through his head when a short, tubby guy wearing a McDonald's uniform tapped on his window. Barlay powered the glass down.

"You like gonna be here long, pal? It's just that we do have regular customers who need parking space. You like gotta pick up here? And, like, your exhaust has been pumping out a whole load of gases like nitrous oxide and carbon monoxide. McDonalds are an eco-friendly, green company, don't you know? You are polluting the atmosphere, like!" The window went up as Barlay gave the Macca D jobsworth the evil eye but said nothing. If looks could kill, the spotty chip friar would be prostrate on the tarmac. Stone dead. Colder than a dodo.

***

Tommy had visited the Blue Umbrella the previous Friday night when the young bucks were in checking out the talent. It had been a cool evening, but most of the girls were dressed for a Mediterranean island like Ibiza; short skirts, skimpy blouses and shoes that made them six inches taller but as wobbly as a house of cards. His trimmed beard made him look swarthy, a hint of half Italian might help him blend in. Not that Boro lads generally looked like Rudolph Valentino, but nonetheless, he hoped he'd be less obvious.

The place was fairly dark, discreet strip lighting around the edges of the coving, small round downlights illuminating just enough to see where you were walking, or who you bumped into. Dark purple patterned carpeting didn't help to brighten the place up, but aircraft-like aisle lighting along the edges of the flooring meant you shouldn't fall down the steps, especially those leading onto the small, parquet dance floor.

At around 8.00 pm the place wasn't busy, but as time went by groups of young people had come in, some possibly related to Neanderthal man by the look of some of them. The lower age limit for entry was 18, but Tommy would bet his Pomfreton cottage on half of them being under that. Young girls these days, hardly out of school, were experts in applying make-up, eye shadow, and mascara. Tommy recalled that Dave Teague had told him at their lunchtime meeting that Steve Attridge and Nicky Barlay used this club where an annual membership fee of £100 was considered good value. Non - members were allowed in, but it was £10 a throw to get past the two burly doormen.

Tommy wanted to get a look at Attridge and Barlay. Not only that, but casually introduce himself and move the conversation toward Gordon Ashby's son, Dick. He needed to keep his story the same as the one he'd fed Dave Teague over a pork pie in The Black Lion a few weeks back . . . he'd been on friendly terms with Dick, played pool with him on Teesside, but hadn't seen him since 2012 and recalled that his father was an estate agent.

Tommy prided himself on reading body language such as the look in someone's eyes, the glance away, a slight touch of the nose, swallowing, fidgeting with a glass, opening their collar a bit more . . . anything to buy time while they considered the question that had been posed. The dimness of The Blue Umbrella was going to make it more of a challenge, but he'd do what he could. Tommy ordered a fresh orange juice from the bar and handed over a fiver for the £3.50 drink. 'Bloody extortion,' he thought. The barman, wearing a black bow tie, gave Tommy his change.

"Excuse me, but do you know a guy called Steve Attridge? Gets in here from time to time, apparently," Tommy had asked casually. Looking around, the barman pinched his clip-on bow tie as if to make certain it was still there.

"No, but his brother Matt is in tonight. I've just served him his fourth drink. With a whisky chaser, too! That's him over in the corner, the one in the grey and yellow shirt." The barman had pointed toward the edge of the dance floor. Tommy saw a guy of average height and build, clean shaven, short hair, his shirt giving him the appearance of looking as if he was considering entering the Mardi Gras carnival in New Orleans. Matt Attridge was on his own looking at the screen of his smartphone, his thumb flicking upwards across the thin glass.

"Hi. Are you Matt, Steve's brother?" asked Tommy, smiling casually.

"Who wants to know?" Attridge seemed guarded. Tommy held his right hand out, seeking a handshake.

"Tommy. Tommy Smith. I'm an old friend of Dick Ashby. I think your brother Steve knows him." Tommy was braced to give him his pre-prepared story as Attridge held out his right hand. His grip was firm. Tommy asked if he'd heard anything of Dick Ashby lately.

"Why are you asking? Are you a copper?" Tommy shook his head and sipped his orange juice.

"No. Dick and I used to play pool together. I moved away for a couple of years and when I returned, he'd moved on. Somebody mentioned that Steve might know where he is."

"Somebody? Like who?" Matt Attridge tensed slightly. Tommy smiled in a reassuring manner.

"Don't remember their name – some guy I had a brief chat with at the David Logan centre over a coffee. I mean, nothing serious, and it's not that important . . . just like to catch up with Dick again. That's all." Tommy leant back against the bar and glanced around in a layback manner. If he'd been any more relaxed, he'd have fallen down. Attridge took a long gulp of his pint then placed it on the bar before catching the edge and spilling some of it.

"I don't know you. How can I trust you?" Tommy wondered what Matt Attridge might tell him. Asking if he could be trusted gave Tommy the distinct impression that Attridge was about to share a document from MI5 or some secret fetish no one knew about. He'd taken in a deep breath as he finished his drink, his eyes glazed. "Let's sit down over here." Attridge slurred his speech, pointed to an alcove with a fixed table, and stumbled slightly as he missed the one step up.

"Ashby is into drugs. Some say his father is to blame. When he was in the young offender's institute, he was instrumental in bringing drugs into the centre – smuggled in by drones flown close over the cell windows. You wouldn't believe it. They say his old man has some connections with the local drugs scene." Attridge quickly added the word 'allegedly.' He looked down at his empty beer glass. Tommy held his hand up then pointed at the teaspoon of froth in the bottom. Matt Attridge nodded, and within less than a minute Tommy had placed another pint in front of him.

"Connections?"

"Yes, I thought you would have known that. Gordon Ashby, respectable estate agent, fingers allegedly dusted with white powder." Attridge slurped his beer. Tommy recalled Dave Teague mentioning Dick Ashby possibly having had a spliff when he'd crashed the stolen Nissan on the Whitby road.

"Anybody else involved with Dick's father?" Tommy decided on the direct approach. Attridge was well oiled by now and his tongue loose.

"Don't know. Could be somebody local. If you asked Gordon Ashby, he'd deny it anyway. But to answer your question . . . no, I haven't seen Dick Ashby. He could be anywhere now. I need to go to the loo . . ." Attridge tottered away from the table, his face slightly ashen. Tommy imagined he'd be talking to the toilet bowl very soon, his grey and yellow shirt possibly in need of a clean when he'd finished. It was time to leave The Blue Umbrella.

So that was the outcome of Tommy's club visit a week back. It had given him food for thought. Gordon Ashby involved in drugs! Surely not? Some drug cartel? Tommy had a few more questions that could wait, but he was no nearer discovering the whereabouts of Dick Ashby.

No wonder his father wanted ThomArch Investigations to find him before Cleveland Police.

***

Tommy parked his VW Golf a couple of hundred yards along Tees Street in Grangetown. A few pedestrians walked along the nearby shopping parade with its post office cum newsagents, a Greggs' baker, a butcher, two charity shops, a unisex hairdresser, Subway sandwich outlet and a Taylor's pie shop. No wonder the local population were skewing the overweight statistics for north east England as large rugby-type building contractors with Wimpey written on their jackets tucked into jumbo sized pasties and pies.

On the corner with River Lane, Tommy spotted the taxi office. Large red letters on a white background read BARLAY'S TAXIS AT YOUR SERVICE, a Teesside phone number shown below. Tommy had prepared himself that morning, talking at his bathroom mirror for a few minutes before he left home. Being sunny, he wore darkened glasses and decided to leave them on for added anonymity. 'Please let Mavis be on her own' Tommy repeated to himself over and over as he strolled the last few steps. His wish was granted. The clinking bell tinkled as he entered, reminiscent of a shop in a Charles Dickens novel. Mavis was sitting at a desk on the other side of the counter, an open packet of chocolate biscuits near the computer mouse. The chair was a good fit, the metal arms pressing into her ample waistline, the navy - blue dress revealing a few inches of cleavage. Her rotund stomach suggested a liking for food and a pair of long, pearl earrings gave her the look of a television soap actress. Mavis spoke first.

"Good morning! I'm Mavis. What can we do for you on this sunny day?" She prised herself out of the chair.

"Hi, my name's Jim Stevens. I'm looking for a taxi firm that can help with a wedding coming up in a couple of months. You know, taking guests to the church, then to the reception, home at night, that sort of thing." Was it becoming easier to tell lies, Tommy wondered?

"When's the wedding . . . have you got the dates to hand?" Tommy fumbled for a pocket diary, opened it and pretended to check.

"Yes, here we are, Saturday October the first. It's in Middlesbrough." Mavis shoehorned herself back into the chair, the springs groaning as she did so. Her porcine eyes scanned the computer screen.

"No problem. The three taxis we have are all available. Do you want me to book them for the whole day? That would be best, wouldn't it?" She smiled and Tommy wondered if she was on commission. "We'd have them valeted the day before, inside and out, and we can buy some white ribbons. Might be best to take the roof sign off the main wedding car, you know, make it look really classy. They're all Mercs so you'd have that extra bit of kudos that only comes with German cars. Well, apart from a Roller, of course." Mavis was a saleswoman and she was selling her product. "Nicky, the boss, he could wear a peaked cap – look smart, you know, do a proper job." Tommy could see Mavis was loving this, her chest reddening slightly with her enthusiasm.

"It sounds good to me. What about costs? The wedding couple have a limited budget so it needs to be within their scope. How much are we talking?" Chubby fingers flitted across the keyboard as Mavis did some calculations.

"Maximum nine hundred pounds, could be as little as seven hundred, depending on the journeys." She smiled at Tommy waiting for his response. Tommy wrote the details in his diary and then put it away. He'd tell the couple later that day, he told Mavis, and let Barlay's Taxis know if it was suitable. He told Mavis he thought it sounded a really good deal.

"You've been very helpful, Mavis. So helpful, in fact, that I'd like to buy you a cake, or a sandwich or pie. What do you say?" If there had been a prize for the biggest smile on Teesside that day, Mavis Burgess would have won by a mile. "I hear Greggs do a mean pasty, and there's the pie shop." Mavis smiled and nodded – in that order. "Be back in two ticks!" Tommy left the office and marched back to the line of shops. He bought a crusty Cornish pasty and a pork pie, then returned to see Mavis. This was his bargaining tool; he hoped a little charm would ease Mavis' tongue and provide him with any information that could just lead him to get a better handle on the whereabouts of Dick Ashby. The bell tinkled above the door.

"There you go Mavis. Lunch!" Tommy placed the two paper bags on the counter. It was 10.05 am by his watch so too early for Mavis to start demolishing the high calorie pastries. She offered to put the kettle on and make two mugs of coffee. Tommy immediately accepted. "No milk or sugar, Mavis, thanks." A minute later Tommy took his saccharin container from his jacket pocket and flicked one into his mug. "So, do you like working here, Mavis, it must be interesting?" Mavis peeped inside one of the paper bags, licked her lips, and then folded the top over again.

"Yes, I love it. Occasionally a bit quiet, like now, but I get to talk to some interesting customers . . . and then there's the gossip. Can't keep up with it sometimes . . ." Tommy knew he ought to say as little as possible, and that's just what he did. "It was sad when Mrs. Barlay, er Judith, went off with Harry Nevin 'cos he was a regular customer, but Nicky didn't seem to care. But I think he did really, didn't want to show it. They went to live in Redcar. Nicky and his wife didn't have any kids. I haven't seen him with a woman, but I don't think he's one of *them,* you know - gay. Divorce hasn't been finalised, yet. Anyway, he keeps busy what with this job – his own business – and his hobby." Tommy listened intently. Mavis was loving the opportunity to talk. It made sense. Sitting alone in a quiet taxi office, a computer screen to stare at and an ample supply of biscuits . . . "And he's had some interesting customers lately. Told me about a Russian millionaire he's collected from Durham Tees Valley a few times. He does some regular runs – schools and that – but likes doing business down at Tees dock. That Mr. Sewell from the shipping company is a real gentleman. I've spoken with him several times. He once told me I've got a sexy voice over the phone. Me! A sexy voice for goodness sake!

Anyway, whatever turns him on. Maybe that's why he rings up instead of that stuck up tart of a secretary. What's her name . . . oh, yes, Gillian Finch. Now there's another interesting thing, our Gertrude said that Finch's father moved into the area about eighteen months ago from the Costa Blanca. Blimey, why move to North Yorkshire when you can have all the sun and cheap Spanish plonk you want on a Spanish Costa?" Tommy kept expecting the phone to ring. It didn't. He smiled and listened. Mavis stopped for breath and sipped her coffee, now cold.

"Do you know of anybody called Dick Ashby?" Tommy changed tack quickly.

"Dick Ashby. Why yes. He's a bit wayward if you ask me. I've heard Nicky mention him on a couple of occasions. Gone missing, hasn't he? If memory serves, and it doesn't always, he's the son of an estate agent somewhere in this area. I hear he'd got mixed up with a bad lot – even with that Gillian Finch. Rumour has it that he was friendly with a pub landlord somewhere in North Yorkshire who runs a pub with an odd name. Frog and something, I think. Sometimes Nicky has stopped by there for an orange juice if he's in the area. Anyhow, Nicky says he's still on the run after stealing a car and writing it off on the Whitby road a while back." The office phone rang and Mavis answered it. A client needed a taxi from Grangetown to North Tees Hospital. Mavis told them it would be there in ten minutes. Tommy glanced at his watch. It was time to go. His phone had double beeped twice so he knew there were text messages for him. Mavis put the phone down.

"Well, Mavis, you been more than helpful. I have to go, but enjoy your lunch. By the way, you mentioned Nicky having a hobby. Do you know what it is?"

"Yes, of course. It's taxidermy. He loves stuffing dead animals . . . making them look as if they're still alive. It's a bit gruesome if you ask me."

Tommy reached to his top jacket pocket and switched the microphone pen off as he left the office and walked briskly back past the shopping arcade. He smiled to himself as he reflected on the irony of a taxi-driver liking taxidermy.

***

Tommy checked his two text messages. The first was from Joe Blackwell.

Two of our hotels have had three East Europeans check in from tomorrow. Separate bookings. If interested phone me for details. J. IN CONFIDENCE as usual.

The second was from Paul Dawson who'd been quiet for a while. Perhaps Maria was being her normal self. No alleged girlie meetings, no dinners with Alan Clarke. But Tommy now had that same gut feeling . . . if he followed Maria, was it going to be the same pattern as the two previous tails?

Hi Tommy, can we meet at Sugar & Spice tomorrow at 1.00 pm. Thanks, Paul.

Sat in his VW Golf, Tommy checked his Dawson account on his smart-phone. So far, he'd clocked 11 hours 35 minutes and he'd be sending Paul an invoice soon. Another meeting with Paul meant one thing, although Tommy cursed himself. 'Not necessarily!' He recalled the old saying 'Never Assume,' because 'assume' makes an 'Ass of U and Me.' How trite, but true. No, he'd wait until tomorrow at one o'clock in the cafe to see what Paul wanted.

And of course, Tommy often thought about Looby-Loo. Who'd have imagined it – following his childhood sweetheart? His beard helped keep him from being recognised, he hoped, and Tommy had recently bought a pair of plain spectacles that could easily be slipped on and off. It was all part of the PI strategy of being trying to be anonymous. Tommy checked the Ashby account, too. Gordon was nearly one thousand pounds in debt to ThomArch Investigations. Just as well Tommy had a few pounds in his HSBC bank account, thanks to a lottery win about six months ago. Of course, he hadn't left it all in the bank. An offshore account was giving him 2.5% so he'd put half of it in that.

Tommy sent a text to Joe to thank him for the 'in confidence' information he'd received, but wasn't going to ask him for any details yet. Not until he'd had a chat with Paul Dawson. For now, he simply wanted to absorb what Mavis had told him. His key objective had been to find out more about Dick Ashby, and the one thing that Mavis had said was about 'rumour has it that he was friendly with a pub landlord somewhere in North Yorkshire.' And Mavis couldn't recall the name, but 'Frog and something' strongly suggested it was the Frog and Ferret in Pomfreton. Tommy listened to part of his recording on his microphone pen. Hell, right on Tommy's doorstep! In *his* village . . . could Gordon Ashby's son be in Pomfreton? No, somebody would have spotted him. All the reports that had been in local newspapers and on TV news some weeks ago showing photos of the still - missing Dick Ashby strongly suggested that he would have been noticed by the *'I'm a member of the Neighbourhood Watch Group'* that live in the village. Blinkin' nosy parkers Tommy called them.

It wouldn't do any harm to stop by for a drink soon, though, see how Roger was keeping, raise the subject of young Ashby and watch the landlord carefully for signs of embarrassment or a flustered reply. Tommy might even get to meet Mark Finch in the pub. Although he'd had nothing to do with Finch directly, he'd picked up enough local gossip, pub and shop, to know something about him – his so-called business dealings, a high maintenance wife, and of course, Gillian, their daughter who was now having to survive without the credit card her parents had issued for her, as well as drive her Suzuki Swift instead of the Beemer. Mavis had mentioned Gillian with distaste in her mouth, and revealed that she worked as a secretary at the docks. Tommy recalled Dave Teague telling him that Gillian was a PA to one of the big bosses at Teesport so she's probably still there. He hadn't managed to get to see

Gillian Finch, yet, but he'd work on a plan. It wouldn't be a problem finding out exactly where she worked, and he'd have to use an alias. Tommy didn't want Finch rushing home telling her father that she'd been interrogated by a private detective!

"You going to be sitting there all bloody day, mate?" Tommy looked up to see a thickset workman who had tapped on his half open window. Wearing a Wimpey hi-vis jacket and a muddy white helmet perched on his head he continued. "We're trying to get a park, know what I mean, and to be honest it's chronic round here this time of day. Can't leave the ambers flashing all the while! It's time to be collecting us snap." Tommy nodded, smiled, and powered up the window. He was thankful the doors were on auto lock. No way did he want the lookalike gorilla dragging him out of his Golf for a bit of a hiding. When the Wimpy lads want their 'snap,' it's time to let them have it. He started the engine, indicated to pull out, and drove away as the builders Ford Transit pick up slipped into his parking space.

***

"Maria says she's having a night away with Rachel and Becky. Going to do some shopping in Middlesbrough on Saturday afternoon and then take in a show at the theatre and be home by Sunday teatime." They were sitting in a café on Normanby Road. Paul picked up his mug of tea as Tommy recalled the names of the two girls Paul had just mentioned. Paul had met them at a wedding some months ago, but apart from that knew little about the two friends except that Becky lived in Norton. When he'd asked Maria, she calmly told her husband that they were purely girlfriends - he really didn't need to know any more. Were they the perfect foil for Maria, these two people whose identities were sketchy to say the least? Did Maria need to be so secretive? Did she like being clandestine? Paul put it down to her personality, her passion for maths, and her astrological star sign – Leo. Tommy sipped his coffee.

"What do you want me to do, Paul?"

"Follow her, of course. Maria is meeting up with some guy, I'm sure of it. She says she's meeting the girls on Saturday in town for a light lunch. Apparently, they're staying in a triple room at the Travelodge hotel in Newport Road." Tommy mentally worked out the hours and his expenses for this surveillance. "I think she's lying. First, it's some guy at The Seaview Hotel who ends up in the boot of his own car, then the dinner at The Cleveland Bay Horse, where later that night some foreign guy is found dead in his room at The Queen's Head. Where the hell is this heading, Tommy?" Paul took out a hanky and wiped his nose. Tommy leant forward over his mug.

"You haven't shared any of this with anyone, have you Paul? It's best you don't, you know that?" Paul shook his head as he replaced his hanky, his nose now dry, eyes a little red.

"Course not! Hell, it's my wife that's involved with this . . . well, involved somehow. I dread the day when the police come calling with their 'we're just here to ask a few routine questions, sir' bit. I wake up sweating some nights. I'm beginning to wonder why I married her." Paul reflected on his first meeting with Maria at the library; the knee-length brown leather boots, her confident swagger, the blonde hair that spelled out late summer corn fields bathed in evening sunshine.

"Look. I'll do what you want. I'm here to do a job for you. It may be best if I book into the hotel, too, and then follow the three of them over the week-end. Are you OK with that, Paul, if I put it on expenses? I'll get the best deal for a room I can."

"Yes. Go for it. I'll text you any additional information between now and Friday, but let me have a report as soon as possible. Hell, who knows what they'll be getting up to . . . if indeed Maria is going to meet with Rachel and Becky at all!" Paul wiped his nose again and looked at the clock on the cafe wall. 1.30 pm. "By the way, there's something else you'll find very interesting. This morning a guy came into the library to enquire about membership – said he was just passing the door. It was for a friend of his. He didn't give his name, but you'll recall his appearance from the photos you took at The Cleveland Bay Horse . . . just over six feet in height with thick, blond hair. I'm sure it was Alan Clarke. What your photos didn't show was the look in his eyes. The sort of piercing stare that a sparrow hawk or falcon might have for its prey. Really scary."

Neither spoke for a while as they looked out at the raindrops that began to streak down the cafe windows. Paul's face was stony as he stood up.

"Tommy, I must go. There's a delivery of books in half an hour and then a meeting with the chairman of the local libraries committee." He rose, shook Tommy's hand and started to walk to the cafe door but before he got to the exit he stopped and turned back. "Tommy. Be careful." Was Paul warning Tommy? If so, why? Maybe he thought this might be Tommy's last few days of the surveillance project?

"OK, Paul. I won't let you down. We'll catch up soon." Tommy drained his coffee mug and wondered why he hadn't ordered a bacon sandwich as his stomach grumbled. He'd admired the new, tan leather jacket that Dawson was wearing as he watched him walk across the road.

***

"Now, I've checked the registrations of vehicles after our observant hotel guest at the Queen's Head, Peter York, middle name David, noticed the number 65 and the letters PDY on the plate for obvious reasons, his initials! It was a blue 2015 Audi A4 Sportback with the registration number NT 65 PDY. York reckoned it was about 7.00 pm when he noticed the Audi at the hotel. He thinks there was only one man inside when it stopped near the entrance, but he didn't take much notice of the occupant." Straker was briefing Adamson over a cup of cold coffee. "The car was on a 24 -

hour test drive – booked out from the Audi dealer in Stockton. I spoke to the manager yesterday and he confirmed that the car is logged with them. Their details show that a man had driven it from the dealer mid - afternoon on the twelfth and returned it the following day, the 13th. July. They always obtain driving licence details, and a £300 returnable deposit, before they allow any vehicle to be taken away. He paid cash and got cash back when he returned the car. So, there isn't a record of a cheque being paid to him. Problem is, there was a fire in the office two days ago that destroyed some paperwork, and they've lost quite a bit of admin stuff. There's nothing on their computer. They can't trace details for a number of test-drive customers, including our Audi Sportback driver, and the young girl who handled it can't remember what he looked like. It was a busy time, apparently."

"Good work, Kev. So, it was an Audi dealer's car that was seen at The Queen's Head that evening. Find out if anybody else saw that vehicle on the evening of 12 July. Check fuel station cameras – he may have put some petrol or diesel in, but that's doubtful. Any town centre CCTV from this area, and get some more background on Kodric's movements between Gateshead and Yarm." The DCI blew his nose, the hint of a cold coming on. "And, we haven't found his wallet or blue rucksack, have we?" Straker shook his head.

"Nor have we got the wallet of Ivo Stavinsky or his car keys, or mobile phone if he had one. Needles and haystacks come to mind, sir," replied the detective sergeant.

"Well, Kev, time to start playing the bloody farmer, then!"

***

The two credit cards were held side by side. One from the Bank of Estonia in light green, the other a black MasterCard issued by a Lithuanian finance house. So similar, but totally different. Both were almost new, the gold numbers as clear as the Pole Star on a frosty night. And what was interesting to the person holding the cards was that the CV numbers on the reverse of the cards contained the numbers 1,2,3 and 5. The start and expiry dates were easy to read and the two wallets were nice, one calfskin, the other leather. The holder replaced the cards exactly where they came from, closed each wallet and placed them into the blue rucksack from which came a slight jingle of keys as the bag was zipped up.

***

Hello Nejc! You haven't called me for a while. Your phone is obviously switched off. How were your few days in Gateshead? Is it a nice place? Did you meet any nice people in the bars? I hope you haven't been a naughty boy? Anyway, let me know what's happening, especially when you get to London! Give Alan my regards, and give him a kiss for me. Look forward to hearing from you. Miss you. Yuri.

***

A glance at the small screen fitted on the stairwell showed him laid on his dirty bed. Appearing to be asleep, the grainy image revealed him curled up in the foetal position. He hadn't moved for a while now, not that he was being observed all of the time. The thin cardboard plate was near the door, an empty plastic bottle close by, and the plastic spoon that had been used for the breakfast porridge looked dirty.

The walls were still damp, the atmosphere dreak. With little air circulation everything got musty, the smell of month - old mushrooms hung in the air. The toilet bucket was close to capacity. He avoided smelling himself, because he knew he'd wretch if he did.

The question now was . . . how long could he go on?

He'd been to the Outward Bound School on Ullswater in the Lake District, completed the three week course, got the badge and the certificate. What was the school motto?

To Serve, to Strive, and Not to Yield

He wasn't going to yield. Give up? No way. But there had to be a way of getting out of there. The next time someone pushed some food and water through the door flap he'd shout and tell them that the shit bucket was full! Surely, they'd empty it? Wouldn't they? But if he carried on losing weight like he had done, there wouldn't be much to fill the bucket with.

His head was hurting. Not a normal headache such as he'd get after drinking six pints of cider with his mates on a Friday night but more of a throb, a piercing thrust. Like a hot spear slowly being pushed into his brain. And it was so easy to count his ribs now . . . one, two, three, four . . . Then suddenly he heard that noise again - a melodic tune. Dah, dah, doh, doh, dah . . . and a tinny, jangling sound. Then the monitor was switched off.

***

Tommy had agreed with Paul that he'd tail the girls after they'd booked into the Travelodge until sometime on Sunday afternoon, but that excluded the shopping. No way did he want to be joining other furtive-looking men hanging about in the lingerie department of M & S. He parked his Golf in the hotel car park as far away from the main door as possible at just after 1.30 pm. He reckoned that they'd check in after lunch but before going shopping. He registered at reception, keyed in his car registration number for the free 24 - hour car park, and was handed his plastic key card. But within a few minutes Tommy heard giggles coming from behind him. It was Maria and her two girlfriends and they headed straight for the bar. Each was carrying light luggage but it seemed they were in need of a glass of wine first. His darkened glasses were in his top pocket, ready to be put on if needed. Tommy went up to his room on the second floor, unpacked the few items he'd brought and used the loo. After washing his hands and face, combing his hair, and dabbing on some aftershave, he went down the stairs to reception and ambled over to one of two girls on the desk and noted her name badge. Lydia. Tommy switched on the charm.

"Hi, Lydia, I wonder if you could help? I'm meeting with a group of people for a birthday celebration this week-end and just wondered if a female trio have checked in, yet? A blonde girl, Maria Dawson, and a couple of gorgeous beauties?" He grinned mischievously. Lydia looked at the screen in front of her, and then back at Tommy.

"No, not yet." Lydia left her reply hanging in the air. Tommy leant forwards, a spearmint in his mouth, and lowered his voice.

"Do you have a room allocated . . . maybe a room number so I could call them later?" he whispered as he winked at her. Lydia looked around her for a split second, then back at the screen. Lowering her voice, she replied with over-lipsticked, pouted lips.

"I really shouldn't do this, but it's three – two – seven." Tommy smiled and thanked Lydia with his eyes. He headed for the bar. It was fairly busy, with shoppers and friends meeting up to share their trials and tribulations of the week. Sitting in a corner, the three girls each had the same drink. A tall glass contained an orange-yellow liquid, a straw and one of those silly umbrellas; a large slice of cucumber hung over the glass edge. Tommy ordered a J2O and sat in the opposite corner, near an old guy with a girl young enough to be his granddaughter. He ignored them as he flicked through a house magazine pretending to be interested in hotel deals and offers.

Tommy began to wonder what he was doing here. Apart from the fact that Paul had asked him to track Maria over the two days, she was with Rachel and Becky after all. A girl's night away wasn't going to result in Maria chatting up some Italian stallion, surely, unless they were heading for a night club to find the three most eligible bachelors on Teesside? Thinking about it, Tommy was pretty confident that after shopping they'd return to the hotel, have a couple of drinks, shower and change, and find a place to eat. Tommy had checked the theatre – the Jersey Boys tribute band were touring the UK and were the star turn at the theatre on Saturday night. The show started at 8.00 pm so he guessed the three of them would probably be dining around 6.30 pm.

Now that Tommy had the room number for the three girls it would make it easier to keep tabs on them, but he had to be discreet. Avoiding the lift was the first priority; he couldn't share a lift with them, that was for sure, and using the stairs would help his fitness. As the place was becoming busier Tommy was certain he wouldn't be out of place wandering about on the third floor, pretending to hold a key card in hand as if he was searching for his room or looking for someone. His plan was to be in the foyer half an hour after the girls left the bar. That should make it soon enough to tail them when they left the hotel. But this was all assumption, of course. Tommy knew that. But without an assumption, he had no plan. A challenge would be if they got into a taxi, then he'd have a problem; walking behind them would be easy.

At 6.10 pm he walked along the thickly carpeted third floor corridor and slowed at room 327. He could hear laughter and the odd shriek coming from the room. Another drink, perhaps, Tommy wondered? Finishing touches to lipstick and make-up, maybe? He stopped and looked down. A white envelope was protruding from the gap at the bottom of the door. Glancing both ways Tommy didn't see anybody, and quickly slid the envelope out and straight into his jacket pocket in one deft movement. In seconds he was on his way down to the ground floor heading for the Gents. In the first cubicle he took the envelope from his pocket and slit it open.

Maria

Don't have your mobile number.
Meet me in Chambers bar on Albert Road at 21.00
Slavko

'Who the hell is Slavko?' Tommy wondered. How did he know Maria was there? Why didn't he knock on the hotel door if it was him that put the note under it? Was this going to be ground hog day all over again? Tommy wouldn't have to worry about following Maria in a taxi. He'd ask at reception where the bar was and make it his objective to be there at the time suggested. No need to wait for Maria in the hotel bar, he'd find a cafe or restaurant for a quick bite and then head for Chambers.

So, was Maria having an affair with this Slavko guy? Why take the trouble to make up a story about a girl's week-end away? But then, why not? A perfect foil, especially if Rachel & Becky were in on it! Suddenly Tommy realised that, as he had the note, Maria would not be aware of the arrangement. Sod it! He had to put the note back under the door as soon as he could. In less time than it takes to watch Usain Bolt run the 100 metres Tommy, breathless but silent, walked along the corridor and slipped the folded sheet of paper back under the door sealed in a new envelope from reception. He was back in reception seconds later, the original crumpled envelope tossed into a bin.

Lydia was helpful. A street map showed Tommy the exact location of Chambers. It was within walking distance and Lydia had circled an eating place called Bunter's Diner with a ball-point pen. He'd stop off there for something simple such as chicken nuggets and fries, and maybe a Diet Coke with ice. Tommy left the hotel and turned right on Newport Road. But as he was walking toward the diner, he noticed a guy across the road, perhaps a hundred yards ahead, who resembled Paul Dawson. About six feet two inches tall, of medium build, and wearing a dark knee-length coat. The man suddenly turned left down a narrow alley. Walking briskly, Tommy crossed over the road. The alley was gloomy, grime covered walls either side. He took a few strides along it but there was no one there. Shaking his head, Tommy decided he must have been mistaken so he headed off to find Bunter's as it began to drizzle, trying to decide whether to have ketchup or barbecue sauce on his chicken nuggets. He also wondered what Maria would do with her theatre ticket?

***

"Have you got a minute, sir?" DS Kev Straker entered Jim Adamson's office with a folder under his arm.

"Come in, Kev, I was going to give you a shout in the next ten minutes anyway. I'm dying for a coffee, any chance of popping down to the machine? Here's fifty pence." The DCI reached into his trouser pocket but Straker held up his hand.

"No, on me today, sir." Adamson smiled as the sergeant dropped the folder onto a chair and strode off along the corridor to the drinks machine located just inside the canteen door. He was soon back with two white coffees. Adamson took a sip and grimaced.

"Ooh, this doesn't get any better, does it? But it's hot and wet. So, Kev, what have you got for me?" Kev Straker sat down and opened the folder.

"Well, sir, I've been following up on some CCTV images. The Audi A4 was seen at a major crossroad junction near Stockton at 6.47 pm on Tuesday, heading towards Yarm. A previous camera had picked up the vehicle in Acklam at 6.34 pm. I've checked with the Audi dealer again, and they do know that the total distance covered by the car was 52 miles. Knowing what we do about the movements of the Audi, I'd say the driver lives within a ten - mile radius of the Boro."

"This is all very interesting Kev, but is it getting us anywhere nearer to finding the mysterious driver of the Audi, who may or may not be implicated in the murder of Kodric?"

"Well, we may yet get further information from the public on a sighting of the car. Can we get the details on the local news? Tonight?" Adamson nodded.

"OK, Kev, contact the BBC and Tyne Tees offices. Minimum information, but give them the registration number and ask for responses on Crimestoppers."

***

Blue lights were slashing through the darkening sky; grey rain clouds rolled in off the North Sea. Three police cars were parked on Albert Road, about a hundred yards from Chambers bar. Tommy made his way past onlookers and reached a POLICE DO NOT CROSS tape. A narrow snicket was being guarded by two police constables. Tommy craned his neck and could see a couple of SOCO's in their white suits kneeling down. One had a camera.

"What's happened?" Tommy was standing next to a guy taking a couple of photos with his smart-phone.

"Dunno. I heard some shouting and ran down here. Somebody must have phoned the police – they were here in no time, a couple of cars at first, then a third. I reckon somebody's had it . . . there, down that alleyway." Minutes later a black Mercedes Sprinter van eased under the raised police tape and within moments a stretcher was eased into the back but because of the poor view Tommy couldn't make out if there was a body on it and, if there was, if the face was covered. The van doors slammed shut as the crowd grew. Tommy turned to another guy to his right.

"See anything? Has someone been killed?" Tommy glanced at his watch - it 8.50 pm. He was seeking another opinion, a different viewpoint on what had occurred.

"Well, my girlfriend and I had just left the pub along there," he pointed behind him, "and I saw a woman walk along that alleyway. I thought it strange that she was pulling a wheeled suitcase, I mean you don't see people doing that in Albert Road on a Saturday night normally. Then I heard a shout, well, more of a shriek I suppose, and a guy comes running out of the passage shouting 'get the police!'

"Where's the guy now, did you see him run off anywhere?"

"I don't know . . . it all happened so quickly, a bit like a dream. I think he just sprinted – he looked scared." The couple that Tommy was talking to held hands tightly. "Someone must have called the cops 'cos they were here in no time." Tommy inched to his left. A woman with a tattoo on her right arm was also taking photos using her smartphone.

"Hmm, you don't expect to see these things going on in Middlesbrough, do you?" she said to Tommy in a casual way. "It's not a rough place. The odd domestic and of course, a bit of street fighting at the week-end, but otherwise it's all right around here." The couple drifted away, as most of the crowd were doing now – the excitement over. Out of the corner of his eye Tommy spotted DCI Jim Adamson getting out of a black BMW. He hadn't spoken to the detective for quite a while. Ambling over, Tommy thought he'd try and have a quick word.

"Hello, Jim, how's tricks? Long time, no see. How's Helen?" Tommy didn't want to hit Adamson with *'what the hell is going on here?'* Adamson, hands thrust deep into his pockets, turned to Tommy.

"Hi, Tom. She's as well as can be expected. And you?" Tommy knew the DCI was being polite, considering what had just happened off Albert Road.

"Yes, fine. What's occurred here? Another mugging?"

"Worse, Tom. I had a radio report as I was driving over. A guy has been loaded into a private hearse, dead as a dodo. I can't say too much obviously, but we'll probably have a meeting with the media at police HQ on Tuesday or Wednesday when we've got some facts. I'll ask my Sergeant to let you know when it is." Tommy was about to enquire about the two other cases that he'd been involved with when a uniformed policeman shouted for Jim Adamson. So that was that.

Tommy sauntered down to Chambers bar arriving at a quarter past nine. He squeezed past a crowd of young people, found a barman, and ordered an apple and raspberry J2O. Maria was nowhere to be seen despite Tommy searching the whole place. He sat on a bar stool sipping his drink but if Maria wasn't there, then what about Slavko? It was nearly 9.30 pm and there was no sign of her with the 'phantom note leaver.' Tommy began to reflect on events of the past hour. Not the fact that his chicken nuggets were slightly undercooked, or that the chips were too greasy, or that the plastic, tomato-shaped ketchup dispenser was empty. No, it was the fact that the eye witness account of a woman seen with a suitcase *could* have been Maria, and the dead man in the alleyway *could* have been Slavko. No, surely not. That wasn't the plan. They were meeting in Chambers at 9 pm. But Tommy felt as if he was floundering. Tommy had relied on the details on Slavko's note for his surveillance that evening. Had he been duped, he wondered?

If Maria had not gone to the theatre, where was she now? Back at the Travelodge? Tommy finished his J2O and left the bar. On the third floor of the hotel, Tommy stopped outside room 327. Listening very carefully, he placed an ear against the door. There was no sound, no TV or radio. No running tap or shower. No toilet flushing. The room had to be empty – unless Maria was laid on the bed asleep or between the sheets with Slavko? He discounted the latter; there'd be some grunting and groaning, wouldn't there? Tommy got down on one knee and looked under the door. The room was dark. So that was that, at least for now. He'd have to play the waiting game.

Brushing his trouser knees as he walked away, Tommy decided to get a drink in the hotel bar. He went down the stairs and thought about Paul Dawson. The man he'd seen in Newport Road . . . had that been Paul? Same height, similar build. Or just a coincidence? Was Tommy's brain playing tricks? Some kind of association factor between the woman he was supposed to be following and her husband? He dismissed the thought but instantly had another. With his iced orange juice, orange wedge on the edge of the glass and a striped paper straw, Tommy texted Paul.

All OK at this end. Were you in the Boro town centre tonight? Thought I saw you? Regards, Tommy.

After eating half of the orange wedge and stirring his juice with the straw Tommy got a reply.

No. Been home all evening with Hawaiian pizza and DVD! Keep up the good work. Looking forward to the report next week. Paul.

***

"You don't seem to be taking much notice of your daughter these days. Have you thought about talking to her sometimes? I know she's your stepdaughter, but please try to and treat her like she's your own!" Mark Finch's wife, Louise, was cheesed off with her husband. "You paid for a good education but now it seems you've almost abandoned her! And yes, I'm aware that she was only one year old when we got married, but *she is your daughter*! She'll be moving out next! You spend too much time down the pub with that Grimes fellow. Getting friendly, are we?" Mark Finch picked up the folder and went to the foot of the stairs. His study would give him some peace from this tirade. He turned.

"When you calm down, we can have a sensible discussion about this. I try to have a talk with her but she seems to be in her own world. She doesn't seem to bother with boyfriends, ask her yourself. As for moving out, why would she leave her home comforts? And why do you have to be so concerned about Roger Grimes? He's OK. You don't think I'm having an affair with him, do you?" Without waiting for a reply, he laughed as he climbed the thickly carpeted staircase two at a time, entered his study and slammed the door. He heard Louise shout that dinner would be ready at seven thirty. Why did his wife have to question everything in this way? Mark Finch had made an effort to sit down with Gillian but she always had other things to do, and a drink at the Frog and Ferret was a form of release. Maybe if he'd carried on with his medical studies he'd have retired by now as a consultant surgeon? And found a younger wife?

He wondered if he'd need a food taster; perhaps he'd get into the habit of offering a morsel of his evening meal to their black Labrador, Nessie. It would be an hour before he'd be sitting at the dining table so Finch had time to go through the contents of the folder still gripped in his right hand. He threw it down on his desk, knocking a desk diary off the polished surface. Firstly, he scanned plans for the new houses in Wynyard – sixteen detached properties, each walled with a sliding electric gate. The houses were complete with roof, the plumbing and electricity connections almost finished, and the interior fittings, especially the luxury bathrooms and kitchens, were currently being installed. Although Finch had sold property himself some time back, he had appointed a small estate agent named Hunters as the sole seller. Gordon Ashby was pretty cheesed off when he'd heard that but there was no love lost between Finch and him.

Mark Finch had tried his hand in the Spanish property market on the Costa Blanca. He'd had some success with a builder constructing detached villas in the Murcia region despite cursing the local bureaucracy on a daily basis. Everything was *manana* and approval for building work took ages. That was until he'd got the hang of the Spanish 'backhander.' It was surprising how a good long, lunch with the mayor seemed to oil the wheels of administration. He'd given it five years and then decided, somewhat to the chagrin of his wife that he'd return to the UK. Louise lapped up the ex-pat existence with regular dinner parties and shopping trips to El Corte Ingles in Alicante, but all good things must come to an end. Perhaps she was peeved about that?

Originally from Berkshire, Finch felt that the north of

England was a good bet for him in spite of what Louise wanted, so almost a year and a half ago they'd ended up in Pomfreton. Their daughter, Gillian, had got an excellent grade in Spanish at Benenden School and managed to get a job doing some translation work for a local business near Murcia. Finch knew she missed the way of life as well as the sunshine.

Mark Finch looked at a bundle of invoices, each pencil-marked with the latest date by which they needed to be settled. He put the invoices to one side and slid out a dog-eared, ragged envelope from a poly sleeve in the back of the folder. Once he regularly used a silver letter opener but it was now his thumb that ripped open most of his correspondence. Mark Finch folded the letter twice, replaced it in the envelope and popped it back into the plastic sleeve. The mention of 'goods' in the letter reminded him to check on his six hundred bottle collection of Sassicia down in one of the three cellars below the manor house. It was ageing nicely and increasing in profit by the day. He decided to do it now, before his 'darling wife' shouted for him to sit at the oak dining table for dinner.

Descending the stone steps, Finch took out his keys and unlocked the door. Switching on the neon strip lights, his dusty wine bottles were laid sleeping like glass corpses in their racks. Walking along the centre aisle, there was little to do except admire them. Finch hadn't opened one yet, not at fifty pounds a bottle. This cellar was optimal for his wine, the other two adjacent one's being too cold and musty. He knew he ought to get the dampness seen to, and stop a small leak from one of the water pipes that ran across the top of the alcove in one of them. But there was no hurry. Nobody ever came down those steps into the bowels of the building except Mark Finch.

After locking the door, he placed his left foot on the first step. There was a slight noise from one of the dank cellars but Finch paid little attention to it. Probably a rat scurrying about . . . or some poorly stored broom or garden tool had dropped off its loose bracket. Then a voice came from above.

"Dinner's ready." He shivered for a second then climbed the lead-grey steps. Before he reached the top his smart-phone had beeped twice.

***

"I don't believe this!" DCI Jim Adamson was looking out of his office window at a denim blue sky, thumbs tucked into his trouser belt like a cowboy. "Bloody flowers, Kev! You're telling me that the dead guy was stuffed with two bunches of bloody flowers! Both with their stems tucked into a condom! One in his mouth and the other up his . . . (Adamson stopped short of saying one word and used another) . . . backside!" DS Straker gave his boss a few seconds to come down from the ceiling.

"Yes sir. I had one of the forensics guys contact a botanist at Durham University. The flowers rammed down his throat were corn marigolds - *Glebionis segetum* - and those up his . . ." The sergeant coughed. "Ahem, the others were asters - *Aster amellus*."

"Corn marigolds and bloody asters! What are we dealing with here, somebody from Gardener's World?" Straker grinned to himself as the DCI sat down. "And you say no ID on him?"

"No sir. No wallet, no driving licence, no phone, nothing. He's got a small tattoo on his right forearm with the initials SD. That's it. He definitely looks as if he's from Eastern Europe, you know, that sort of grim, determined appearance like a Bulgarian weightlifter or a pig farmer from Hungary." Adamson lay back, lacing his fingers across his stomach and creasing his polyester tie in the process. He tried hard to imagine what a Hungarian pig farmer looked like.

"I know the Super is going to be walking into this office sometime soon and we need some answers to his questions, Kev. So far, we've got three murders on our hands. Ivo Stavinsky from Estonia and Nejc Kodric from Lithuania and this third guy. Is there a connection? Then we've got bodies with their wallets missing, assuming they had a wallet in the first place, which would in all probability have contained some form of ID. No phone either. We've got these bloody numbers on Stavinsky's arm, followed by a domino and octagon pushed into Kodric. And now, and I can't believe I'm saying it, but a third body stuffed with flowers! Corn something and . . ." Adamson hesitated but Straker quickly added 'Corn marigolds and asters, sir.' The DCI continued.

"The cause of death has been recorded as asphyxiation. And . . . the first two were reported as having a piece of luggage that disappeared. The suitcase that Stavinsky had and a blue rucksack belonging to Kodric as well as the green holdall from left luggage on Darlington station. We don't yet know if the third victim was in possession of anything similar, but we're still questioning several eye witnesses in Albert Road." Straker scanned his notes again. "One woman says she thinks she saw a man matching his description walking north on Albert Road and pulling a small case of sorts – 'on wheels with a handle.' It had a beige tartan or Burberry style of pattern on it. He seemed to be in a hurry. Then we have a chap, let me see, Jimmy Banks, who has told us that SD almost bumped into him as Banks came out of a pub on Albert Road. Mind you, he smelt of booze so I've taken that with a pinch of salt. However, what's of more interest is this!" The detective sergeant took a sealed medium sized polythene sleeve out of a large brown envelope. Inside was a luggage tag – a Burberry pattern on the edges, its narrow, brown leather strap broken but the buckle was intact. "It was handed in yesterday."

"My theory, sir, is that this luggage tag came from the bag that SD was pulling along behind him. And . . ." Straker paused for dramatic effect. "The initials SD stand for Slavko Dalopov, a Ukrainian." Adamson jumped up like a firecracker.

"Bloody hell, Kev, you don't half like to keep the best bit 'til the last! And?" The DS grinned cheekily.

"Sorry sir. The tag has an address and phone number on, too! I've also checked local hotels and we now know that Dalopov stayed at the Crimdon Grange Hotel in Blackhall last night." Right at that moment, Superintendent Harry Charlton walked into the room. He looked at his DCI.

"Well, Jim, anything on this latest case?"

***

Tommy. Got your report. Few points to clarify. S & S cafe tomorrow? 1pm. Paul

Tommy had sent his report from the week-end surveillance in Middlesbrough. It was in Paul Dawson's post office box by 8.00 am on the Tuesday but if Tommy was honest with himself, he wasn't pleased with it. Included were several photographs - the three girls in the hotel bar early evening, the front of the hotel, Maria's car in the Travelodge car park, the note from Slavko, the number 327 on the hotel door, and the three of them having a drink in Chambers bar at 10.44 pm. All photos were taken on the Saturday.

On the following morning Tommy had risen early and popped out to buy a Sunday newspaper. The Boro had lost at home to Norwich City and he reluctantly wanted to read the match report as well as check on some other sports stories. The nearest newsagent was a five - minute walk away. Tommy had got back to the Travelodge at two minutes past nine and was feeling hungry. He thought it a safe bet to use the restaurant for a bit of breakfast as the three girls had not got back to their room until around midnight and would be having a lie-in. Bunters chicken nuggets had been OK but he had felt hungry as soon as he'd showered that morning.

As Tommy got back to the hotel, somewhat out of breath, he'd looked across to the car park. Maria's red

Mazda MX-5 was where she had left it. Tommy had made time for scrambled eggs and bacon, scanned the Boro report and checked some tennis scores from a WTA competition in Japan. He'd gone up to the third floor and eased past their room. He could hear girlie voices coming from inside. Tommy wondered if Maria was now aware of him following her. Was she smart enough to be playing some kind of cat-and-mouse game with him?

Just supposing that Maria knew all along that her ex-boyfriend from school was stalking her! For that's how it could be seen . . . stalking, surveillance, scouting, following, shadowing, trailing. It was all the same, wasn't it? And didn't people who felt they were being stalked report it to the police? What if PC Foot Patrol rang Tommy's doorbell and asked him to accompany him to the station. 'We've had a complaint, sir, from a young lady who says you've been keeping an eye on her and she wants it stopped right away.' He'd slapped himself hard on his bare neck to bring his daydreaming to an end.

Tommy had waited in the lounge bar area, checking the BBC news on his smartphone, making a coffee last as long as possible. Lydia had texted him from reception. He'd slipped her £25 to let him know when Maria and the two girls were checking out of the Travelodge to be certain he didn't miss them. It was just before 11.00 am. They'd crossed over to the car park, put a small bag into each of their cars and within seconds the three cars were leaving. Tommy had pulled his coat collar up, put on his sunglasses and moved quickly. It was the elusive Maria that was his objective so he kept track of the red Mazda. It soon became apparent that the two cars were in convoy. 25 minutes later the cars slowed outside a semi-detached house in a smart suburban area of Norton and the lead car parked on the drive. One of the girls unlocked the front door and walked in, followed by Maria and the other girl. Tommy observed the house for over an hour when a woman with short dark hair wearing spectacles came out and drove away in the red MX-5.

***

On a damp Wednesday lunchtime Tommy met Paul. They both ordered a mug of tea and a bacon sandwich. It was a few minutes after one o'clock.

"Thanks for the report and the photos, Tommy. It makes for interesting reading." Paul hesitated for a few seconds. "But it doesn't seem to cover much on Sunday? How long did you follow Maria on that day? Where did she go, what did she get up to?" Tommy swallowed hard. "And, let's see, you've now spent 28 hours on this job at £50 per hour and covered 285 miles at 45p per mile. I make that £1,528.25p." Tommy felt his ears go warm and hoped they weren't turning red, too.

"Paul, I understand what you're saying. Let me explain." And with that Tommy took a large bite of his sandwich, chewed it rapidly and gulped down a quarter of his mug of tea. He went on to tell Paul exactly what had happened, including the incident in the alley off Albert Road that had now appeared in the newspapers and on regional television. He insisted that Maria's movements had been awkward, and had made a decision not to follow the black - haired girl who left the premises in Norton in Maria's car. On that point Paul Dawson smiled enigmatically but said nothing. Tommy had made assumptions about Maria's activities but he had lost track of her and apologised. As a PI, Tommy had to report the truth about what he'd observed – and that's what he did. Paul had eaten half of his bacon butty and pushed the crusts aside. Paul held his mug with two hands and, for the first time, Tommy noticed how big and strong they seemed. Maybe library books were heavier than he remembered.

"Well, Maria didn't come home until 4.15 pm on Sunday and went upstairs to look at her doll collection after we'd had a brief chat. She wanted to clean them, or check them, or something. She said she'd had a good time with Becky and Rachel and enjoyed the Jersey Boys tribute band, even told me the songs they'd performed. Then they'd been shopping at Dalton Park shopping centre on Sunday. But you didn't tell me in your report where Maria was between leaving the hotel on the Saturday evening and the time you photographed her in Chambers bar at 10.44 pm. You made no mention of her at the theatre. Then there was Sunday. You didn't know whose house she went to. And you decided not to follow Maria's car when it was driven away?" Paul paused. "Listen, Tommy, I'm paying you good money to follow my wife and to tell you the truth I'm very disappointed. There are other private investigators on Teesside, you know." Tommy hadn't seen this side of Paul's character before. Tommy needed the income from this job. Apart from the Ashby case, he only had two other small investigations on the go – a philanderer and someone copping off work.

"OK, Paul, point made. Don't you see that your wife is probably lying to you. There's no way she went shopping at Dalton Park. I'm reporting what I observe but I'll reduce my fees by 25% for the week-end just gone and promise to be more diligent in future if it keeps you happy. Maybe I took the meeting with the Slavko guy at 9.00 pm for granted. My mistake . . . schoolboy error." Paul appeared to calm down and drank his tea. After another ten minutes of discussing the possibilities of Maria's whereabouts on Sunday, Paul stood up and Tommy quickly got to his feet. Tommy had paid for lunch, which made him feel a bit better, and shook Paul's hand. "Paul, give me a call when you want me to follow Maria again. I think we're getting closer to understanding what's going on. Three murders interlinked with Maria's three meetings. That's downright incredible! I feel the police are not telling the public as much as they know. We've agreed to keep this to ourselves . . . my work for any of my clients is always confidential." Paul nodded, thanked Tommy for the tea and sandwich and moved towards the door. He turned.

"By the way, Maria has changed her hair style. It's

black and shorter than before. Becky is a self-employed hairdresser – works from home." With that the café door closed behind Paul.

Tommy sat back down on the hard, wooden chair. Changed her hair style! He could have kicked himself. Not in a million years did Tommy recognise Maria when she'd left what he now realised was Becky's house. He'd have to sharpen up. Was Paul testing him? And hell, if DCI Adamson and his team knew that Tommy was so close to the three deaths, they'd be very interested in talking to him! He'd almost got a ring side seat! But he had to keep it to himself, client confidentiality and all that. There was sharing information *and* sharing information. And Tommy hadn't shared everything he knew with his client, Mr. Dawson.

Lydia was most helpful on that Sunday morning. She'd also told Tommy that a gentleman with a foreign accent had come into reception around 7.30 pm and asked the hotel to ensure a note was given to Miss Dawson as he'd lost his mobile phone and so was unable to contact her. He'd added that he knew she was with friends and didn't want to disturb her. The receptionist had put the note into an envelope and arranged for it to be slid under the door of room 327.

But it hadn't answered one basic question – had Maria really gone to the theatre or was she doing something else? Where had she been when the man was found in the alley off Albert Road? Tommy glanced at his watch. He'd taken a call from DS Straker the previous day; Adamson had asked his sergeant to let Tommy Archer know that a press conference had been called at Middlesbrough police station on Thursday at 3.00 pm.

But he hadn't mentioned *that* to Paul Dawson.

***

After his meeting with Paul Dawson, Tommy had driven home via the David Logan Leisure Centre. He had decided to say 'hello' to Chris Butler, the Centre Manager. He felt he owed Chris a courtesy call after he'd been so helpful a few months ago when Tommy had called in and asked questions about Dick Ashby and ended up with information on Dave Teague and Gillian Finch. Butler's body-building coach, Carl Williams, had also been helpful. Parking his VW Golf in the corner of the car park, Tommy strolled across to the front glass doors and walked in. Clare, the receptionist was on duty again.

"Hi Clare." Tommy placed both palms on the front edge of the desk and was about to remind her of his name. Clare smiled.

"Hello, Tommy, how are you?" She'd remembered. It made him feel good. But then maybe she had a memory for names and knew everyone who came through the door?

"Mustn't grumble, you know. I was just passing and wondered if Chris was in? I just wanted to say 'hi.'" Clare lifted the handset in front of her and very shortly afterwards Chris Butler appeared and the manager invited Tommy into his office.

"Chris. Thanks for seeing me. I wanted to say another thank you for your help back in May when I was making enquiries about Dick Ashby. I'm afraid to say he hasn't been found yet. Police believe he's either still on the run or he's come to a sticky end. As I told you in confidence, his father asked me to try to find him and so far, I've had no joy." Tommy left his comments hanging in the air. Chris Butler leant back on his chair as if to collect his thoughts.

"Well, Tommy, it's fortuitous that you've called in because Carl and I were chatting over a coffee only yesterday. It seems that Dave Teague might know something about Dick Ashby. Teague was in here about a week ago and talking to a guy in the lounge, all sort of pally and close up. I don't know who he was, but Carl was sitting nearby after having ended a body building session with some bloke who wants to enter the Mr. England contest next year and couldn't help but overhear their conversation . . ." Chris stopped abruptly. "This is all off the record, Tommy, right?" Tommy gave an assuring smile and nodded as Chris bent forwards. "Well, Teague runs his own business called HighVisibility and uses an office at Film & Video in Victoria Road. Apparently his HighVisibility work is a bit dodgy . . . gets asked to film an odd collection of goings on, put stuff on DVD, some undercover activity but it's not illegal, no porn or anything like that, and he gets well paid for it." Tommy hadn't turned on his microphone pen on, and was beginning to wish he had done.

"What can you tell me about Teague's current photography assignments? How much did Carl hear?" Tommy took out a small notepad and turned to a fresh page and clicked his ball-point pen.

"Well, somebody asked Teague to install a camera in their basement to capture the movements of anybody that entered the place. The filming was set to a time lapse exposure of five seconds per frame; something about items going missing and this person wanted evidence of any thieving that was occurring. You know, for the police." Tommy paused.

"This is interesting so far, Chris, but none of this makes my neck hairs stand up. This is pretty routine with a number of premises I would have thought? Stuff being nicked . . . set up a camera. Catch the villain." Chris Butler grinned.

"Yeah, but when he's asked to set up the camera in an unlit basement while the client holds a torch for him in complete darkness, don't you think that sounds odd? He gave him some story about a blown fuse and the electricity being off down there." Tommy swallowed, his throat becoming dry.

"This guy, the one that Teague was talking to, did Carl recognise him?"

"No, he's not a regular, and nobody signed him in. It's not that difficult to wander in here and grab a coffee. Clare can't watch everyone coming and going."

"Did Carl describe the guy, I mean, did he have any notable features. Would he recognise him again?" Tommy eased forwards in anticipation. Chris closed his eyes for a few seconds.

"I don't think so. He was your pretty average guy off the street – medium height but with a chubby build, clean shaven, dark hair, no specs." Chris hesitated. "Oh, there was one thing. Carl said he wore a cravat. Now you don't see that very often these days - a bloody cravat!"

***

Two elderly couples were sat chatting in the lounge bar as Tommy wandered into the Frog and Ferret. Three young men were sat on bar stools, each with a partly consumed pint in front of them. He recounted what Mavis had mentioned about the 'friendliness' that existed between Grimes and Dick Ashby. That could mean a heap of things, and Tommy wasn't going to jump to any conclusions. Perhaps young Ashby had called in a few times with some pals for a drink. He may have gone in with his father, Gordon, who called in from time to time, but Tommy had a plan as he eased up to the quiet end of the bar.

"Evening, Roger! How are you keeping?" Roger, one known to easily perspire, mopped his brow with a spotted handkerchief. His mustard waistcoat was a size too small for him.

"Fine . . . can't grumble. A pint of the usual, Tommy?" There were five real ales. Tommy eyed the enamelled metal tag on each beer pull. He normally liked the Theakston's Old Peculier but he decided on a pint of Ruddles. Tommy thanked him and took a long, slow draft. Roger stayed near the end of the bar.

"They don't seem to have found the Ashby boy, yet, Roger? It's been a while now." The landlord wiped his bushy eyebrows.

"Aye, there's no telling where he is. Maybe he's run away . . . gone down south. London, even? He could be anywhere. I know his old man is fretting for him – you'd expect that."

"He used to come in here, didn't he?" Tommy probed.

"Yes, a few times. Nice young man. He popped in with some of his pals from time to time, they were harmless youngsters." Tommy quaffed his Ruddles.

"I heard somebody say that you got on well with him," Tommy lied.

"Well, er . . ." Roger looked around the bar. "We had the same hobby. He's a numismatist. You know, coin collector. It just came out in conversation one evening. I mentioned my collection of Roman coins which he said sounded very interesting. He collects Georgian silver coins in particular, but my two hundred odd display of Roman coinage took his fancy. Said he'd like to see them sometime when it was convenient . . ." Tommy soaked up the information.

"And did he ever see them?" Roger shook his head.

"No, it wasn't long after that when he was put into that detention centre . . . Hartsup or Hardtop or something like that." Tommy corrected him. Hartshot.

"Ah, well, he'll turn up sometime. By the way, do you know a taxi driver called Barlay?" Roger nodded and told Tommy he popped in from time to time for a soft drink. Roger didn't ask why Tommy was enquiring. "Changing the subject, Roger, a friend of mine who's just bought a pub down in Essex tells me that running a place like this is hard work. He reckons the beer cellar is the heart of the business. A good cellar is what brings the customer back time and again, apparently." Lowering his voice, Tommy leant forward. "Any chance of a quick look down there, Roger?" The landlord's face flushed slightly.

"I don't think so," he exclaimed, and then apologised. "Sorry, what I mean is that it isn't appropriate right now. You see a pub landlord prides himself on his cellar and I can't let any old Tom, Dick or Harry down there!" He began wiping the bar surface. "Didn't mean to be off with you, Tommy, but there's the barrels and pumps and other equipment down there. In any case, it isn't that interesting really. Tell your friend down south that everything is as it should be in this part of North Yorkshire." With that, Roger turned to serve another customer. So, Tommy's ruse hadn't worked . . . a look down those stone steps had been thwarted and he wondered again about the comment from Mavis.

Tommy downed the last of his pint, wiped his mouth on the back of his hand and put the glass down on a beer mat. As he moved to the door, Mark Finch entered the pub. Finch ignored Tommy as he waved at a man sitting near the brick fireplace. 'Arrogant sod!' thought Tommy. As he was closing the heavy wooden door of the pub, Tommy heard piano music. Roger had probably put a classical music CD into the Sanyo player on the end of the bar.

***

The conference room at Bridge Street West, Middlesbrough was pretty full. Almost 3.00 pm, DCI Jim Adamson and DS Kevin Straker were sitting at the front behind a table covered with a plain blue cloth showing the Cleveland Police logo. Some twenty news media journalists were gathered to listen to the latest update on what was now being labelled as The Three Throttlers by some dyed-in-the-wool newspaper hacks. One cynical journalist wondered if they'd ever released a Christmas album. Superintendent Harry Charlton sat to the left, away from the forthcoming verbal bombardment of questions that would be inevitable. Jim Adamson tapped the table and silence fell. Notepads and recording devices were poised.

"Good afternoon, ladies and gentlemen, thank you for coming today. Our objective is to bring you up to date with our ongoing enquiries regarding the three murders that have been committed in this area over the past few weeks. My colleague, DS Straker, will be giving you information as we go along, but as is normal during these press conferences we may be unwilling, or unable, to answer every question you ask." The screen behind the table changed images. The police logo morphed to a list of the three victims. "As you already know there are three East Europeans that have been found murdered in Cleveland." Adamson flipped his index finger over his left shoulder at the screen where Ivo Stavinsky, Nejc Kodric and Sergio Dalopov were listed. Estonian, Lithuanian and Ukrainian respectively. "You are aware of the MO, modus operandi, of the killer *or* killers but to recap . . . Stavinsky was found bound in the boot of his car in the rear car park of The Seaview Hotel in Marske, left ear cut off, the numbers 01123 cut into his right inner forearm, and no car keys or wallet belonging to Stavinsky have yet been recovered. Cause of death, strangulation with a white 5mm cord.

Kodric checked into the Queen's Head in Yarm on 12 July carrying a blue rucksack that is still missing. He was picked up from the front of the hotel that evening in an Audi A4, registration NT 65 PDY. We have had a report that the vehicle was seen at The Cleveland Bay Horse in Kirklevington that same evening at between about seven thirty and ten o'clock. Kodric's body was found by a maid the following morning in his hotel room with a domino pushed well into his left eye socket. An octagon-shaped lump of marble was lodged in his airway and itself the cause of death by asphyxiation. No sign of Kodric's wallet or phone." Adamson took a long drink of water from a tumbler in front of him.

"The third murder is one of those that make you really wonder about the killer of Sergio Dalopov. His body was found in an alleyway in this town with a bunch of flowers rammed both down his throat *and* up his backside!" Some of the media stifled a chuckle. "The thick stems of the flowers down his throat filled his trachea and choked him. We have witnesses who state Dalopov was wheeling a small, light brown suitcase along in Albert Road, but we have not found this yet. This third investigation is still in its early stages and there are facts that we can't share with you just yet including some aspects of the pathologist's reports. . ." Adamson was interrupted by a newspaper reporter with a *Gazette* ID tag hanging round his neck.

"You're saying that you haven't found the suitcase that Stavinsky had when he checked into the Seaview? Or the rucksack belonging to Kodric? I mean these must be key to your investigations. And the wallets of these guys . . . still missing? What steps are you taking to recover these?" Adamson stood his ground despite feeling that he'd like to slap the guy. Before he could answer, another question. "Has the third victim lost his wallet, too?" Kev Straker placed his hand on Adamson's forearm to indicate he'd answer this. The DS spoke.

"We can tell you that Dalopov's personal belongings, including his wallet has not yet been recovered. Nor do we have a mobile phone, assuming he possessed one." Another reporter shouted from the back of the room.

"Are you looking for one killer – a serial killer, or three murderers?"

"From the look of the situation it would appear that it's the same perpetrator, but we're keeping an open mind right now." A reporter on the front row quickly stood up.

"Have you got a psychological profile of the perp, somebody with a real problem, a psycho with a screw loose?" A brief ripple of schoolboy chuckles wafted across the room as Harry Charlton scowled. Adamson noticed. Then the DCI spoke.

"We don't expect comments like that, Gus, but we are now working with a criminal forensic psychiatrist, Dr Adam Harper." Adamson recognised the guy from the *Newcastle Journal*. Gus Stroud looked suitably embarrassed and mouthed the word 'sorry' at the senior detective. "We are pursuing a number of lines of enquiry, interviewing numerous witnesses and clearly can't tell you everything at this stage. We're checking out more details on the background of each victim, any connections they may have had with anyone in the north east, following up on their exact movements leading up to the time of their deaths. We'd like to find the driver of the Audi that collected Nejc Kodric, and whether the three victims knew each other. What we can tell you is that a blonde woman has been mentioned in five witness statements. Accounts vary slightly regarding her height, we put her between five feet two and five feet six but witnesses cannot be sure if she was wearing high heel shoes. Eye colour uncertain, possibly blue or green, but she has shoulder length fair hair and wearing a heavy pair of spectacles . . . maybe tortoiseshell." A short guy resembling Danny Devito sitting on the second row jumped up and asked if any of the victims had a mobile phone on them. Adamson replied 'As we've said, we are assuming they did, but none has been found, yet,' and then before anybody else could pose further queries Jim Adamson raised a hand and brought the meeting to an end. He thanked everyone for attending the meeting and promised further information would be made available in due course.

Tommy had made notes, but there wasn't much that was new for him. One crucial comment from the DCI had hit Tommy like a soggy wet flannel flung hard across the bathroom and slapping his face.

'A blonde woman has been mentioned in five witness statements . . .'

As he walked outside on a dull afternoon Tommy Archer wished that he'd never started this investigation. But he had. He was involved. Right up to his neck.

There was no wonder that Maria Dawson had changed her hair style.

***

The cellar was still dank, the musty smell of the cold walls seemed close one minute, further away the next. It was an optical illusion, surely. Like thinking you were looking down a dark tunnel and realising that it was an alcove only a couple of feet deep. Time had no meaning any more apart from when the door flap opened and a plate and bottle of water were pushed through. He must have been sound asleep at some stage as the toilet bucket was now empty. What a relief. The bed clothes were dirty, felt dirty, sort of greasy. As he'd pulled the bedclothes over him two days ago his long finger nails snagged on the slits in the material. They kept breaking and he'd had to chew them off, the wall making a good emery board to file them down.

But it seemed that things were looking up. He'd been sat up on the edge of his bed for a while now. Back straight, knees bent, hands clasped together in front of him, head upright. The pose was that of an interviewee ready and waiting for the questions that would get him the job.

Yes, he was ready and waiting.

***

The new coffee machine worked perfectly. Paul had decided to buy it without asking Maria. She wasn't bothered about decent coffee, but he was – especially at breakfast time. But he wouldn't have bought it if one of his colleagues at the library hadn't gone on and on about her new coffee machine. He was jealous. But not only would it provide freshly brewed coffee for him on a morning, but he'd be able to tell his neighbour – brag about it, even. Score points. And if he and his wife met with friends, he'd take pleasure in sharing *his* experience of *his* coffee machine.

***

"Hi, Tommy. It's Paul. Maria has spent almost all evening up in the spare room with her doll collection. What the hell she does up there I'll never know. Anyway, she has told me she's going out on Thursday evening this week. She's says she's meeting a friend in the Crathorne hotel at seven o'clock so she'll be leaving the bungalow about six fifteen. Can you do the usual? I guess it'll be at the hotel there. Do you know it?" Tommy did. "As ever, she hasn't said much. It's an old school friend from her days at Cheltenham, apparently." Paul laughed. Tommy had a feeling that this was going to be ground-hog day but prayed it wouldn't be. Surely not again? Paul continued.

"Tommy. I was a bit harsh with you recently. Sorry about that." Paul sounded almost compassionate. "If you can give me a full report on Maria by end of Monday, with photos, there's a £500 bonus in it for you. How does that sound?" Tommy smiled to himself. That would come in handy for a few outgoings he had soon. "And I'm going to buy Maria a bunch of flowers. I haven't done that in ages. There's a florist near the library."

"Thanks, Paul. I won't let you down. I'll cling to Maria like the proverbial leech!" With that the conversation ended. So, the day after tomorrow, Tommy would go through his routine. Park up, follow the red Mazda, keep his distance, take photos, and – if lucky – get close enough to use the mike. The chances of Maria meeting up with some guy who'd end up dead was about the same a winning the UK national lottery Tommy decided. He was about to make a coffee when his phone beeped on the kitchen worktop. It was Joe Blackwell.

"Hi, Joe, how's my favourite head of hotel security?"

"Tommy, how are you? It's been a while. Listen, I just wanted to let you know that the Northcliffe Group have acquired another hotel, probably the jewel in the crown for us. I've only just heard about it and I'm really pleased. It may be on the local news later." Tommy felt a thump in the solar plexus as if Tyson Fury had driven a boxing glove into his stomach. He knew what was coming next. "It's the Crathorne Park Hotel just outside of Crathorne village itself . . . you know just off the A19." Tommy wasn't sure what to say.

'Congratulations.' 'Will you get a pay rise?' 'Will there be another murder soon?'

"Hey, Tommy, are you still there?" Tommy told Joe that there was someone at his front door and had to go. It was a lie. He wished Joe all the best and ended the call. Tommy made his coffee and sat on a kitchen stool. He needed to take this in. The Northcliffe Group owned four hotels, including The Seaview in Marske and The Queens Head in Yarm. The other two were smaller, one on the north side of Hartlepool near Blackhall called the Crimdon Grange and the other in Richmond, The Riverdale. The Crathorne Park purchase made it five in total.

Joe Blackwell was a good friend. He'd been a sergeant in the Military Police for eight years; solid and upright as they come. A former schoolboy chess champion with a sharp mind, Joe had been helpful with information on the two hotels where the two East Europeans had been murdered but Tommy began thinking back to how he'd first met Joe. It had been at a car boot sale in Bedale one Saturday morning in July about eleven years ago. They'd both been looking at a stall with a Clarice Cliff jug. As Tommy went to pick it up Joe reached for it at the same time. They laughed as Tommy apologised, but Joe said he didn't mind. One of those very British moments when outwardly nobody shows any concern, but each probably wishing the other wasn't there. Eventually Tommy put it down and Joe bought it. A month later they bumped into each other in an ASDA supermarket. Joe was with his wife, Chloe, and they told her about the jug episode. It didn't sound half as amusing as it was at the time. Joe's wife worked as the manageress in Stockton at a flower shop called *Pistils and Roses*. Tommy assumed it was a take on Guns 'n Roses and he'd smiled inwardly.

Apart from that, when they exchanged phone numbers with a promise to let each other know of any Clarice Cliff bargains, Tommy realised that there were things about Joe Blackwell of which he was completely ignorant. He didn't know where Joe lived, his age, unsure about any children. Of course, they'd kept in touch and would meet for a beer or coffee as time went on, but they weren't 'Christmas card friends.' It was Joe who'd suggested joining the police, and Tommy was grateful for that. But as he downed the last of his coffee and rinsed his mug, he came to realise that he didn't really know Joe Blackwell. You could say that he hardly knew him at all. And now Crathorne Park Hotel . . .

***

The enquiries on Slavko Dalopov, the murdered Ukrainian, proved fruitful. DS Kev Straker had put in long hours, the figurative midnight oil lamp nearly empty. The address and phone number on the luggage tag had been followed up. Straker had now received authority to talk with Interpol. The details were of the chemistry department at Sumy State University in the north east of the country. Dalopov was a research student in his second year. The report from Straker was now with Jim Adamson.

Adamson had given his Superintendent as much information as they had, but told him that his Detective Sergeant was still very much on the case. There was no sign of wallets, keys or phones – any or all of which the three murdered men would have had on them, and the only passport they had was that of Ivo Stavinsky found in his car in Marske. 'Doesn't every man and woman carry these kinds of things these days?' the DCI had asked Straker. 'Hell, nobody went anywhere without their lifelines to the outside world!' he'd added. The DCI was convinced that the killer or killers of the three East Europeans had taken these items from the victims, then either kept them, or thrown them away. Interpol had traced credit card details and phone numbers of each victim and none of these had been used since the date they were murdered. Each victim did have a mobile phone registered with a service provider in each of their own countries. A trace on each phone proved useless, suggesting not one of them had been switched on for some time, but phone companies had been asked to alert the Cleveland Police if it should happen.

Dr Adam Harper had spent quite some time drawing up a profile of the killer, and it was the criminal forensic psychiatrist's opinion that it was the same person who had committed all three crimes. He believed the killer was male, but did not rule out a female who was physically strong. In either event, the murders were carried out by someone with a troubled childhood who may have killed small animals or pets, possibly been abused by a parent or other member of the family such as an aunt or uncle and been bullied at school. Likely age? In their thirties. There was a strong possibility that the killer had a 'dark' fetish and it was vital to establish a link between the three victims, if there was one. Once that had been done Harper felt he'd know more about the murderer.

But what was of special interest to the psychiatrist was the modus operandi - strangulation and body mutilation, as well as the apparent desire to thrust objects into the victims – eyes, throat and rectum. The sequence of numbers on the arm of Ivo Stavinsky, the swollen eye orbits of Nejc Kodric stuffed with a domino and a lump of marble down his gullet, and the stems of two bunches of flowers inserted into Dalopov's throat and rectum.

No, Dr. Adam Harper hadn't had a case like this one before. And he was intrigued by it. If he could help solve the murders and find the killer, he believed he'd have an opportunity to deliver a paper at the next annual meeting of the British Association of Clinical Psychiatry.

DCI Adamson had just finished bringing Harry Charlton up to speed when a police constable knocked on his office door. It was 8.25 am. "Sir, sorry to interrupt but we've had a phone call from Crathorne Park Hotel. The receptionist there was nearly hysterical. A dog walker who let his pooch off the lead heard the dog barking near the end of the hotel where a body lay on the grass. The desk sergeant has sent two patrol cars to the hotel. The dead guy is from Latvia, apparently, and he'd booked in for one night." Adamson jumped up, almost knocking his chair over backwards.

"Kev, leave everything. Let's get over there now!"

***

Freddie Sewell had been thinking about a house move from Nunthorpe. A friend at the Corndale Golf Club had told him about a new development at Wynyard some time back. As a result, Freddie had made enquiries, but when Gillian Finch realised that her boss was looking for a new-build house, she told him that her father was in property development. And so, Mark Finch and Freddie Sewell had met at the golf club over lunch one day and discussed matters. Finch wasn't a golfer. He'd heard of Tony Jacklin and Colin Montgomery but that was about the limit of his player knowledge, and when it came to shots to put the ball into a hole, he never could tell the difference between a birdie, an eagle and an albatross.

They'd exchanged cards and talked of the Wynyard development. Sewell went away with a comprehensive brochure listing all the external and internal features, the plan of rooms, and an artist's impression of the finished house and detached triple garage. He'd be able to show that to his wife, Gwen, and she'd read every single word. He also knew that she'd want her own choice of worktop, cooker hood, kitchen island with wine racks, as well as choosing the pattern of all frosted glass doors. And she'd demand a double washbasin in the en-suite bathroom.

It was a month later when, over a couple of gin and tonics at the golf club, price was mentioned. Finch had said that Hunters was the sole appointed agent for sales but he himself would be able to let Freddie Sewell have one of five remaining houses at a 'discount.' For that, Sewell was enormously grateful and presented Finch with a bottle of Rioja from Spain, 1995 vintage. And that was when their friendship took off. Wine! They talked about it for hours, Sewell having laid a couple of dozen bottles of claret down to mature. And the interest that Finch developed in wine, especially as an investment, developed further. His Sassicia collection was now growing in value – down there in his dark, slightly damp cellar.

The relationship between Mark Finch and Freddie Sewell grew. He planned to invest more in red wine. With his Social Member status at Corndale Golf Club, thanks to Sewell, that was where they would meet. To discuss

relevant grape matters and the chosen house in Wynyard.
***

"Oh, my God!" spluttered Jim Adamson as he looked down at the half naked body lying face up on at side of Crathorne Park Hotel close to a sign that read WOODLAND WALK. A police constable had already taped the crime scene with the usual yellow and black plastic ribbon using four tree trunks as posts. Adamson had met the hotel manager briefly on his arrival and promised to keep him informed. He requested that any hotel guests who had not yet checked out remain in the hotel lounge until further notice, and he wanted a list of all guests who'd stayed there last night. Minutes later SOCO's had arrived and began their task – placing numbered markers, taking photographs, collecting any minute items of evidence to attempt to piece together the events that had led up to the crime.

The partially disembowelled body of a white male lay next to a small tree out of site of the main car park. A bunch of flowers were pushed into the gaping hole in his abdomen, the liver, pancreas and large intestine clearly visible - flowers with daisy like petals and blue-lilac flowers, and cone-flowers with a central seed head about two centimetres wide. Blood had flowed across the dry grass turning it black.

"What the hell have we here, Kev?" asked the DCI, noticing the tattoo on the neck of the victim. "Looks like a Jack the Ripper job! And more bloody flowers! Let's get the body identified, then details on this guy from reception, and make sure we have documented every single item from the scene of crime officers' report to really get to the bottom of this whole affair. Somebody is taking us for a bloody ride here. No pun intended! Get the information to Adam Harper to add to his psychiatric analysis of the perpetrator . . . and have samples of these flowers looked at by your contact at Durham university's botanic department. Needless to say, we're looking for a murder weapon so let's get the grounds searched. Check for CCTV here in the car park and take a good look at the victim's hotel room. You know – all the standard stuff." Kev Straker nodded. He knew what was necessary. But when the DS reflected on recent events none of it made much sense. Three previous murders, all Eastern Europeans, killed in a bizarre fashion. What was the motivation, he wondered? All murders are motivated by something, an event, an individual, a circumstance . . . he'd need to go through his notes again and see if there was a common thread.

The hotel manager was most helpful. The Latvian, Marin Bukelis, had checked into the hotel at 4.17 pm on Thursday, August 11. His registration form details showed an address in Riga, his date of birth, and passport number. An imprint of his VISA credit card was taken and he agreed that he'd put any extras on his room. Purpose of the visit – Business. Bukelis had arrived by taxi, a blue Toyota Avensis belonging to Boro Cars had been seen on the CCTV footage at the front of the hotel. He'd carried a medium sized black suitcase to his room. It had a two inch - wide, rainbow coloured strap around it, and a table for two had been booked in the Leven restaurant at 7.30 pm. The receptionist, Grace, stated that she had noticed Bukelis on his own in the bar, on a bar stool with a drink in front of him, at about 7.10 pm. Being a Thursday the place was not overly busy and nothing unusual was seen by any of the members of staff on duty. Grace had remarked, however, that he seemed to have a large piece of luggage for just one overnight stay.

The internal CCTV cameras showed a dark - haired woman, on her own, entering the hotel at 7.12 pm precisely, followed six minutes later by a man, estimated to be in his mid to late thirties, with a beard and wearing spectacles. They were noticed because, as the manager put it, both seemed 'lost', suggesting they had not been into the hotel before. The woman appeared to be searching for someone as the grainy CCTV images showed her looking from left to right as she walked towards the bar area. Outside CCTV, but again not clear, captured the same woman getting out of a red sports car minutes earlier at the far end of the car park. There was no footage of the bearded man having arrived in a vehicle.

DCI Adamson and his DS spent two hours interviewing the hotel guests that had waited begrudgingly whilst the police checked the crime scene. The hotel manager had made the room next to his office available for interviews. By 11.00 am the two detectives had formed a good picture of what had happened on the evening of August 11 and MOCT had issued another crime number.

In the restaurant with about twenty diners, four guests reported seeing the dark - haired woman having dinner with a man that fitted the description of Bukelis. They seemed amicable, but there were no signs of physical contact – no hand holding or arm touching. Two guests suggested it looked like a meeting you'd have with your solicitor or bank manager – factual and to the point. The woman used a wine glass which she apparently filled with bottled Harrogate Spring Water placed on the table, the Latvian preferring a pint of beer, of which he was served three or four. They left the table at about ten o'clock, and no one seemed certain of what happened after that. Nobody recalled seeing them in the bar, neither did they show up on the CCTV camera that covered the reception area. It was dark by around 9.30 pm and it had started to rain heavily. Images from the external security monitors were not clear enough to identify anyone leaving from the car park at the front of the building.

When asked about the bearded man with spectacles, only one of the guests remembered such a person and reported that he sat alone three tables away from the couple, and in between eating was reading a paperback book, although he seemed to take a pen from his pocket from time to time and adjust the lapel of his jacket as though trying to keep it flat. The manager confirmed the couple's bill came to £68.95 and was added to the

Latvian's room account, but there was no record of any individual dining alone that evening that had pre-booked a table, or paid with a credit or debit card. However, one of the waitresses, Nora, did recall the bearded man and remarked that he reminded her of 'David Baddiel off the telly' as she put it. None of the guests interviewed came up with very much more for Kev Straker and his boss to go on.

It was likely that Marin Bukelis had returned to his room after dinner. But if he did, there were no signs to indicate that he'd slept in the bed. The SOCO'S had checked it thoroughly. The soap on the washbasin had been used and was still slightly damp; the hand towel askew on the rail. The shower showed no sign of usage, and the bath sheet was still perfectly folded. A slightly damp toothbrush, and minute splashes of white toothpaste on the tiles behind the handbasin along with his prints on a glass mug suggested he had brushed his teeth, probably before dinner. No clothes had been hung up or placed on the bed or chair. Neither the suitcase nor it's coloured strap that Grace had seen him carry up the stairs, were in his room, and the examination of the clothes of the half- naked body of Marin Bukelis revealed no phone or wallet.

By noon on Friday, August 12 DCI Jim Adamson was sitting at his desk wondering how he'd pitch his report to his Superintendent. The Chief Constable was asking more and more difficult questions and considering involving Scotland Yard. How soon would Dr Harper be able to get a better, more thorough psychiatric handle on the killer or killers, what botanical news would Durham university have on the flowers and when would the PM report be available? Where were the private possessions of the four murdered men? The dark - haired woman that had dinner with Bukelis needed to be found and interviewed. Adamson was aware that five previous statements had mentioned an attractive blonde woman, medium height and build that had been seen at or in the immediate area where the three murders had occurred. Was the one who'd had dinner with Bukelis related to her, he'd wondered?

And what of the flowers? The DCI wasn't the gardening type, but he'd be asking Kev Straker to check out all the florists within a ten - mile radius of Middlesbrough town centre. Adamson prayed for a concrete lead. Something . . . anything that would kick-start the investigation with sound, logical reasoning. Little did he know that there might be a catalyst to the whole sequence of events much closer to home than he'd ever have expected.

***

Nicky Barlay was pleased with his badger work. The animal looked surprisingly life-like. At 67 cm in length with a good, thick black and white coat, its glass eyes gleamed and the polished claws were sharp. A friend who mounted Barlay's work would, at a reasonable price, fix the feet to a cream coloured plinth, add a metal plate with genus and species, and the badger would find a place in Barlay's house. The addition of a glass case could be considered later. Or, if he decided that his collection was becoming too cluttered, he'd take it to an emporium in Guisborough that specialised in small mammals. Barlay had sold five of his taxidermy specimens there over the last two years that had netted him around two thousand pounds. The other option was to send it to an auction mart – perhaps Tennant's in Leyburn or Thomas Watson in Darlington.

***

His taxi business was doing OK but one of the other two drivers, Charlie, was being kept under scrutiny. Mavis, who did all the bookkeeping, had told Nicky Barlay that she was concerned about the mileage versus takings that Charlie's figures showed. She'd had a quiet word with Barlay and suggested that perhaps Charlie wasn't using his meter for every trip. It would be so simple to pick up some old lady bordering on dementia and just tell her the fare was a tenner; then the cash goes straight into Charlie's back pocket. But Mavis had proposed a meeting at which a few issues could be discussed, including the distance against income data she'd compiled. If that was amongst other items such as start and finish times, promoting the business differently, a Christmas bonus, getting more contracts . . . then it wouldn't stick out as being a big deal. The hope was that the miles to cash ratio for Charlie would improve. After all, he was good at his job, friendly with his customers and always had a bit of banter on all matters of low interest to most people – including Sunderland A.F.C. of which he was a season ticket holder. Despite that, Barlay didn't want to lose Charlie.

Nicky Barlay wondered where his taxi business would be in twelve months. He really didn't have to concern himself about his business at the moment. Let it trundle along for the time being. He made a reasonable profit from it, and the three cars were in fair condition and regularly serviced. Mercedes diesel engines were known to be good for at least 250,000 miles. With a couple of mild winters, the local council had used salt sparingly on the roads so body work was OK. Use of a local car wash, always with the wax treatment, kept the cars clean and shiny.

It was as Nicky Barlay drove to pick up a fare in Billingham that his Apple iPhone beeped. He didn't recognise the caller. Switching it off, Barlay headed off to his pick-up address off the A19 flyover. Within six minutes his new customer was sitting in the back seat.

"North Tees Hospital, driver." The Scots accent was harsh. "Yer busy today?" Barlay made eye contact in his mirror and nodded. "You cab drivers are always busy, no peace for the wicked, eh?" Nicky Barlay smiled and said nothing.

***

"Paul, can you talk? Is it convenient right now?" Paul

Dawson moved away from the main desk in the library towards a quieter part of the building. Tommy, sitting in his VW Golf parked up on a derelict industrial site near Stockton, waited a few seconds.

"What is it? I haven't received your report yet from last Thursday's surveillance." Dawson sounded cold. "That's six days ago. It's Wednesday today in case you're losing track of time."

"There was another murder last Thursday evening at Crathorne Park hotel. I'm bricking it, I can tell you! It's been on the news but I would guess the police are keeping their information to the media limited. It's the fourth bloody time that I've followed Maria and there's been somebody killed. It's like a crime drama on television, and I'm one of the characters in it! Don't you see that if the police find out that I've been at every venue, or at least close by, I could be for the high jump! They'd take me in for questioning – I'd have to come clean . . ."

"Now listen to me, Tommy, you're being paid to do a job." Dawson was more assertive than he'd been before. "It was *you* that said we'd need to keep this to ourselves, over a mug of tea and a bacon sandwich recently. Remember? So that's what we're going to do. Don't you think I'm concerned for Maria? Hell, she's my wife! It seems clear to me that they're going to be looking for her if they're not already asking questions. I'm glad she decided to change her hair style. But Maria is the innocent one here. You don't honestly believe she could murder those guys in such a brutal manner, do you?" Tommy looked out at the drab, grey buildings around him.

"You'll have my report by tomorrow, Paul. Two pages and several photos." Tommy recalled it was Maria Dawson's birthday coming up on Sunday. "By the way, are you taking Maria out for a celebratory meal for her thirty sixth birthday?" He tried to lighten the mood.

"No, she's going down to Lincoln to see her older sister, Jane, on Friday afternoon. She hasn't been well. I said I didn't mind. She'll be back by Sunday evening so I might open a bottle of fizz when she gets home. Anyway, look forward to your report, Paul. Must go."

Tommy was grateful that Joe Blackwell had provided some information for him on the events at Crathorne. He'd written his report for Paul Dawson but hadn't posted it. The hotel manager had brought Joe up to speed on what the two detectives had planned - they wanted to keep information to a minimum on the murder details – no victim's name, only nationality, and no description of how the hotel guest was killed.

Sitting in his Golf, Tommy watched two pigeons scrapping on a rusted, grey metal roof top and tried to take stock of the past few weeks, ever since Paul Dawson had asked him to follow his wife because he didn't believe what Maria told him. But who were the four victims? Was there a relationship between them? Who wanted them killed? Where were their possessions? And now most importantly . . . was it time to call it a day on this case for Tommy Archer? He had a couple of other jobs keeping him busy, and was well aware that Dick Ashby was still missing. In fact, he reminded himself that Gordon Ashby hadn't been chivvying away at him for a while. If truth be known, Tommy had no idea where young Ashby was. He promised himself to make more effort.

Tommy considered DCI Adamson. He wondered how his wife, Helen, was doing with her MS issues. He had the detective's direct line number. But there was no way he could call Jim Adamson, was there? If he phoned the DCI and spilt the beans on everything he knew where would that take him . . . to an interview room at Cleveland Police HQ with intense questioning. "Why didn't you contact us after Ivo Stavinsky was murdered. Why did you continue to withhold information from us when the police asked for it? Don't you realise you've obstructed the course of justice?"

Tommy felt nervous. He was between a rock and a hard place. Spots of rain began to fall, the windscreen gradually becoming obscured. No point in switching the wiper blades on yet, the dead flies would only smear across the glass. Tommy was perspiring slightly, his armpits damp. Release would be nice. He took his mobile phone from his inside jacket pocket, pressed Contacts and scrolled down to 'Jim Adamson.'

His index finger, quivering slightly, hovered over the direct line telephone number.

***

They looked so pretty in the dim light. Four credit cards . . . Bank of Estonia, a Lithuania finance group, the third from a Ukrainian bank and one from Latvia Finance. Other cards were there, too. Supermarket loyalty, a DIY chain, coffee shops. Nice wallets, too. Calfskin is such a tactile material. Black leather has a characteristic smell, and so does brown leather, but slightly different. Plastic doesn't do it, even that thicker, shiny sort.

'You can tell the cut of a man by the type of wallet he uses.'

The wallets were put back into the blue rucksack alongside other items. And the keys. So many keys, all dangling on one large, metal ring.

And mobile phones these days, so thin, so light. And they are called smartphones because they're so smart, right? Or maybe we ought to refer to them as cell phones? That's what the Americans still call them. They can do so much, too, with their high - resolution cameras.

Nearly all of your life is on one of these, isn't it? All that data and information. What was on them? And photos . . . they could tell you so much about a person. It was tempting to turn one on, just to see what was there . . . something compromising, maybe.

Best not to. No need to alert anyone.

***

"Tommy, it's Gordon Ashby here. Have you got any news

for me, for goodness sake!" The call Tommy was expecting. And because he was expecting it, he was prepared. He took a mouthful of his coffee, his stomach leaning against the kitchen sink.

"Oh, hello Gordon, do you know you've just beaten me to it. I was about to give you a call." Ashby said nothing. "Well, I've got a couple of new leads I'm following up. Can't say too much about them, got the info in confidence, but they could be promising. I should have something to go on by early next week."

"Are you still clocking up charges for this? I'm not bloody made of money! I've had a copper round telling me they haven't any news on his whereabouts. Even used his words carefully to suggest he might not be alive! Don't know why he bothered. He could've phoned. Bloody hell, Tommy, I have to believe he's OK. Perhaps he's holed up with someone, either around here or down south, maybe?" Ashby sounded frustrated.

"Gordon, if he's down south as you put it, then there's no way I'm going to find him. Let's keep our focus on this area. I'll follow up my leads, and ask more questions in the pubs and bars where he may have been. Is there anybody that *you* know that Dick was particularly friendly with?" The question went unanswered for a few seconds.

"Well, he knocked around with a lad called Steve Attridge, a plumber by trade. Not sure how they met, but Steve came to the house a few times – seemed a nice enough lad, but then something must have happened. When my wife asked Dick about Steve, he didn't seem to want to talk about him. These young people can be fickle when it comes to friendship." Ashby paused as if he was thinking of others that his son hung out with. Tommy waited. "I think he got pally with a local taxi driver, and he sometimes went to a gym in Thornaby. There were people there he knew, and he went into some club in Middlesbrough – the Blue Umbrella I think it was called. Although I wasn't keen on the idea, Dick would go into the Frog and Ferret now and again, said he only had alcohol-free beers. He came home once and said he'd been chatting to the landlord who turned out to be a keen coin collector – Roman coins, I think. Dick has a good collection of Georgian silver coins. That's about all I can think of right now."

"Gordon, that's been useful but I must be honest with you, I've already followed up on a number of leads, including some of those you've mentioned. None have really given me any strong indications of where Dick might be right now. He hasn't been seen since the road accident. Would you consider your son to be the type to steal a car?"

"Of course not! We'd brought him up to be a good person and sent him to a decent school. You can't keep an eye on your children all of the time and giving him a bit of space, we thought, was fine, but you never know who they're getting involved with." On that note Tommy wished Gordon Ashby all the best and reassured him that he'd continue searching for his son. Rinsing his coffee mug, Tommy recalled what the brother of Steve Attridge, Matt, had told him about Gordon Ashby which Tommy still couldn't really believe. That the Yarm estate agent was involved with drugs! 'Drugs baron,' 'kingpin' . . . terms used by Matt Attridge when his loose tongue gave Tommy the information. But how was Gordon Ashby involved?

Tommy was tempted to keep an eye on him, but what would that reveal? Did Ashby have a club somewhere that he frequented? Maybe he was a golfer? Always a useful place to discuss business, walking on the fairway and sealing the deal. What about Round Table membership? Even Rotary? Better still, a Mason? Tommy didn't know much about the Masons, except that, apparently, they had odd initiation ceremonies and a strange handshake.

Picking up his car keys, Tommy straightened a painting of Roseberry Topping hanging near the front door. He hated pictures being lop-sided. Locking his front door, he zapped the VW and got in. Before he turned on the ignition he sat and considered matters regarding his search for Dick Ashby. How much did his father know about his son? And if Matt Attridge was telling the truth, was Dick Ashby in league with his father, somehow? What *really* happened on the Whitby road on the evening of the Nissan car accident? There were still unanswered questions but Tommy felt relieved that he hadn't called Jim Adamson the day before. As he reached to turn the car key his phone rang. The screen showed Joe Blackwell.

"Hi Joe. What's up?"

"Tommy, I'm still getting details from the hotel manager on the poor guy found at the Crathorne Park. He had his belly slit open, his suitcase is missing, and some personal effects have gone. I feel a responsibility obviously, and can't say too much at the moment so please keep things to yourself for now. But you know what? Chloe has just called me to say the police have been to the flower shop where she works asking about what kinds of flowers they sell and if they have any regular customers!"

***

Nicky Barlay had hardly slept, at least that's how it felt. The milky, hot malted drink at bedtime hadn't made a scrap of difference and his Wednesday lottery ticket hadn't won him anything. He had rehearsed things in his mind, and if he wasn't thinking about them, he was dreaming about them. Barlay had a plan, but he had to get the timing right. He would make a phone call and determine the time of the appointment. That would be easy. Then he'd use the false beard he'd once bought for a fancy - dress party, and the heavy, black-rimmed spectacles. After all, he only ever seen the man from a distance, so the chances of being recognised were zero. The added bonus was that the customer would be alone – he didn't want his girlfriend going with him.

So that was the plan, all sorted. What could go wrong? Nicky Barlay, alias 'Peter Johnson,' would be doing his job as a Volunteer Driver, and he would tell the customer that he'd been sent to collect him for a surprise meeting with his girlfriend, arranged in secret by a good friend via a phone call to the Volunteer Office. But, 'no,' he wasn't told who'd made the call.

And that's how it all worked out. Easy really.

***

"Right, Kev, let's take another look at what we've got." DCI Adamson had asked DS Straker to come into his office and go through their information to date on the events over the past few weeks regarding the four murders. The Detective Sergeant had been in touch with police forces in each of the home countries of the deceased and collected relevant information. "We've got Stavinsky from Estonia, an out of work lorry driver, Kodric who was a travel agent from Lithuania, Dalopov, a research student from the Ukraine and Bukelis, who we were told by the Latvian police, was a printer. I can't see a link between any of their jobs. Stavinsky entered the country via a ferry from Amsterdam into the Port of Tyne, Kodric was renting an apartment in Gateshead and collected at Darlington station, then there is still a query over Dalopov's entry into the country, and Bukelis had arrived at the Crathorne in a Boro Cars taxi." Straker checked over a page of his folder, then continued. "All four guys lived on their own apart from Stavinsky, married and who lived with his mother. One question is . . . did these four know each other? Is there a connection between the four countries? All murdered by a person or persons unknown where the cause of death has been strangulation followed by asphyxiation, choking and lastly . . ." Adamson flicked through some recent notes.

"Ah, yes, the coroner's report says a knife to the heart for Bukelis, so, we need to look for that murder weapon in the case of the Latvian. Hell, Kev, if this is one person, we've got a real nut case on our hands." Straker had brought two coffees in with him earlier and Adamson swirled the last dregs and emptied his cardboard cup. "Any

DNA?" Straker shook his head. "Any joy with Dr Adam Harper?" The Detective Sergeant opened another folder.

"Yes, Harper emailed me first thing and I've printed two copies." Passing one to his boss he continued. "He's certain that we have a single perpetrator on our hands, male or female, with psychopathic tendencies. He wonders if the killer has a specific grudge against Eastern Europeans but believes there's something else. Harper puts him or her in their thirties as he told us before, and reconfirmed the killer may have been abused or bullied as a child. The missing wallets, phones, luggage, etc. are almost certainly in the possession of the killer who gets a kick out of touching these items – handling them, probably running their fingers over the wallets, stroking the screens of the phones. It gives them a sense of power, apparently. Not happy with a Boro F.C. season ticket then?" Straker chuckled as Adamson smiled to himself.

"Anything from the mobile phone networks . . . have they been switched on at all?" Straker shook his head. "What does Harper make of the MO of the killer?" Kev Straker continued after checking some other notes.

"He's still looking at that. He's spoken with the pathologist. The numbers 01123 cut into Stavinsky's arm were very neatly done. The killer is a person of precision, perhaps with a hobby such as philately or miniature model making. The bunches of flowers, all neatly tied, stems cut to the same length, and firmly inserted into the killer's victims suggest accuracy in their life and work. The knifing of Bukelis was out of the ordinary, but there may have been a good reason, obviously more direct and instant. The closeness to the hotel entrance meant he or she couldn't risk any shouts for help from the victim. Bukelis was quite well built so the perp didn't want to risk a struggle."

"You've had three constables checking florists? What information there?" Straker scanned his tablet.

"They've checked eleven florists in the greater Middlesbrough area. My contact at Durham University's department of botany has given me the Latin names of the flowers, genus and species, but basically, they were corn marigolds and asters, then pyrethrum, also known as coneflowers, and Michaelmas daisies. Only three of the florists sell all four of those. I would say we can assume that the blooms were bought at the same florist by the killer – at least let's begin with that premise." Straker eased an index finger down the list. "*Bloomin' Loverly, Bouquet Bowl* and *Pistils and Roses.*" Adamson lay back in his office chair and smoothed his slightly wrinkled tie.

"Any news on the luggage they carried, Kev? Suitcases . . . the rucksack? What about the driver of the Audi? Anything on him?" The sergeant clicked to another screen on the tablet.

"We've checked the car for prints and found too many sets to be of any value. Prints were lifted from Kodric in the mortuary which match one set still in the car. As I said, our witness, Peter York at the Queens Head, had seen the Audi arrive to collect Kodric and CCTV images confirm that Kodric left the hotel at 7.02 pm."

"Going back to the florists, we need a list of any regular customers, descriptions of them, anything unusual about anyone. It might be worth phoning some garden centres, too. See if they sell those types of flowers. Have they got any CCTV footage? Try and find out more about Dalopov and Bukelis entering the UK. Keep looking for the Bukelis murder weapon. Once we've more to go on, we'll consider another press conference."

"We're on it, sir." Straker closed his folders, switched off his tablet and stood up. As he walked to the door Adamson leant forward and spoke again.

"And another thing, Kev. We need to find the woman that has now been mentioned in eight witness statements at three of the murder scenes. She was described as blonde earlier on, then dark haired later. I'd bet that it's the same person who's either changed her hairstyle or is using a wig. Who is she? We need to find out . . . try to get the photography guys to get a best image shot of her from any

CCTV footage then get a picture onto local television with the usual invite to ring MOCT or CrimeStoppers on the usual 0800 number." Straker gave a reassuring smile as he closed the office door. DCI Jim Adamson knew that if he didn't get some answers for his Superintendent soon, he might be moved sideways onto another case. That was the last thing he needed.

***

There was more regular maintenance at HBF Shipping than Freddie Sewell at first thought. Steve Attridge had been offered a twelve months contract after his initial plumbing work on valves, pipes, etc. so he kept the key to the brick building that acted as a workshop and a small hide-a-way, with the lower basement cool enough to fend off the spell of hot weather that had crept across northern England. Half of Attridge's income came from HBF Shipping, and although he tolerated Gillian Finch, he thought Freddie Sewell was a bit of a tosser. Still, he couldn't look a gift horse in the mouth, and there was the emotional link between Sewell and Les, Attridge's father, who'd played golf together before he passed away.

Gillian Finch continued to make coffee for Attridge with cream and brown sugar 'just as you like it' she'd say to him. But Attridge wasn't really bothered about the cream or whether it was brown or white sugar. It was hot and wet, that's all that mattered. She'd look deep into his hazel eyes as she handed him the mug, a mug she'd bought specially for him. *When All Else Fails Smile* on the side in red letters. There was no doubt about it, Steve Attridge had no feelings for the female sex, but he felt he had to be polite and always thanked Sewell's secretary with, if not a smile, a grin. Finch, although preferring the company of women, had once suggested an evening out with the hydrostatic operative, but she'd been gently rebuffed. 'Purely Platonic' she'd said. Gillian wasn't concerned about the fact that Attridge had a slight limp, a remnant from a car accident he'd said. It was his feminine side, his gentle aura, the way he walked – male-model like, and shook his hair back. She'd noticed his Rolex watch but never dared ask if it was genuine. How could she? And when Gillian requested to take a peek into the brick building on the edge of the Teesport complex where he kept his tools and things, she got a quick and firm 'no.'

But the ankle of Steve Attridge was much better now after the car in which he was a passenger had gone into an oak tree on a dangerous bend near Boulby on the main A174 road to Whitby. He cursed. Why hadn't he driven? The guy at the wheel was buzzing, his head all over the place after an evening in a Middlesbrough night club. Neatly rolled marijuana and tobacco cigarettes had been smoked out back with beer and whiskey adding to the feeling of a 'great night out.' A number of customers had been arguing and one in particular had been standing on a table shouting 'I'm the king of the castle.' He was told to shut up a few times by fellow smokers and drinkers but took no notice. If *he* hadn't been the one supplying the marijuana, he'd have been pushed off the table and told to get the hell out of there.

And when the guy dancing on the table had issued a challenge to steal a car and go to Whitby for fish and chips, there was only Steve Attridge who'd accepted his offer. Down the road from the night club was a fuel station. Quiet at eleven o'clock at night, with an occasional careless car owner who left the keys in the ignition, it wasn't difficult to sneak up out of the shadows and hop in.

So, that's what had happened. The fully fuelled Nissan car had been nicked off the forecourt by two men 'away with the fairies' but with the inane desire to head to the coast for a fish supper, thankfully on the correct side of the road, seat belts secured. But forget aspirin and paracetamol; there's nothing quite as sobering as an air-bag smacking you hard in the face to bring you back to your senses. Attridge had bust his ankle but both managed to get out of the Nissan before the full tank exploded and turned the car into a fireball that could be seen for miles around.

The fuel station CCTV where the Nissan was parked hadn't been working for three days and the guy on the till was busy watching a film on his i-pad to take any notice of anybody on the forecourt.

***

The hospital corridor was busy. Patients and visitors were milling around like a colony of ants travelling to and from their nest. The man from the Volunteer Driver organisation waited close to the exit from the Renal Dialysis unit at James Cook Hospital. Then he saw him. Harry Nevin, the bastard who'd stolen his wife, walked toward him. It was exactly 3.25 pm.

"Excuse me, Mr. Nevin? I'm Peter Johnson, a volunteer driver. My office asked me to collect you. Apparently, a friend of yours has set up a surprise for your wife. It's Judith isn't it?" Nevin nodded. "She's at the Hilton Hotel with a couple of girls having afternoon tea and it's the birthday of one of them. Judith doesn't know that, so it was suggested that you join them and take a gift with you on her behalf!" Barlay smiled, enough to make it all sound genuine.

"A gift? What gift?" Nevin enquired.

"Some flowers. I've got them in the car. They were paid for by your friend over the phone – I'm afraid I don't know who this person is, but they thought it would be a nice gesture for the 'birthday girl.'" Barlay eased his spectacles up the bridge of his nose, looking at Nevin through the plain glass. Nevin seemed to hesitate. Barlay continued to smile – but not too much.

"And a surprise for Judith!" Nevin beamed. "Ok, let's go! But what do I owe you?"

"Nothing, it's a volunteer service. We get funded by Teesside council," he lied.

Now wasn't that useful? Nicky Barlay had known for some time that Nevin had his renal dialysis on a monthly basis – the third Tuesday in the month. And reception had been very helpful in giving Barlay the time of the appointment and length of treatment.

"This is a nice car, Peter!" said Nevin as he got into the back of the black Mercedes Benz, the removable taxi sign stowed in the boot.

***

It was still damp down there. A slight odour like a forest floor with fungi hung in the stale air. The darkness was constant, only the narrow slit under the door allowing a little light in during the day. The unmade bed stayed rucked up, the smelly blanket creased on the lumpy mattress as a rat scuttled along the rotten skirting board hunting for any food remains.

He hadn't used the toilet for a while now nor had he touched the bottled water or skinny pizza. He'd read about meditation and how it calmed the mind, settled the soul. Transcendental meditation, wasn't that what the Maharishi Mahesh Yogi performed? Sitting in a fixed position for hours on end, focusing on the key factors in your life. Clearing your head of every possible thought that might mar the process. Or you could imagine that you were alone on a desert island, laid on your back on the white sand, in the shade of a palm tree with large waving leaves that gave you shade. The only sound was the lap, lap, lap of the warm azure blue sea intermittently tickling your heels and calves. Your fingers dug gently into the coral sand, scooping it up and throwing it down with no purpose other than to help you drift away into a state of rapture.

He hadn't done much of late but sitting on the edge of the bed. Upright, hands clasped together, staring into the void, no longer hearing any of the slight sounds that emanated nearby from time to time. Some would call him lazy but under the circumstances that would be harsh.

If there was an upside it was that he hadn't coughed for a while now.

***

The sale of the red Mazda MX5 had been painless. Without telling Paul, Maria had been on the Autotrader web site and checked out cars for sale within a fifteen - mile radius of Eston. She chose a three - year old black Ford Fiesta, the ideal unobtrusive colour. She'd been in touch with the garage owner, Chrissie Mackintosh, and the price agreed. Maria had asked for two new tyres to be fitted to the front, a new set of mats and a complete service and valet. When she called in that Friday afternoon the car was parked near to the small office. The paperwork didn't take long, and a phone call to Maria's insurance company to amend the policy was done in a couple of minutes. The garage owner handed Maria two sets of keys and showed her to the Fiesta gleaming in the afternoon sun. Before she drove away, Mackintosh helped her to move three cardboard boxes and a suitcase from the Mazda into the boot of the Fiesta.

Having taken the day off work, she'd told Paul that her sister, whom he'd never met, wasn't feeling well. Lincoln was only a couple of hours drive down the A1 towards Newark and then across on the A57. The car had sat-nav and Mackintosh had shown her the basics, and, although she didn't much care for the sat-nav voice, the screen map would get her to her destination even with the volume turned down. Maria wasn't going to rush. She wanted to get used to sitting higher up than in her sports car and make certain that she knew where all the controls were. No, she'd take it easy on her drive south. And she wanted time to think.

The afternoon was dull but dry. Maria travelled down the not-too-busy A1 with her own thoughts. She was an intelligent woman with good academic qualifications, and a career mostly in teaching. Brought up by caring parents initially in St. Petersburg and then in England from the age of six, Maria had always been encouraged to do well. Her father, a Colonel in the Intelligence Corps who'd been posted to Russia for a three - year period, was her driving force. There had been times when she'd wanted to give up on her A levels and BA course at Durham University but her father would take her aside and tell her that *'second best counts for nothing.'*

Maria needed coffee and stopped at a small diner just south of Blyth Services. Half a dozen cars were parked in front and Maria pulled up a few yards away. Taking a seat near the window, she ordered a latte and a chocolate wafer bar. Removing the red wrapper and silver foil, she reflected on the past few months. How it had all happened. How she'd come to be in this position. The latte was hot; she sipped it slowly. With the police now involved in the four murder cases – Maria couldn't help but wonder how soon they'd be asking her questions. After all, she works for Alan Clarke, and been out for dinner with him, albeit with an old friend of his from Lithuania. Would the police have been talking to him, yet? When would they be asking her awkward questions? She'd watched enough crime dramas on TV to have a good feel for how things went.

"So where were you on the evening of . . . what time did you get home . . . can you give us the names of the people you were with . . ."

Maria was going to have to trawl through her diary, the one kept hidden at home, and make absolutely certain of the facts. She had a good memory, and, like an actress preparing for a stage play, she'd learn her lines, checking and double checking every detail, visualising in her mind's eye the times she met with the four East Europeans. But why would they enquire about her link with Ivo, Nejc, Sergio or Marin? Is it a crime to have a meal and catch up with someone you knew? Maria didn't want to believe that the police knew of any connections between these four. As far as she knew there was no incriminating evidence; no one had spied on her, she hadn't been followed. Maria realised, however, that the odds of her meeting with four men all of whom were murdered were better than winning the Irish Sweepstakes.

So, if that was the case, then did someone know that she was meeting these men? Her husband, Paul, didn't know, did he? As far as he was concerned, she was meeting a girlfriend for a drink and bit of gossip, or having a weekend in town for some retail therapy, or an innocent dinner with her boss and an old friend of his. She never gave much away when she got home. Was there somebody else who could have known? She'd made some arrangements by email and text, but no one had access to her smart-phone. She wasn't important enough to have her phone hacked like some international celebrity, was she?

But as much as Maria thought about matters, it was the right time to change her car. The red Mazda was too conspicuous. The last time Maria had looked in a mirror she'd wondered if she could alter her appearance if she decided to? She'd already had her hair cut short and dyed dark brown, the sunglasses she carried hid her eyes, high heels or flatties could change her height by six inches, and her friend Becky had once used botox injections around Maria's mouth and eyes which had made her look more youthful. Maria was aware she'd be 36 years old on Sunday and her sister had promised a cake with that many candles! Selfishly, she didn't think she looked too bad for nearly 36. Maria's phone showed she had an incoming call. It was Becky.

"Hi Maria, it's me. You OK?" Before Maria could reply Becky rapidly continued. "Have you seen or heard the news? Your manager has been taken in for questioning in connection with the murder of the Lithuanian guy." Shortly after this bombshell, the phone call ended. Maria sat stunned at the Formica table. Alan Clarke questioned by the police?

"You finished, darling?" The skinny waitress smelling of stale cigarette smoke stood next to Maria, stained tea towel in her hand. "It's just that we close in five minutes, and I need to tidy up."

***

"I think all this town twinning stuff must go on all over the world," remarked Helen. Jim Adamson finished his coffee and pushed the cereal packet aside. It was nearly time for him to go. His wife had been reading an article in the Daily Mail about the subject in some parts of Europe. "Didn't you say that the men you were dealing with were from somewhere like that?" Jim sometimes told his wife the outline of a few cases he was working on, but she'd also seen the television reports. He nodded and smiled.

"I suppose it does. Why, what have you read now?" Helen often chirped up with news items that took her fancy and her husband only thought it right to hear her out – on most occasions that is.

"Here look." She passed the newspaper across the breakfast table, almost knocking the cereal packet over. "It says that there was a town twinning conference held in St. Petersburg - the city has the most twinned places in the world. The focus was on countries close to Russia . . . there's a list somewhere . . . anyway, there were over two hundred delegates from towns and cities that included Riga, Minsk, Bratislava, Tallinn, Vilnius, Kishinev, Helsinki, Kiev . . . the list goes on. It looks like they had a good time – a three - day meeting just to talk about your twin town. Probably lots of eating bratwurst sausage and drinking vodka I should think. Whatever next." Helen slowly pulled the Daily Mail away from her husband's grip. Her eye had caught a headline on current attitudes to taking vitamin supplements.

Jim Adamson sat for a moment and pondered what his wife had said. *A town twinning conference attended by over two hundred people and held in St. Petersburg.* He picked up a notepad and ball-point pen and wrote down the towns and cities mentioned. There were twelve in total. It was a long shot, but he'd have Straker go over the information and, if necessary, ask Interpol for assistance. Adamson was never one to get his hopes up on hunches, but at least two had paid significant dividends in his twenty - year career. This might be the third.

The DCI was at his desk early that morning but there was already a buzz in the place. By the time they'd finished their second cup of coffee, Adamson and DS Straker had identified a number of facts. A biannual town-twinning event was held in St. Petersburg aimed mainly at the Baltic States and neighbouring countries. It began in 1999 and had initially been run by a small enthusiastic group, several of whom enjoyed travel. Contact with the mayors of a growing number of towns and cities had snowballed and by the 2015 conference it had grown to fourteen towns and cities which had the same objective of approaching other urban areas with a view to establishing a bond between them. The dates of the last event were Tuesday to Thursday, 15 to 17 September 2015.

Enquiries had revealed that 206 delegates had attended the conference. Hopes were raised with their enquiry when three of them were identified as Ivo Stavinsky, Sergio Dalopov and Marin Bukelis. The greater majority of the attendees were from the northern and eastern area of Europe, but fourteen British delegates had also been there. Topics discussed included new medical developments, education initiatives, drug abuse and proposed green strategies on recycling and reduction of plastic waste - the usual topical issues that various countries would be interested in hearing and learning about.

After contact with the conference organisers, Kev Straker discovered that the three East Europeans had stayed in the Corinthia Hotel. Three British delegates were also booked into the same hotel. Their names were Karl Lamb, Andy Young and Maria Dawson. Checks with airlines showed that Dawson and Lamb flew from Leeds/Bradford via Amsterdam Schipol, Young from Newcastle airport – all return scheduled flights. CCTV footage was still available from the venue, the Expoforum Conference Centre, although not for the whole of the event. Straker would be able to have access to that, but he didn't hold out much hope of gaining much from it. It would take hours to go through the images showing a melee of individuals to-ing and fro-ing from place to place, but it would have to be done. The DS knew he shouldn't make assumptions, and the three British delegates did not necessarily have any connection to the three victims.

By mid-afternoon, with a sandwich and coffee for lunch, Adamson and his detective sergeant had sufficient information to plan their next move. Names, addresses, contact details, flights, dates . . . Superintendent Harry Charlton knocked on Adamson's door at 3.30 pm.

"Hello, Jim, any news? I've got the Chief Constable on my back wanting a progress update." Adamson smiled confidently.

"You'll have a report on your desk by five o'clock, sir. I think we may have something to give us a lead on the murders." Charlton gave Jim Adamson a sideways glance and then looked at Kev Straker. The DCI had his fingers crossed under his left armpit.

"I hope so, Jim. I do hope so."

***

Two days ago, DS Straker had asked two detective constables to visit the three florists that he now knew sold the flowers that had been identified in the East European murder investigation – *Bloomin' Loverly, Bouquet Bowl and Pistils and Roses.* They assumed that the florists probably knew one another, and the sooner they got around the better . . . to reduce the 'jungle drum' effect. Not all of the blooms were necessarily stocked at the same time and occasionally some had to be ordered from a Dutch based company who delivered weekly. None of the managers of the florists could recall an individual buying all types of flowers they mentioned - the corn marigolds, asters, cone-flowers and Michaelmas daisies. Various regular customers were mentioned and their names were taken; also, the method of payment – cash, card or cheque. A handful of buyers ordered over the phone and paid by card at the same time. In those cases, it wasn't always the customer who necessarily collected the flowers, perhaps a son or daughter might call by. At the end of the three - florist investigation, the DC's weren't much better off. The senior detective constable, Martin Jones, left a business card and, as usual, asked if they remembered anything that may help the police to get in touch. Joe's wife, Chloe, had told him all about it when she got home that day which made him feel uneasy; Joe was aware that different kinds of flowers had been found stuffed into Dalopov and Bukelis from the newspaper and TV reports.

When Kev Straker received a report on the flower shop trip it was as he expected, and hadn't pinned his hopes on getting much information. But now he had three names to follow up from the Expoforum convention that might offer a lead. By the end of the day, DS Straker had some more potentially useful information. There was a listing of which delegates had attended the various presentations. Of eight talks delivered over the two full days of the convention, the one entitled Current Misuse of Drugs Across Europe had been attended by all three murdered men, plus the three from Britain. It was the only presentation that fitted that pattern of the six together in one place at one time. Straker allowed himself a smile. Was this the clue to the murders? But if there was a link between them, what was it? As he had mug shots of each one, he'd be able to check out the archived CCTV material and search for any signs of liaison between them. He needed to visit the three British delegates as soon as possible, too. Young lived in County Durham, Lamb on Tyneside and Dawson resided on Teesside. Straker looked at a map on his wall.

'Where to first?' he wondered.

***

Tommy drove along Yarm High Street past Barnacle's fish and chip shop, turned right, and parked in the supermarket car park. It gave him two hours free parking. He'd decided to visit Gordon Ashby Estate Agents for a face-to-face conversation regarding his son, Dick. Tommy had hit a stone wall with his enquiries on the wayward youth, and felt it was time to close the search for him. Tommy had brought an invoice for the work done with a view to handing it over after his brief meeting. He hadn't phoned Ashby, so Tommy prayed he was in.

The estate agent was half way along the High Street, close to Costa Coffee. Tommy looked in the window for a few seconds, interested to see what properties were for sale. A bungalow in Eaglescliffe looked nice but not at the asking price shown! Through the gaps in the display boards Tommy spotted a man talking to one of the two girls sat at desks, computers almost hiding their faces. He'd never met Gordon Ashby despite having bought his little cottage in Pomfreton through the estate agent. The purchase had been handled by an assistant who had since left. All of the contact regarding Dick Ashby had been via phone calls or email. Tommy felt certain he was looking at the owner. Smartly dressed, coloured tie, waistcoat buttoned up, no jacket. He looked slightly familiar.

Tommy recalled what Matt Attridge had told him in the Blue Umbrella about Gordon Ashby – that he was a 'Drug Baron.' Hell, if that was true Tommy had better tread carefully. But he'd try to put it out of his mind for his meeting. Tommy entered and was met with a joyful 'good morning' from one of the girls. Tommy replied but eyed the man stood behind her.

"Can I help?" he asked.

"Are you Mr. Ashby?" Tommy enquired. The man looked slightly uncomfortable for a second.

"Yes. And you are?" Tommy handed Gordon Ashby a business card in silence. Glancing at it, Ashby ushered Tommy into a back office and closed the door. Ashby offered him a seat and Tommy sat precariously on a rickety wooden chair that should have been taken to a tip ages ago. "Well, it's good to meet you at last. Have you brought me some good news on Dick?" Tommy wished he had but there was nothing so he was going to be honest.

"I'm afraid not, Gordon. I've asked around all the places where Dick might be, spoken to a number of people that have given me the odd lead . . . but nothing." Ashby leant back contemplatively on his chair. "It's taken up quite a bit of my time and I regret to say that I feel it's time to close the case." Tommy watched the estate agent closely. Ashby twitched.

"But surely you can't have covered everything, yet. There must be people out there who know something? You don't think he's dead, do you?" When asked questions like that, Tommy tried to be positive.

"No, of course not. My gut feel is that he's keeping his head down somewhere. But where, I just do not know. I've observed a few places where he might be, but haven't seen any signs."

"I mentioned Barlay and Attridge. Any joy there?" Tommy shook his head. "What about the club in town?" Again, Tommy could only indicate a negative response. "You ought to know that his coin collection has gone – he was keen on Georgian silver coins – and kept them in a case in his room. They're not in their usual place. He once had them valued at Tennant's. Three thousand pounds he was told by their coin expert." Tommy recalled Gordon had mentioned Roger's interest in coin collecting at the Frog and Ferret, and Roger himself had also mentioned Dick's coin interest to Tommy.

"He may have sold them to somebody? Three thousand pounds would be interesting to a young man." Tommy reached for the envelope in his jacket pocket. He placed it in front of Gordon Ashby. "Gordon, here is my final invoice for the case. I'm calling time on it. It's not fair on you. Perhaps you could try another PI? There are a few in the telephone directory." Ashby looked surprised. He eased the envelope back across toward Tommy. He didn't want to start over again with another private 'tec.

"Tommy, let's give it another four weeks or so. I'll pay

you well to stay on it. Let's agree the end of September. I don't really want to brief another private eye. If you haven't found him by then we'll call it a day." Tommy hesitated.

"OK, Gordon, it's a deal. But I'll leave the invoice with you. It is work up to date, and I need to keep the building society and my bank happy." Ashby stood and held his hand out. They shook hands. Tommy noticed a hint of bath salts in the air as he got up, a sort of clean, bleach type smell.

***

"Thanks for coming in, Mr. Clarke. We thought it was best for us to talk with you here. As we said over the telephone, we were able to trace you as the driver of the Audi, registration number NT 65 PDY." Adamson was sat opposite Alan Clarke in the interview room, Straker to his left. "You'd taken the vehicle on a test drive as offered by the Audi dealer in Stockton, is that correct?" Clarke nodded. "Did you purchase the vehicle?" He shook his head. It wasn't what he was after, so he'd be keeping his BMW for now.

The girl who'd taken the £300 cash deposit for the test drive at the Audi dealer had put the money into an envelope overnight. The next day when Clarke returned the car, and after she'd examined the car for any marks or scratches, she took the money from the same envelope in her desk drawer and had given him the fifteen £20 notes back. The envelope had Mr. A. Clarke written on the front. She'd then, absent-mindedly, slid the envelope under her desk-pad. It lay there for a while until she moved the desk-pad . . . and there it was. As she'd been interviewed by DS Straker she called him to let the sergeant know. Straker followed up the lead and found three people with that name in the area. He'd already assumed from the Audi's mileage that the test driver probably lived within a ten - mile radius of Middlesbrough town centre.

The detective sergeant had visited two men called Clarke, an Alfred and an Andrew, before finding Alan Clarke in Ormesby. And here he was, answering questions on Nejc Kodric.

"Can you tell us about your relationship with Mr. Kodric?" asked Adamson.

Alan Clarke explained that he'd been on a two week visit to Lithuania, and spent most of the time in Vilnius. He'd met Kodric in a down-town bar that the hotel had recommended when he said he wanted to find some 'fun.' Clarke had spent some time with Kodric, visiting the zoo, museum and theatre. They'd enjoyed each other's company. Clarke had given Kodric his business card and suggested that he call him if he came over, especially as the Lithuanian had never visited the UK before. Kodric had phoned Clarke from Gateshead on 9th. July, three days before he caught the train to Darlington from Newcastle, and told Clarke he had booked into the Queens Head in Yarm. As Clarke had already arranged the test drive in the Audi, he decided to use that to collect Kodric.

"And after you collected Kodric, you drove to Kirklevington to have dinner with Kodric. Was anybody else with you?" Clarke went on to say that he'd invited one of his staff, Maria, to add a bit of bonhomie to the evening, and that she could speak Lithuanian. She had driven there on her own, they'd had a very enjoyable evening, and then Maria left while Clarke dropped Kodric back at the hotel. He had gone into the hotel with Kodric for an orange juice, but only stayed about an hour. They had planned to meet the following evening.

After a few more questions, the detectives were satisfied with Alan Clarke's response. It seemed to make sense. It was time to go.

***

DCI Jim Adamson and DS Kev Straker had left Middlesbrough early on a Wednesday morning and travelled to Whitcliffe near Durham city to speak with Andy Young. The town - twinning delegate lived in a small detached stone cottage where two cars were parked on the drive. Straker rang the doorbell; a woman in her early thirties opened the front door.

"Mrs. Young?" She nodded, as both detectives showed their ID. "Is Andy at home?" Hesitatingly she stepped back and opened the door wider. They stepped over the stone step. Andy Young's wife shouted for her husband, who came into the low beamed lounge within a few seconds. He was neatly dressed, and had an academic air.

"Yes, what's this about?" asked Andy Young. Straker explained the reason for their visit. Young glanced at his watch, but the DS quickly assured him they'd only take a few minutes. All four remained standing as Straker confirmed that Young had been a delegate at the Expoforum convention in September 2015. His answers to questions about the flights, hotel, and town twinning theme all tallied with the information that the detectives had.

"Do the names Karl Lamb and Maria Dawson mean anything to you, Mr. Young?" They didn't. "What about Ivo Stavinsky, Sergio Dalopov and Marin Bukelis. Do those names mean anything at all?" Again, Young shook his head. "What was your interest in attending the event in St. Petersburg?" Andy Young, a geography master at Durham School, explained that he'd been involved in town twinning when he and his wife lived in Frinton-on-Sea. He'd taken up his teaching post in January 2015 and had met the mayor of Whitcliffe at a local fete that summer. The mayor was interested in getting the small town twinned with a European town of a similar size and asked the geography master if he would attend the September meeting on behalf of Whitcliffe. Young had agreed and obtained leave of absence from the headmaster for the three days.

And so that was it for now. Young's explanation seemed sound; aspects could easily be checked out if needed.

Before leaving, Jim Adamson told Andy Young the real reason they were there, the murders of the three East Europeans who'd attended Expoforum convention. He did not reveal any information that hadn't already been given to the press at the media briefing. At that, after a second's hesitation, Young did confess that he'd recalled the surnames of Stavinsky and Bukelis from news reports. His wife shrugged her shoulders as if to suggest the names didn't mean anything to her. Jim Adamson moved toward the door.

"Well, Mr. Young, thank you for your time. We may have to speak with you again, but, in the meantime, you may want to keep things to yourself. Here's my card – if there is anything you remember from the Expoforum that might throw any light on things don't hesitate to give me a call." With that Mrs. Young showed the detectives to the front door. They got into the unmarked Vauxhall Insignia and eased off the gravel drive. Straker tapped the sat-nav screen to bring up their next call, an address in Hadrian Road, Whickham, near Gateshead, where a Mr. Karl Lamb lived.

***

Judith Barlay was distraught. Harry Nevin hadn't come back from his renal dialysis appointment at James Cook hospital. Routine checks had been made, his departure time from the unit, he'd been seen on a CCTV camera – but only alone. The bus route he took had no evidence to suggest he'd got on the 55 service back home.

***

Adamson and Straker were in luck. Although it was just after 9.30 am, the door of the semi-detached bungalow was opened by a man in his dressing gown who yawned as he peered at their ID.

"Karl Lamb?" With eyes widened, Lamb held the door.

"May we come in?" Sweeping his hand low across his stomach Karl Lamb invited them in. About five feet six inches in height with a mushroom of corn coloured hair that may have been dyed, he led the way into a small kitchen. Lamb sat on a stool without offering either of the detectives a seat. He sipped from a dirty looking mug.

"Nasty looking eye you've got there, Mr. Lamb?"

"Yeah, I walked into a bloody door!" Jim Adamson repeated his opening lines used with Andy Young, and after explaining their reason for the visit, he began.

'Did he know Andy Young or Maria Dawson?' No.

'Did he know any of the three mentioned East Europeans?' No.

'Had he attended a town twinning event in St. Petersburg?' Yes.

Asked about his trip, Lamb stated his flight was from Leeds Bradford but he couldn't remember the exact departure time, or the airline. Then he recalled it was Jet2. Adamson asked him which hotel he stayed in. Lamb could not remember but thought it began with the letter C. And the reason that Lamb was there?

"I'd read about the convention in a magazine somewhere, it sounded interesting. I mean Newcastle upon Tyne is twinned with Bergen, for example, and Middlesbrough with Dunkirk. Hartlepool is even twinned with Sliema in Malta! My dad died eighteen months ago and left me some money. Thought I'd give it a go, especially as it was in Russia! They serve decent vodka there! The hotel was a bit expensive but what the heck, you can't take it with you." Straker asked Lamb if he attended any of the presentations? "Yes, I'm interested in green issues, especially the use and misuse of plastics. Our north east coast needs tidying up I can tell you. I also met some fascinating people while I was there." Lamb sipped from his mug, with the message LETS ALL GO GREEN on the side, as Adamson spoke.

"What do you do for a living, Karl?"

"I work at the local funeral parlour as an embalmer."

Adamson shivered momentarily.

"Sorry to ask but have you ever been in trouble with the police?" Lamb smiled quizzically, looked into his empty mug and shook his head. "Do you ever get down to Teesside?"

"I've got a couple of friends who live in Haverton Hill and see them from time to time. I might go into Middlesbrough sometimes and I've got an uncle who lives in the area." The DCI explained the reasoning behind their questions. Lamb seemed laid back. "I'm afraid I can't help you. Whoever is involved with this nasty business needs locking up and quickly!" The two detectives left Lamb's home, tempted to wipe their feet on the way out. Once belted up in the Vauxhall, Straker spoke first.

"Not sure about him, boss. He seems an odd guy with a poor memory which may be convenient. And he was lacking personal hygiene, too. Embalmer! Blooming hell, I don't think I'd want him touching me when I'm dead!"

"OK, Kev. Now we need to talk with Maria Dawson." Straker suddenly sat up. Adamson searched his face.

"Maria Dawson! That's the name of one of Alan Clarke's office staff." The DS took a note book from his inside jacket pocket. "Yes, here we are . . . Senior Administration Executive at GoWorldTravel."

"Got her address there?" asked Adamson. Straker flipped over a couple of pages. He read out Dawson's details. 89, St. Roseberry Close, Eston. The detective sergeant tapped the screen to enter the address. "Could be worth a chat at her place rather than at the travel agent's? Let's if she's in." They headed south on the A1 then drove east onto the A19. Within thirty minutes the Vauxhall was pulling up in front of the Dawson property. At this time of the morning it was unlikely that Maria Dawson would be home. The detectives knew she was married so perhaps her husband might be home? They heard the bell chime and waited. Straker hit the bell push again. No response. As they turned to leave, the neighbour, who was pruning his roses, spoke.

"Good morning, gents. Not sure if they'd want JW's calling at their home at this time of day!" Adamson hid a grin. Did they really look like Jehovah's Witnesses?

"We just wanted to see Mrs. Dawson. It doesn't look as if she's in."

"No. They're both at work. She's at the big travel agents in Middlesbrough, and he's a librarian – Middlesbrough Central Library. Shall I say you've called? You can leave a brochure . . . I'll pass it on."

"It's OK. Don't worry. We'll try another time, but thanks anyway." Adamson and Straker managed to get into the unmarked car and close the doors before each burst into laughter.

"Jehovah's Witness! Hell!" exclaimed the DS. "I'm going to have to take a serious look at my wardrobe!"

"Maybe it's the way you walk!" guffawed his boss. After they'd controlled themselves, sides aching slightly, Adamson suggested a visit to the central library. "Let's go and have a talk to Mr. Dawson, Kev. See what light he can shed on matters."

***

The Frog and Ferret had been fairly quiet lately; customers seemed to be dropping off. The odd newcomers would stop by for a drink but the regulars that Roger Grimes had built up over several years were declining. His beer was kept in good condition, there was a decent range of wines, and over twenty whiskies above the bar including a decent Glenmorangie and an Isle of Jura malt. Those that did call didn't stay as long as they used to. One of his infrequent customers from Tyneside nicknamed 'Carlos the Jackal' suggested an industrial cleaning machine would come in useful to clean the flagged floor. Roger was pissed off at that.

It didn't help that Roger Grimes had lost his sense of smell following an industrial accident in the warehouse where he worked. A heavily loaded palate had slipped from a forklift truck driven by an employee who shouldn't have been driving it. The accident had left him with a scar on his scalp and right leg and the two smaller fingers were missing from his left hand. The compensation payment was enough for him to buy the Frog and Ferret with a bit left over. His loss of digits wasn't too much of an issue, though, as the landlord was right - handed and strong with it. And although he'd lost his wife ten years ago, he managed his own laundry and cleaning with the occasional help of his sister, Iris, who did his ironing and helped with the shopping.

But it was a close friend of Roger's who called in one night that mentioned an odour. Nothing too unpleasant, not a drain smell or anything lavatorial in nature. Simply something that might be off-putting to some of the punters in the pub. One of those battery - operated devices that sprays a fine scented jet every two minutes was high on a shelf about ten feet from the dartboard, and a couple of gel air fresheners were placed around the bar. But none of this meant anything to Roger. Being nasally challenged he couldn't tell a sewer from a bunch of roses! Had a disgruntled customer deposited a kipper in a brown paper bag hidden behind a radiator somewhere? Or stuffed a dead mouse into the compost of a plant pot? But his friend firmly suggested that Roger do something about it – and soon.

It was a Thursday and Roger always popped down to the cemetery in Pomfreton to visit his son's grave on that day before he opened up. Ian had taken his own life one evening in his bedroom at home, leaving a note for his father. Roger still had the note, a sore reminder of days when he and Ian had enjoyed life together especially after his mother had been killed by that drunken bus driver in Middlesbrough. It pained him to read it, but he took another look at it after he'd got back from the cemetery.

Dear Dad,

You probably won't understand but life has become too difficult for me. I've let you down by failing some of my exams and not mixing well with others at school. But the real problem has been the bullying. One of the boys in the form above me has been getting inside my head. Nothing physical, but comments about my stammer, my mother's disability and my inability to integrate with other boys has become too much.

Your loving son, Ian.

Roger Grimes had never shared this note with anybody else, and now, as he prepared to open the pub on a Thursday morning, he wiped away a tear with a tissue and looked in the bathroom mirror. His face was blotchy, bags under his eyes. He brushed his hair, buttoned up his mustard waistcoat and stumbled down the stairs to meet the first customers of the day. At the entrance to the bar was another small mirror. Roger glanced at it. A slight adjustment was required. He tightened and tugged at his cravat a little; Roger loved his cravat - it complimented his waistcoat. It was 10.59 am. He unbolted the heavy, wooden pub door and turned the key. As he'd finished, a Beethoven's piano concerto ringtone told him he had an incoming call on his smart-phone. He tapped the screen.

"Hello, Roger Grimes."

"It's me. You haven't paid me for the job, yet. I'll call in tomorrow for the payment. One thousand pounds cash as we agreed. See you then. Bye."

***

Jim Adamson was busy. He wanted to talk with Maria Dawson. She had taken the previous Friday off to visit her sister in Lincoln, but it was now Tuesday 23rd, August and she still wasn't back.

***

Tommy had woken earlier than usual. The sun was coming up over the village, painting the sky a shade of gold tinged with pink. He'd been dreaming, but as he woke the content of those dreams were hazy. A black coffee helped waken him. He noticed an old coin on the kitchen windowsill, one he'd found on the edge of a field outside of Pomfreton some time ago. Suddenly, he recalled one of his dreams. In it a man was trading coins . . . old, silver coins. He recalled what both Roger Grimes and Gordon Ashby had said regarding Dick's Georgian collection. The pub landlord had told Tommy of Dick Ashby's interest in collecting, and Gordon had recently confirmed that the silver coins were missing from his son's room. Tommy sat on a kitchen stool and held his mug with two hands. Was there a connection between them? Tommy put his brain in gear and began to think.

After the car accident on the Whitby road had Dick Ashby managed to somehow get back to the Middlesbrough area? Needed a place to find sanctuary? Knowing Roger Grimes lived alone above the Frog and Ferret he might feel that was the only place where he'd be safe for a while, rest his ankle. It would be late after all. Maybe around midnight. Grimes probably wouldn't be asleep by then, not after doing what landlords have to do after getting rid of the last drinkers around 11.00 pm. Dick could have hitched a lift to the pub, banged on the door, and the kind Mr. Grimes might have let him in. It was all possible. Tommy recalled his conversation in the Frog when he asked Grimes about his cellar, using a lie about a friend of his in Essex who'd just bought a pub. The way he'd refused to let Tommy take a look down there seemed more vivid in Tommy's memory now.

Was Roger hiding something? Did he have a good reason not to want Tommy going down the cellar steps? Perhaps it was untidy . . . needed cleaning? As Tommy rinsed his mug, he also remembered the conversation with

Chris Butler at the David Logan Leisure Centre a few weeks ago . . . 'somebody asked Teague to install a camera.' Had Dave Teague placed a surveillance device in the cellar of the Frog and Ferret? It was possible, but was it probable? Chris had also grinned when he'd told Tommy that Teague had been asked to install it in the dark while the client held a torch!

As the day brightened, Tommy's thoughts became clearer in his head, but if he was right, how was he going to check it out? By the time Tommy had showered and dressed he knew he *had* to do it. He *had* to find a way to get into the cellar of the Pomfreton public house.

***

It was nearly noon by the time DCI Adamson and DS Straker left the library. They'd parked up off Emily Street and walked round to Central Square. Paul Dawson had been slightly surprised to see the two suited men stride up to the desk as he was checking a list of new deliveries. Most visitors were bordering on scruffy. After Adamson had introduced himself and his DS, Paul asked them to follow him. In his time at the library it was the first time he could recall plain clothes police coming in. Being a public place, none of them wanted to discuss anything with the 'elephant's ears' of Teesside all around. Paul had shown them to an office beyond a frosted glass panelled door marked STAFF ONLY. He'd asked one of the library assistants to let him know if there was anything urgent, otherwise not to disturb them. He'd offered the detectives tea or coffee, but both had declined.

"May we call you Paul?" Dawson nodded and smiled weakly. "We'd visited your home address but there was no reply. A helpful neighbour told us you worked here. We're here to ask a few questions about your wife, Maria." Paul sat forward with a quizzical look. "We understand that she attended a conference in St. Petersburg in September 2015." Adamson fixed his eyes on Dawson; Kev Straker held open a note pad, pen poised.

"Yes, that's right. Is there a problem?" The DCI ignored that specific question.

"And we understand that she flew from Leeds Bradford airport to St. Petersburg?" Dawson nodded. "Do the names Karl Lamb or Andy Young mean anything to you?"

"No. Why, should they?" Jim Adamson explained that the two men were from the north east and both attended the same conference. Dawson shrugged his shoulders. Adamson continued.

"Why did she attend the conference, Paul?" Dawson told the DCI that Maria had been born in the city and was keen to see a couple of old friends as well as attend the Expoforum. She'd had an interest in town twinning from an early age. "How old was Maria when she left St. Petersburg?" Dawson stated that she was six. "Six! Would she have 'old friends' to visit if she was only six?"

"She found them on the facebook website. They've kept in touch for the last three years or so." Straker made some notes.

"Are you aware of the four murders that have taken place in the Cleveland area in the past weeks?" Dawson replied saying he'd read the papers and watched TV news so yes, he was aware. "In case you've forgotten, the names of the four are Ivo Stavinsky, Nejc Kodric, Sergio Dalopov and Marin Bukelis. They're all from East European countries. Three of them attended the conference in St. Petersburg. Do you think your wife knows any of these men?"

"I wouldn't have thought so. I'd remember names like that, I think. I suppose it's a possibility that she may have had some contact with one or all of them in St. Petersburg, but no, I'd say she didn't know them." Straker chipped in.

"Do you have any photos of your wife with you here at the library – either in your wallet or perhaps in a frame?" Dawson eased himself on his chair. He replied 'no.' "Has your wife changed her hairstyle in the past couple of weeks, Paul?" Dawson explained that she had, what else could he do, he'd thought to himself. He told Straker that she used to be blonde but had tired of her hair colour and style and decided to change it.

"In our investigation of the four murders, and from the evidence we have so far, it appears that your wife may have been at the scene of the crime in at least two cases. What do you have to say to that?" Dawson felt his neck redden. Standing and turning around, he opened a window to let some air in. Then, composing himself, he placed his hands on his lap as he sat down again

"That's impossible! What the hell are you suggesting? I know she's been out a few times for a meal or drinks with girlfriends. What *evidence*?" Adamson quickly explained that he wasn't at liberty to divulge the source of their information. Paul Dawson tried to relax as visions of photos taken by Tommy Archer flashed through his head. "This is ridiculous." Adamson carried on.

"We understand that your wife works at GoWorldTravel. What does she do there?" Paul Dawson told the two detectives that Maria was a Senior Administrative Executive. "And remind us of the name of the MD there?" He confirmed it was Alan Clarke. Adamson knew, of course. "And as you've said, you are aware of the four recent murders in this area . . ." Dawson breathed out slowly and sat forwards. Adamson waited for him to volunteer anything more.

"Of course, it's been all over the news. I feel sorry for these East European victims, but what's all this got to do with Maria? I don't understand."

"It would be very helpful if we could talk to Maria herself, Paul. Is she at the travel agent's today?" Dawson moved on his chair again, eased it back and crossed his legs.

"No. She's taken a few days off. Let me see. It's Tuesday today. She went down to Lincoln last Friday to see her sister, Jane, who hasn't been feeling too well lately. I'm not certain of her sister's address." Adamson enquired as to her return plans. "Not sure," replied Dawson, "but I'll be phoning her tonight. I can let you know." With that the two detectives stood up and thanked Paul Dawson for his time. Kev Straker gave Dawson a business card and asked that if there was anything else that Dawson might think was helpful to contact him. And with that they left the library, breathing in the tangy Middlesbrough air, tinged with tones of an ICI Billingham distillation process and aromas of commercial traffic nitrous oxide fumes. Sitting in the Vauxhall five minutes later, Adamson chirped up as he slipped a Polo mint into his mouth.

"Well, Kev, what's your take on that?"

"I think he's protecting his wife. But then, wouldn't you do the same?"

"Probably. We need to talk to Maria Dawson as soon as we can . . ." said the DS.

"Sooner than that!" replied Adamson with a smirk.

***

"Hello, Mavis, is Nicky there?" Freddie Sewell was sitting on his leather office chair, swivelled so that he could look out at the bank of cranes handling goods on the dockside. Mavis squeezed her backside out of her chair in the taxi office and tapped on Barlay's door.

"Nicky, it's Mr. Sewell at the docks. Think he wants a word." She held the cordless telephone out for Barlay who took it from her firmly. Mavis closed the door as she went back to her desk.

"Hello, Freddie. How are you?" Sewell cut to the chase. He told Barlay that one of his customers had asked that he no longer be his taxi driver to collect him from the airport, or anywhere else for that matter.

"Is there a problem, Freddie?" Barlay recalled a Russian who'd been awkward. Someone who'd asked Nicky to do a 'special job' for him, as he called it. The taxi driver had refused.

"I don't know. He phoned me half an hour ago to discuss some shipping matters and before he hung up, he told me what I've now passed onto you." It sounded as though Sewell wasn't up for a discussion. "As simple as that. . ." Barlay butted in.

"Freddie, I'm hoping this doesn't affect our existing working relationship. I mean, I've handled a number of your clients for a while now as well as doing local runs for your staff." There was a pause.

"To tell you the truth, Nicky, I've been considering a number of aspects of the business here. One of them is transport and we feel it is time to switch taxi companies. No hard feelings, Nick, but that's the way it goes sometimes. Listen, I need to go, but take care and good luck with your taxi firm." Mavis asked if all was OK.

"No, it bloody isn't! Sewell's terminated our contract with him. Just like that. Not so much as a bloody proper explanation, either!" Barlay was annoyed; really annoyed. He needed time to think things through. Was the Russian getting his own back? He had an uneasy feeling in his gut.

"Nicky, there's a fare waiting to be picked up at the railway station. He says it's urgent. Can you do it now?" Barlay swallowed hard.

"Er, no, Mavis, I need to go out. Get one of the other lads to do it. Try Charlie." As Mavis left Barlay switched on a small fan. It was feeling warm. *He was feeling very warm*. Barlay opted to go out in the Mercedes and pick up fares that were not by request. It was safer that way. Either of the two other drivers wouldn't be a target of some deranged Russian, he was pretty certain of that.

Nicky Barlay's day went OK. He'd picked up fourteen fares since he'd left the office – bus stations, high streets, supermarkets. A couple were worth over thirty pounds each and by the time he got home around 6.15 pm he had a decent wad of cash. Parking the Merc on the drive he let himself in, tossed the keys on the semi-circular hall table and went to the fridge for a can of beer. Nicky Barlay was damned annoyed. What was it with Sewell? Barlay had never had a complaint, nor done anything wrong – as afar as he knew, anyway.

***

Kev Straker had gone through seventeen hours of videotape from the Expoforum conference. His eyes ached with too little sleep. But the detective was able to identify the three murdered men, as well as Maria Dawson, Karl Lamb and Andy Young who appeared from time to time throughout the footage. The clarity of the footage was good enough to see that all delegates wore a name badge with the flag of their country on it. After he and his DCI had spoken to Paul Dawson, they were provided with a photo of Maria by her husband which he assured the officers was a good likeness. He was looking to see if any of the East Europeans were in a face-to-face relationship with Maria or any of the other British visitors, and whether the dead men seemed to spend time with other delegates. Not taking their word for it, he also wondered if Dawson, Lamb and Young interfaced for longer than it would take to say 'hello' to one another.

His conclusion, which he shared with Adamson, was that there wasn't any obvious communication between any of the Brits apart from a short chat, probably after spotting the Union Flag on their name badge. He'd seen Dawson speak briefly to Stavinsky and Bukelis, but there was no videotape evidence indicating she'd had contact with Dalopov. On the occasions Dawson was seen talking to Stavinsky and Bukelis it was for no more than a few minutes at a time, and the body language suggested what looked like merely a convivial greeting. Lamb and Young were spotted talking to only one of the victims – Bukelis. Again, it appeared that pleasantries were exchanged, but nothing more sinister than that. Each of the three East Europeans had been seen interfacing with several other people but there was nothing that Straker observed to give him any hint of anything sinister, apart from a tall man with a moustache who had an air of authority that wandered around chatting to many of the delegates. So basically, the Detective Sergeant wasn't much further forward in terms of understanding whether there had been any collusion between those on whom he focused.

The computer programme that Straker used could stop, fast forward and rewind at different speeds and magnify any of the images. After nearly two full days of staring at a screen and going 'goggly-eyed' Straker decided to go back to the videotape on which he'd placed a marker where there was interaction between any of the six delegates. The silent images didn't give much away. Straker went through eighteen minutes of recording where it was possible to zoom in on the face of one of the murdered men or one of the three key delegates when any of them interacted, either as a pair or in a group.

Of the eighteen minutes which were of particular interest to the DS it turned out that there were two minutes and forty-five seconds that turned out to be worthwhile. He made notes, forwarding or rewinding the recording, zooming in when required. An hour later Kev Straker was back in his office taking a long look at what was in front of him.

It was all beginning to make some sense to Straker – the whole reason why the three East Europeans were at the Expoforum convention. Straker tapped his ball-point pen on his desk jotter, almost playing a tune. They must have been there to meet and discuss the supply of drugs into the UK via one main person - Maria Dawson. The only problem was that Dawson had only been seen talking to Stavinsky and Bukelis but not Dalopov. Straker couldn't find any VT evidence that showed Lamb or Young had contact with anyone of significance.

The DS was slowly tying the loose ends together. He knew that Stavinsky had driven off the DFDS ferry at Port of Tyne from Amsterdam and travelled to the Seaview Hotel in Marske in the silver-grey Skoda Fabia. Further enquiries revealed that Nejc Kodric, who wasn't at the Expoforum, and who'd rented an apartment in Gateshead, had arrived at Newcastle airport via a Lufthansa flight from Vilnius. His activities in the Tyneside area were still sketchy but Straker had found that Kodric had visited two gay bars in Gateshead and used his rented apartment for a LBGT party one evening. Enquiries with UK Border Agency showed Sergio Dalopov, the Ukrainian, had flown into Leeds/Bradford airport from Kiev the evening before he was murdered in Middlesbrough. He'd hired a car from the Avis rental office at the airport and stayed one night at the Leeming Motel on the A1 near Bedale in North Yorkshire. The car was found on the top floor of a multi-storey car park in the town centre. Bukelis was picked up on CCTV arriving at Harwich from The Hook of Holland on a Stena Line ferry, then taking a train to Norwich and onward to Darlington. He's seen on station cameras at Darlington where a Boro Cars taxi took him to the Crathorne Park hotel.

Apart from an interest in town-twinning, and the obvious connection with Maria Dawson, Straker had nothing to link the three men, nor the trio to Kodric. Different countries, varied jobs, living on their own apart from Stavinsky. It didn't make sense. He believed that in all probability they did not know each other, at least not before attending the September convention. But there was one thing that Kev Straker now *really* needed to do. Talk to his DCI, bring him up to date with his progress, and then find Maria. Having not heard anything from Paul Dawson, Straker telephoned the central library.

"Hello, please may I speak to Paul Dawson?" It was Dawson who'd answered the call. He recognised the detective's voice. "Hi, Paul, any information on when Maria is coming home? It's just that we do need to talk to her, if only to eliminate her from our enquiries."

"Sorry, not yet, sergeant. I'll be phoning her early evening, so I'll let you know as soon as I have any news." Straker put the desk phone down. 'Was Dawson playing for time?' the DS wondered. He didn't seem to have any sense of urgency about his wife's return. Dawson had already given Straker the Mazda car details, and he'd considered putting out an 'attempt to locate' request with the Superintendent. He wasn't going to hang around too long waiting for the librarian to call him. Within a few seconds the phone rang.

"Hello, Kevin. It's Sergeant Wayford here. We've found a knife with a ten-inch blade in some undergrowth about twenty yards from where the body was found at the Crathorne Park hotel. Looks like an ordinary kitchen knife. It's been bagged and it's now with the scene of crime guys."

***

The man walked into Yarm police station and put the thick brown envelope on the front desk.

"What's this then?" asked the sergeant.

"Found it in a lay-bye on the A19. I'd stopped to check my tyres – the car seemed to be veering to one side a bit. Decided to bring the package in," replied the man.

"Better log it in, then, hadn't we?" said the sergeant, bending down low to get the ledger. It took a few seconds to get the correct one, then he raised himself back up onto his swivel stool. "Now, what's . . ." The man had gone.

Sergeant Clayton Williams lifted the flap of the jiffy bag and peeked inside. He slipped on a pair of nitrile gloves and removed the contents. It was a smartphone, a Samsung iPhone.

***

Tommy had enjoyed a couple of soft drinks in the Frog and Ferret. Lime and lemonade with ice and a slice. He'd been chatting with someone who'd moved into the village recently from east London. The newcomer, Ken, had dropped his beer mat and Tommy had picked it up for him. Ken couldn't believe that anybody would do that, explaining that in Stratford where he'd lived nobody, but nobody would bend down to pick up your beer mat, or anything else for that matter.

"My wife and I never got to know the next-door neighbour despite living there for ten years," Ken retorted, "and if you looked anyone in the eyes travelling on the underground you were asking for trouble." Tommy's eyes widened in amazement. "You can't believe that a human being is living among his fellow homo sapiens and doesn't communicate!" Tommy sipped his sparkling drink.

"Well, it's not like that around here, Ken. Most folks are friendly enough but there's often a bit of give and take, a favour here and there. There's usually something going on in here – tonight is darts night for example. I see the opposition from the King William IV has just arrived. They start at 8.00 pm prompt so be prepared for a bit of noise. On Monday night there is a quiz. One of the local know-it-all lads prepares it . . . six rounds often with a GK round to begin, then a potpourri of different subjects. If you're any good and want to come you and your wife will soon fit in with one of the teams." Ken smiled a smile suggesting that he'd give that some serious consideration. It was one way of easing into the local community.

Tommy glanced at his watch. The darts was about to begin, and he'd offered to score for the Frog and Ferret team. They were playing 501 with a double to finish, five players per side. Nothing too difficult in that but Tommy made several errors in the first ten minutes.

"Come on, Tommy, sort yourself out!" shouted the skipper of the home team.

"Sorry!" shouted Tommy. "Must be that lime and lemonade. Roger, did you put something in it?" Tommy tried to catch the attention of the landlord as a dart hit double seventeen to win the game.

"Well done, Mick," bellowed Colin, the skipper. "Tommy, finish the scoring will you! Bloody hell, did you fail O level maths or what? Seems you've got your mind on other things tonight!"

The thing was, Tommy Archer did have concentration issues. He'd been calm enough talking to Ken from east London but as the evening wore on, he could feel those butterflies in his stomach. Not certain whether to have a proper meal or simply snack before he'd set off for the pub, a crunchy cereal bar and a pear hadn't satisfied him, but he'd decided that he wasn't going to eat too much because he had things to do. Tommy would rather be peckish that have a full stomach and need the loo.

It was 10.20 pm before the final game was finished, the away team winning 6-4. A half time break, with some of Roger Grimes' famous pickled eggs and quartered pork pies had made for a pleasant time. The landlord was happy, the takings for beer well up compared to a normal evening. The door would be locked at 11.00 pm sharp and folk began to drift away from the pub at a quarter to the hour. Tommy made a point of speaking to the Frog and Ferret darts skipper just before closing time.

"Goodnight, Colin. Sorry about the scoring tonight. I'm off to the loo so if I don't see you when I come out, I'll be in next week . . . and bright as a button!" Tommy hastened to the gents as stragglers made their way out. Once inside the toilets Tommy went into the middle of three cubicles, closed the door but left it unlocked, and stood on the seat. Within a few minutes he heard Roger Grimes come in and shout.

"Anyone here?" Silence. In seconds he'd switched the lights off and closed the outer toilet door. Tommy held his breath as he fumbled for the mini-torch on his key ring. He checked his watch. 11.15 pm. The oak door of the pub had been shut and bolted, the noise of the locking eerily permeating the silence of the old public house.

Gingerly stepping down from the firm, wooden seat, Tommy sat on it. He'd give Grimes another quarter of an hour before he started what he'd come for. It seemed odd, sitting on a loo when you didn't want to do anything associated with toilet matters. He locked his fingers together to stop himself fidgeting. It was dark, save for a small shaft of moonlight coming through the closed window above him. Tommy breathed carefully; slowly, in small intakes of the musty air. His heart beat increased, the thought of finding something in the pub cellar thrilling, yet scary. It was now 11.33 pm and the whole building itself seemed to have gone to sleep.

Tommy slowly got up and eased the cubicle door back. He prayed that the outer gent's door wouldn't squeak as he carefully lowered the handle. Silence. His soft soled, denim shoes were ideal for his plan. A vehicle drove past the pub, its headlights bathing the lounge in pale, bright yellow light for an instant. Tommy knew where the cellar was. He'd made a point on the last few visits to get his bearings and so far, the mini-torch was unused. He eased past the two hanging racks of pork scratchings at the end of the bar into the small area with two doors leading off. The wider of the two, painted dark green, led down to the cask beer storage area with the carbon dioxide cylinders and piles of bottled ales. Tommy opened the door and arced his body through. He fumbled for the key ring and switched on the torch, it's white pencil-like beam piercing the gloom. A loose hand rail to his right aided him in his slow descent. He counted the steps . . . one, two, three . . . fourteen. Once on the cellar floor Tommy stopped, his breathing heavy. The ray of light showed an untidy arrangement of aluminium and oak barrels, CO_2 cylinders and pipes and tubes in disarray. He had to be careful here – no tripping over and bouncing a steel cylinder onto the concrete floor. That would wake the devil, let alone Roger Grimes.

The area was about four by six yards; larger than Tommy imagined. Dampness was here, and the sort of smell you sensed in your grandma's house as a child when she was ill. At one side of the cellar Tommy spotted a studded metal door, recessed into the wall by about twelve inches. There was a small gap at the bottom and a secure lock fitted. Tommy moved across and tried the steel handle. It moved down but the door would not budge. His torch beam scanned the immediate area and he spotted a key hung on a cord loop to the left of the door. Lifting the key off the hook, Tommy inserted it into the lock and slowly turned. A tiny click told him it could now be opened.

Needing more force than he expected, Tommy pushed at the metal door. He entered a room about half the size of the main cellar and quickly shone his torch from left to right and up and down. He gasped, putting his hand to his mouth to stop himself screaming, his bladder almost emptying involuntarily. There, sitting upright on a dirty mattress staring at Tommy as if about to speak, was Dick Ashby. Tommy had a clear picture in his mind's eye of Gordon's missing son, from a photograph shown to him weeks ago when Tommy started out on this case. Dark curly hair, good looking, rugged features. His hands were clasped together on his lap.

"Dick. How are you?" whispered Tommy. "It's Tommy Archer. Your father has asked me to help find you. I'm going to get you out of here. OK?" He moved closer to the bed and placed his hand on his right shoulder. Tommy's hand brushed Dick Ashby's face. The ashen skin was ice cold. Tommy recoiled and as he did so the corpse fell sideways, the head banging on the iron bed frame like the sound of a walnut being cracked open. Holding the torch unsteadily, Tommy heard a crystalline thwacking noise as a glass eye bounced on the concrete floor.

***

On the A19 near Thirsk a police car had pulled over a red Mazda MX-5. DS Kev Straker, believing that Maria Dawson would be back from Lincoln, had put out a request for this vehicle to be traced. A police Ford Transit with rear camera had picked up the vehicle on the ANPR system. The sports car was flagged over by the waving index finger of the observer and safely pulled into a lay-by.

"Good morning, madam. Is this your car?" asked the bearded policeman. The police driver had stayed behind the wheel.

"Why, yes. Is there a problem officer?" He assured her

that it was only a routine check on the tyre conditions of all passenger vehicles on a certain stretch of his main road for the current week. He lied convincingly.

"How long have you had the car?" Seven days was the reply. The traffic constable then pretended to examine the tyres, crouching down to inspect each one. "I need to take some details. Name and address, please." He was ready with his notebook. Three minutes later, having assured the female driver all was well, she eased away from the lay-by and continued south. The officer phoned Straker as soon as he got back into his white, marked BMW estate car.

A white female by the name of Cynthia Harding who gave an address in Maltby had bought the red Mazda MX-5 from a car dealer called Chrissie Mackintosh a week ago having part exchanged it against her previous car, a Renault coupe. Within minutes of ending the call, the detective sergeant was on his way to see Chrissie, the garage owner who might have some interesting information on Maria Dawson. Kev Straker parked his Vauxhall Insignia at the edge of the forecourt and entered the small showroom. The owner was sitting at a desk in the far corner. The DS introduced himself and sat down.

"So, Chrissie, you sold a Ford Fiesta to Mrs. Dawson on Friday August the nineteenth who put a red Mazda in part exchange." He nodded as he opened a file on his desk with paperwork relating to car sales for the month. He turned the folder toward the detective so he could see the details. "I'm sure all is in order, Chrissie. I'm not here to check on your VAT returns or anything. But tell me, Mrs. Dawson . . . did she seem OK at the time of the car purchase . . . was she nervous at all . . . anything odd about her behaviour?" Mackintosh shrugged.

"Not really. She struck me as a go-ahead type of woman, paid with a credit card, signed off on the bill of sale in a sort of fluent manner with her own fountain pen. Not many folks do that! She'd asked for two new front tyres and a new set of mats, plus a service and valet. She checked that all that had been done! Mrs. Dawson was a thorough lady, I can tell you. Wouldn't want to cross her. Pretty, too. Nice eyes."

"Did she happen to say where she was going when she left these premises?"

"Let me think . . . ah, yes. She was driving down to Lincoln. The Fiesta is fitted with sat-nav and she asked me to enter the address for her, that was it."

"You don't happen to recall the Lincoln address, Chrissie, do you?" Straker crossed his fingers under the desk.

"Yes, I do actually. I had an aunt who used to live in Tower Street in Richmond, North Yorkshire and Mrs. Dawson was going to number one, Tower Street, Lincoln. That was it. 1, Tower Street, in the beautiful city of Lincoln. I'd entered that in her sat-nav."

***

DCI Jim Adamson had looked at the videotapes from the Expoforum convention. He'd told his DS that a fresh pair of eyes might spot something that may have been missed. Sipping machine coffee at his desk, Adamson slowly scrolled through the footage. After about ten minutes he noticed a tallish man, with a bull neck and a broad nose, that appeared every so often in the background. The DCI allowed the images to run and noticed the same man on several occasions. He decided to call him Mr. X. He stopped the footage and zoomed in on the target. There was a small tattoo on his right ear lobe. Adamson couldn't quite make out what it was but guessed at a bird or something similar. Mr. X could be seen talking to each of the three murdered East Europeans every so often, but unfortunately always with his back to the camera, almost as if he knew it was there. Had his detective sergeant missed this? Perhaps Straker was concentrating too much on interactions between Maria Dawson and the three. It was only a gut feeling, but Jim Adamson decided to make a telephone call to Inspector Gasquet at the head office of

Interpol at Quai Charles de Gaulle, Lyon in France. He'd last spoken to Gasquet a fortnight ago.

"Hello, Ricard. Comment ca va? C'est Jim Adamson ici." Asking how the Inspector was stretched Adamson's knowledge of the French language. He'd only managed a bare pass at O level.

"Ah, Jim, mon ami. Qui, je suis tres bien. Et vous? Et tu mari?" The DCI just managed to pick up on the query about his health and that of his wife. It was time to use English!

"Ricard, we are both well, thank you. Ricard, I have been looking at the videotape of some of the St. Petersburg conference on town twinning at the Expoforum. You'll remember that my sergeant, Kevin Straker, was speaking with you a short while ago." Gasquet managed a brief 'oui.' Adamson continued. "I've noticed a tall man, perhaps a little under six feet tall, with a thick neck like a wrestler, and a flattish, broad nose. You have a copy of the same VT and he can be seen several times but at the point where the clock in the bottom right hand corner shows eight minutes and 23 seconds, you'll see him talking to one of the murdered East Europeans. If you have time have a look. Do you think you could find out who he is? It may be of importance."

"Oui, one moment, Jim, I have my computer here . . . and I can . . . just a moment . . . ah, yes, I see him. And again . . . let me get closer, ah, there is a tattoo on his earlobe." Adamson held his breath. "Non, I do not recognise this man. But I have two colleagues who may know. Leave this with me, Jim, and I will try to get back to you today."

"Merci bien, Ricard. A bientot!" The DCI put the phone down, happy with his effort at pigeon French. So, Ricard Gasquet, who sounded a good honest policeman, would reply to Adamson's question in due course. The DCI flipped through about twenty minutes worth of VT, making a note of the clock times when Mr. X was seen talking with Stavinsky, Dalopov and Bukelis. He'd have something to share with his DS when he got back.

Meanwhile Kev Straker, sitting in his Vauxhall at a KFC where he'd finished chicken nuggets and fries, had been liaising with Lincolnshire Police and spoken with DS Robin Green. Straker had smiled to himself when he first heard the name of the detective sergeant from Lincolnshire. Didn't Robin Hood wear clothes of Lincoln Green? Perhaps his parents had a sense of humour?

"Robin, I feel it might be useful if you could put a watch on number one, Tower Street? Let's not assume anything right now. We don't want to put the frighteners on Maria Dawson's sister or Dawson herself. Surveillance for the next 24 hours should prove something. What do you think?" DS Green agreed with the logic and confirmed with Kev Straker that he'd have one of his detective constables keep an eye on the house from 6.00 pm that evening. "Also, Robin, can you look out for a black Ford Fiesta, registration number alpha zebra, one three, whisky, foxtrot, tango. It belongs to Dawson." Green told his Cleveland counterpart that he'd let him know the outcome as soon as anything useful came to light.

Kev Straker had phoned Paul Dawson twice in the past 48 hours asking about his wife but with no joy. Paul Dawson had told the DS that he hadn't heard from Maria, neither was she answering her mobile phone. Straker was bemused . . . if *his* wife was going away to see her sister who hadn't been too well lately, he'd have made damned certain that he knew where she was going. 'What kind of relationship did the Dawson's have?' wondered the detective. He also reflected on the words of Chrissie Mackintosh at the garage.

'A go-ahead type of woman.'
'A thorough lady.'
'Wouldn't want to cross her.'

Straker opened his smartphone and thumbed down to an image of Maria Dawson that her husband had provided. It was a head and shoulders shot, not quite a passport style photo, but with a hint of a smile. Steel blue eyes looked at him; searching, amiable, but not penetrating. Her hair was blonde on the photo, although Straker knew that it was now short and dark brown. From his research he knew almost as much about Maria as he did his own wife – almost. Except for one thing. He'd never met her. But all of the evidence indicated that she knew each of the four dead men and had been seen on VT talking with two of them at the convention in September last year. Not only that, but she had met with each one individually between June and August. Met then left a dead body - the remnant of each meeting. Straker simply had to talk to Maria Dawson. She was needed to help with their enquiries which were progressing slower than a drunken snail. He knew the Superintendent was being harried by the Chief Constable, and that they needed a breakthrough.

Everything seemed to be happening at once. It was worse than the London bus syndrome – nothing for ages then several come along at the same time. Straker had to get back to the station. His chicken nuggets and French fries would put him on until he got home, but he had things to do. He wanted to call Dr Adam Harper again, get an update on the profiling of the perpetrator, see if Harper had any further developments on the MO of the murderer. Straker thought about the deaths again – strangulation with a cord, the domino and lump of marble, bunches of flowers, virtual disembowelling . . . 'what the hell have we got here?' he whispered as he drove away from the KFC. Before he'd hit the main road, his phone rang. He saw Jim Adamson was calling. The DS pulled over.

"Yes, boss?"

"Kev, get yourself back here asap. I've got something that is very, very interesting!" Straker floored the accelerator but decided against the blue lights hidden in the front grille and at the top of the rear windscreen.

***

"What! Wiped clean? How could that happen?" Jim

Adamson was talking to one of the technical guys, Ray Johnson, at police HQ in Ladgate Lane. He'd looked at the purple Samsung iPhone with a view to checking the data on it.

"It is possible to delete information remotely, Detective Chief Inspector. I'm afraid it's been done. But I've removed the SIM card and I can tell you this phone, from the internal product code number, was not bought in the UK. I've checked the numbers and the case colour, and this particular Samsung iPhone was bought in Latvia. The shade of purple is described as *Gentian Violet* by the manufacturer, and is usually on sale only in east Europe. Probably purchased in that area at the beginning of 2016. We've checked it for finger prints. Nothing." Adamson wondered who'd owned the smartphone.

"Are you sure you can't obtain anything that may still be on the phone?"

"Well, sometimes it is possible. Leave it with me and I'll do what I can."

"OK, thanks Ray." DCI Adamson left the room along a corridor, turned left at the end and went into his office. He stood looking out of his window that faced toward Stewart Park and remembered playing there as a kid, enjoying one of Rea's ice creams, with a free chocolate milk flake that Mr. Rea gave him for washing his ice cream van wheels and windscreen on a Saturday morning. Adamson had stopped to get a coffee on the way. He put the cardboard cup on a coaster he'd once brought back from Skegness and sat down.

***

Tommy Archer couldn't remember how he got home that night. He'd broken two finger nails and badly grazed his right knee. There was a nasty lump above his left eye. He recalled hearing part of the 2.00 am news on Radio Two when he'd turned the radio on in the bathroom as he examined his bruised face. It was now 6.34 am, a watery sun rising, and he cradled a mug of black coffee in front of the unlit log-burner in the lounge. He felt like cow dung, and if he was honest with himself, looked like it.

Tommy tried to piece together the events of the evening. The conversation with the Londoner, scoring at the darts match – albeit badly – and hiding in the Gents toilet. But that was the gentle part of the evening. He never realised, despite his suspicions, that he'd find the body of Dick Ashby down in the pub cellar. Maybe a collection of silver coins, but not a corpse. And certainly not one that looked alive! And he didn't know why he did what he did before getting the hell out of there.

How long had young Ashby been dead? Tommy recalled an unusual odour in the cellar, sort of medicinal but not unpleasant. But what freaked him out the most was seeing Dick sat upright on the edge of the bed for all the world as if he was alive! Just sitting there, staring into the black void. If he hadn't had his mini-torch with him he'd shuddered at the thought of walking into young Ashby and falling onto him, touching his cold flesh, feeling his matted hair. Screaming. Wakening Roger Grimes. Staring fixedly on the log-burner as if hypnotised, Tommy sipped his coffee. He opened the curtains of his cottage, the sun brighter and warmer now. He squinted, realising how tired he was, as he pulled the drapes fully back at each window.

The coffee finished, he ambled back into the kitchen, rinsed the mug and gripped the edge of the worktop. What the hell was he going to do about it? He had two choices he told himself. Say and do nothing, or, inform the police. Tommy unclenched his fingers and went into the bathroom. He had to shower right there and then, he felt filthy. Standing under the hot water might soothe his head, give him time to decide. Weighing up his two options was important.

The broad power-shower head did its job. Standing still for a few minutes, water cascaded over Tommy's body easing away his anxiety. He used a bar of olive oil soap and, eyes tight shut, washed himself vigorously. He felt that some of his built-up tension was now draining away down the plug hole. But this this was only temporary . . . he knew that. He was going to have to come to a decision and soon. Towelling himself down, but mindful of his grazed knee, Tommy got dressed quickly, pulling on a pair of clean leisure trousers and then a freshly laundered polo shirt. He slipped his feet into his flip-flops, combed his damp hair and put the kettle on again. Turning to a kitchen shelf he altered the wooden, block cube calendar – today was THURSDAY 01 SEPTEMBER – the year was flying past.

He revisited the whole event, from the first email on 13 June with Paul Dawson to here and now. He'd told himself often enough that he was getting in too deep, but he had to admit there was a thrill to it. Not so much the 'cut and thrust of the chase' but the 'living on the edge' aspect. Being so close to the action as if he was in a film without the cameras. Following Maria, being a witness to a host of events, having knowledge of things that others didn't have . . . including the police. Hell, why had he allowed himself to get here? But Tommy put his philosophical hat on – he was where he was, and that was that.

He hadn't heard from Paul for a while now and assumed that Maria was not in need of further observation. He hadn't been near Eston to see if her car was on the drive or called by the library. Perhaps he'd send Paul an email to check whether the project was closed, in which case Tommy would send his final invoice. But more important than that right now was the fact that Dick Ashby was stone dead and in the cellar of the Frog and Ferret. There were questions . . . who had killed him and why? Tommy had long since given up on 'assuming.' He wasn't going to jump to any conclusions. Roger Grimes may have been the murderer, but Dick had been missing for nearly four months. Had he been in that damp place all this time? Was the portly landlord the type of person who'd kill a young man and hold him in a cellar? If so, why? Tommy recalled the silver Georgian coin collection that Dick had and the common interest in numismatic matters shown by both Grimes and Gordon Ashby's son. Would the landlord kill for a few coins?

So, there was still the dilemma . . . leave things or tell the police. Then he remembered what he'd done before he left the cellar. Why, in the cold light of day, why? Tommy went over to the coat hooks near the front door and fumbled in his light jacket pocket, the jacket he wore last night. He braced himself as he slowly pulled out the glass eye. It slipped from his grasp and rolled across the entrance hall carpet. Coming to a stop next to the umbrella stand, the black pupil stared at him. In an instant Tommy grabbed a flat cap from the top of the stand and threw it over the eyeball. Shit! He shivered a few times as he went back into the kitchen. Tommy looked out of the window as two wood pigeons were pecking at seed on the small patio outside.

In Tommy's mind he pictured Gordon Ashby. Did Tommy have a moral duty to tell the estate agent about his son? After all it had been a case he'd been working on, so perhaps he should?

"Hello, Gordon, it's Tommy Archer here. Got some bad news I'm afraid. Your son, Dick, is lying on a bed in the cellar of the Frog and Ferret in Pomfreton. Dead as a dodo. Nice glass eyes, though. I picked one up as a souvenir. Anyway, you'll find him there when you've time to get over. Sorry to be the bearer of bad news but maybe he had it coming?"

No! He couldn't do it, no way! But as Tommy's mind raced with such thoughts another thought came into his head.

Tommy got changed, quickly filed his broken nails and looked in the mirror to check the lump on his forehead. It wasn't as bad as it had been earlier. His hair would do. Glancing down at his flat cap, he decided to leave it there for now. Tommy grabbed his car keys from the hall table and walked out into the bright sunshine.

***

"What have you got, boss?" DS Kev Straker had knocked on Jim Adamson's door soon after leaving the KFC and driving quickly across town. The DCI pointed to the chair opposite his desk and the detective sergeant sat down.

"Well, where do I start? OK, let's begin here." Adamson glanced at his notes. "The phone handed in belonged to Bukelis. The tech guy was able to retrieve two texts, both sent to the same mobile. It's a Pay-As-You-Go so we're unlikely to find out who owns that. The messages are both short.

Hi, I've checked in. See you in the bar in thirty minutes. MB

I'm here with a drink. Where are you? MB

Can we assume they were sent to Maria Dawson on the night Bukelis was murdered? For some reason the killer decided to throw it away on the A19. By the way, any news on Dawson yet? She should be here to answers a few questions." Straker brought his boss up to date on the liaison with DS Robin Green in Lincoln who'd be arranging a 24 hours surveillance on 1, Tower Street, her sister's address. Adamson pushed his sergeant to keep on top of it. "How did you know she was in Lincoln?"

"Well, Dawson has changed her car. A traffic officer stopped the red Mazda MX-5 that her husband told us about. He found another woman driving it who'd bought it from a garage where Dawson had traded it in against a Ford Fiesta. Now here's your answer . . . the garage owner, a Chrissie Mackintosh, had put the address into the car's sat-nav for her. Thankfully he remembered the details." Adamson nodded approvingly. "The other news is that the knife found at Crathorne Park Hotel has been dusted for prints and forensics have a perfect set of four fingers and thumb on the stout wooden handle. Left - handed user. The prints don't match any we have on file."

"It looks as if we might be getting somewhere, Kev. Slowly but surely. I don't suppose there's anything on the florists, is there?" Straker smiled.

"DC Martin Jones phoned me earlier. He'd visited three florists who'd sold the types of flowers that are of interest. He's had a call from Chloe Blackwell who runs *Pistils and Roses* in Stockton. She told Jones that she remembers a guy that bought a few different blooms from them – always paid cash. Couldn't say much about him – average height and build – but always wore sunglasses, even if it wasn't bright. She did notice that the specs were RayBan brand, though. He was in yesterday asking about some daisies with large heads, something with an odd name, loads of petals around the centre. He never stays long apparently, a quick in and out job. But . . . and here's the interesting part, he has telephoned the shop before and Chloe noticed the caller's number show up as an 01642 land-line number which is Teesside as you know. She's given me the phone number which she had scribbled on a jotter pad near the phone." The DCI leaned back, then breathed out through his nose slowly like a bull thinking about charging a hapless trespasser across his field.

"Great! So, can we liaise with this Chloe woman and set something up? Ask her to order the big daisies, tell him they've arrived, and wait for him to collect them? We could hide behind the bamboo," chuckled Adamson.

"We could!" Looking down at some notes and stifling a grin, Straker continued. "Going back to the kitchen knife, boss, the forensics guy, who'd seen a similar knife before, checked the brand on a database of weapons. It's a type called 'Belle Cuisine' endorsed by Ricky Sadler, a well-known Michelin starred chef apparently, and you can only purchase them directly from a company called Smart-Cut Blades who sell that specific knife in five blade lengths and only as a set. Sheffield steel and three-rivet handle. They come complete in a beech, wooden block."

"Have you been onto them, yet?" Adamson had sat up quickly. The DS shook his head.

"It's on my to-do list, boss."

"You mentioned talking with Dr Harper again. Any joy with that?"

"It's on my . . ." Before Straker could finish the sentence, Adamson did it for him.

"To-do list, boss." They both chuckled. "And the 01642 number?" Straker threw his hands in the air. "Kev, great work. You're doing a good job here, let me tell you, and I know you've got things in hand. The metaphorical jigsaw is coming together. We've almost finished the border, and when that's done, we'll start putting in the little pokey bits. Let's pray that it's not a charity shop jigsaw . . . always a few parts missing!" Adamson held his head back as he laughed, Straker noticing a couple of dark fillings in his upper jaw.

***

"Joe, it's Tommy. Can you talk?" The PI had parked up in a lay by past Judges Hotel going out of Yarm. I need to talk to you, are you around this morning?"

"Hi, Tommy. I'm going to be at Crathorne Park in about a quarter of an hour. Is that any good?" Tommy confirmed that he'd be at the hotel then; it was less than five minutes away. "Ask for me at reception when you arrive. Bye." Joe Blackwell had known Tommy for a long time. He'd been the one who'd suggested Tommy join the police force after his days in the R.A.F. and then from there he'd become a private detective. So, in a way, Tommy was where he was because of Joe, but Tommy wasn't sure if it had been a blessing or a curse. At least not at that moment.

Tommy sat for a while reflecting on his dark journey down to the pub cellar. Hell, what a surprise he'd got! It almost reminded him of going on the ghost train in Blackpool with his father when he was about six or seven and had gone on a week's holiday with his parents. The little trucks whizzing round a track in the darkness, mock cobwebs brushing your face, and being scared out of one's skin when a seemingly dead body, instantly illuminated, suddenly jumped at you with a scream piercing enough to curdle milk. Roger Grimes must have murdered Dick

Ashby and kept him in the damp cellar, thought Tommy. But why – was it because he wanted his coin collection? Hardly. Did the landlord and Dick Ashby have a relationship that went wrong? Perhaps they were gay lovers. There must have been another reason, surely? And was Ashby's body preserved? Hell, it was enough for him to have had a heart attack! But did Grimes do the evil deed? He'd have known about it for certain, but maybe he'd used someone else to do it? If so, who was it?

Tommy ran his fingers through his tousled hair as he looked at himself in the rear-view mirror. What a sight! Bags under his eyes, a lump on his head, his hair in need of a trim. Poking his tongue out, it had a yellow tinge like the remains of last night's curry. Ugh! He looked awful. A Tesco delivery driver in a Ford Transit eased past Tommy's Golf and stared at him. What did he think, Tommy wondered? It didn't really matter. Tesco drivers must see much worse delivering groceries on Teesside, especially early morning!

Turning the ignition key, Tommy pulled away from the lay-by and headed toward the A19, passed over the dual carriageway and turned right. The entrance to the hotel was two hundred yards on his left and he turned in. The thoughts of his evening here on 11 August came flooding back, but as if through frosted glass. Motoring along the drive to the hotel entrance, parking up, entering the hotel, going into the restaurant, watching Maria and Marin Bukelis. But for Tommy, this meeting with Joe had quickly become a conundrum. When he'd first considered meeting Joe his thoughts were along the lines of 'I want to tell him everything I know.' But as Tommy pulled up in the main car park of the Crathorne Park he wasn't so sure. He switched off the car engine and stayed in the Golf.

OK, Joe was his friend. A good pal, and yes, Tommy would admit that he didn't know him that well. But that's life. Everybody has their skeleton in the cupboard. Tommy had his, which he kept below his 'psyche radar' as he put it. So *how much* was he going to share with Joe? Maybe it would be better to do some probing . . . ask Joe what he knew about the murders. After all, three had taken place in or very near to his hotels and Sergio Dalopov had stayed at the Crimdon Grange in Blackhall! Taking his hand off the interior door handle for a few seconds, that image hit Tommy like a fuel-injected steamroller driven by Lewis Hamilton, followed by a Mike Tyson slap across his drawn face.

All the murders were associated with hotels in the Northcliffe Group.

Coincidence, wondered Tommy? Had the police picked up on that? Did Jim Adamson *even know* that these were part of a hotel group? Tommy surmised not. And so, as he calmly got out of his car and closed the door, he decided that he wasn't going to confide in Joe Blackwell. At least not yet.

***

Kev Straker had just finished reading a phone text from DS Robin Green in Lincoln.

Hi Kev, sorry for the delay in getting back to you. Been busy here – shit hitting the fan and all that. Got a new Chief Superintendent who's a stickler for bloody meetings! We'd kept an eye on the house as you requested. Saw a dark - haired woman, pretty, mid - thirties entering the premises on several occasions. A Fiesta with the number plate you mentioned was parked in a side street. A short man wearing a baseball cap with NY on it rang the bell on two occasions. He went straight in as soon as the door was opened but it was impossible to say who had let him in. No sign of any other persons there. We did a check on the property which is being rented out. The owner is a Mr. S. Ladd. Never saw the guy leave, but he could have sneaked out of the back door which led into a yard with access to a narrow alleyway. The lighting in Tower Street isn't very good. Couldn't spend too much unofficial time on this but hope it helps."

***

Tommy had met with Joe Blackwell at Crathorne Park hotel. A short meeting, with a decent pot of coffee, had resulted in Joe sharing some information with Tommy. Joe told Tommy he had looked through the hotel CCTV footage, albeit a bit grainy, with DCI Jim Adamson. The police team had finished searching the room of Bukelis and the grounds of the hotel. There were no further clues as to what the Latvian was doing at the hotel, apart from having dinner with a woman. They'd found a kitchen knife in the long grass at one end of the hotel, of which Joe knew little else, and the DCI had asked Joe and the hotel manager to keep the matter confidential. The police had told the hotel manager his luggage hadn't yet been found, nor his wallet or phone.

Tommy had been surprised at the information Joe had shared with him and realised that the Security Manager was in possession of facts that had not been made public. And when it came to it, Tommy could have found it easy to open up and tell Joe what he knew. Share and share alike, perhaps? But Tommy was in for a surprise. Joe had told him that he was certain the man he'd seen on the closed-circuit images was Tommy. Black beard, but wearing spectacles. Tommy remembered slipping on the plain specs just in case he'd be seen on CCTV. He looked sheepish.

'But I didn't say anything to the police, Tommy,' Joe added quickly. The PI smiled awkwardly and had stayed quiet as he sipped black coffee from a china cup. Joe reminded Tommy that he'd helped him some weeks ago with information on the 'foreign sounding' guests staying at the Northcliffe group of hotels, but that he'd never told him why he wanted to know.

'It's just some private investigating work I'm doing for a client, Joe. You know how it is, there is a clause in all my work stating that what goes on between a client and myself is totally confidential. I'm grateful for the leads, of course,

Joe. You'll have picked up quite a bit from the news reports, anyway.' Joe hadn't been impressed with Tommy's comment – he expected more of a volunteering of information. Joe's tone changed.

'So, I gave you specifics about the Seaview and Queen's Head hotels as regards two East Europeans staying there. Both murdered. You were here on August 11 – another murder. And an East European was found in an alley in Middlesbrough. Were you there?' Tommy had nodded. He felt Joe Blackwell was trying to make a point, and Tommy was becoming uncomfortable. He sat upright.

'Joe. You're Head of Security, right?' Blackwell smiled in agreement. 'There have been three murders at *your* hotels. Now where's the *security* in that?' Blackwell's demeanour changed. 'What steps did you take after Ivo Stavinsky was found in his car boot in Marske? A dead body in the room at the Queen's Head! And Dalopov stayed at Crimdon Grange hotel. Has DCI Jim Adamson asked *you* any questions, Joe? Does he know the hotels belong to the same group? And you told me that Chloe had been visited by the police regarding sales of flowers at her florists. Don't you think that the detective has considered that there might be a link?' Joe Blackwell was stony silent; a whiter shade of puce. Seconds passed.

'Tommy. We've been friends for about eleven years now and I don't want that to change, do you?' Tommy shook his head.

'OK. So, do you plan to tell Adamson about my appearance on the hotel CCTV here? That you know it's me?' asked Tommy.

'What appearance?' replied the Head of Security, smiling, as both stood and shook hands.

Tommy motored down the drive of Crathorne Park realising that he now had a different relationship with Joe Blackwell. An understanding. But he needed to be careful. As long as Joe kept his word DCI Adamson shouldn't connect Tommy with the visit of Marin Bukelis to Crathorne. But there was now one thing that was certain.

No way could the PI tell Jim Adamson anything. His moral dilemma of a few weeks ago had gone. He had to keep matters to himself. At least for now. Tommy turned right at the end of the drive and re-crossed the A19. He was parking in the Yarm supermarket car park ten minutes later. Tommy had decided that he would see Gordon Ashby and talk to him in private – tell him everything about Dick. But walking into the estate agent's offices wasn't a good idea. Tommy sat in his Golf and took out his phone. He'd entered Gordon Ashby into his Contacts some time ago.

"Hello, is Gordon Ashby there, please?" The girl that answered asked who was calling. "It's Tommy Archer." She asked him to hold. Ashby answered the phone as Tommy took in a deep breath. "Gordon, I need to talk to you. Preferably in private or somewhere very quiet. I've got some news on Dick." Ashby agreed and proposed meeting at the Links View hotel on the Eaglescliffe road opposite the golf course. Tommy had been there before and knew it was rarely busy during the day. The only problem might be if Gordon Ashby had a turn, started raving or totally lost it. "Gordon, it may be better if we sat in my car. In the car park of the hotel?" Ashby was silent for a few seconds, probably fearing bad news. "I drive a grey VW Golf that's in need of a wash. I'll be there in five minutes, stay in the car, and wait for you around the back." Gordon Ashby put the phone down.

All Tommy had to do next was be clear on just how he was going to tell the estate agent that his son had been murdered.

***

There was a buzz in IR4 at Cleveland Police HQ. Harry Charlton was there along with DCI Adamson, DS Straker and four DC's. Kev Straker had been 'board monitor' and an early start for him ensured that all the known facts were on that display. Photos, postcard notes, post-its, some elements connected by wool strands of different colours, and an adjacent white board with half a dozen marker pens on the narrow shelf below. A laptop was connected up to a fifty - inch television screen so that any CCTV footage could be shown.

Superintendent Charlton was there to chair the meeting and to take a 'helicopter view' of matters. He hadn't been too close to detail so enabling him to adopt an impartial view as regards some of the facts. He'd asked Jim Adamson to handle matters and so, at 8.30 am prompt, the DCI called the meeting to order, thermos jugs of coffee and tea on the table. A couple of plates of chocolate biscuits would keep the blood sugar levels up. Adamson had been at his desk at just after 7.15 am that morning, re-read the details on the four dead men, the Expoforum convention information, and reports from the SOCO's that had visited all sites of the murders.

DS Straker had pulled together information on Maria and Paul Dawson, Karl Lamb and Andy Young who'd been to the St. Petersburg conference. He'd also got answers to a handful of key outstanding issues about the Bukelis murder weapon, a Teesside phone number and his latest information from Dr Adam Harper.

The four detective constables – Hardy, Howison, Robinson & Hodgson, had a wide spectrum of data including eye witness accounts from the scenes of crime, statements taken from staff at the hotels and visits to florists, as well as a number of follow up activities relating to the travel schedules of the four murdered men.

By 10.30 am and several coffees later a clearer picture was beginning to emerge of the movements of those that were listed on the large board . . . twelve photos, eighteen note cards and 32 post-it notes. Twenty minutes of video had been shown, and several trips to the loo – at allowed moments – had been taken. The biscuit plates were empty, apart from a few crumbs.

"OK, everyone, let's take a 10 minutes break." Harry Charlton looked at the large clock on the wall. "Everybody back here at 10.45 sharp." A rustling of papers, ball-point pens being clicked and some stretching ensued. The Superintendent walked across to Jim Adamson and leaned over. Speaking quietly, he said, "It's going well, Jim. There's a lot of info and it's coming together. It seems we'll have a few i's to dot and t's to cross by the time we're done today but I'm certain the Chief Constable will be pleased with the progress. Be good to have a priority list when we conclude." Adamson turned toward Harry Charlton and showed him his folder. One page had a heading 'Top Ten Things To Do' and the numbers one to ten down the left hand side.

"I've got my TTTTD list ready to complete, sir," replied the DCI with smug satisfaction. The Super looked embarrassed and wandered off to use the internal phone. He asked for more hot drinks and biscuits to be brought in. Charlton told himself he ought to have known better. Adamson hadn't been a copper for twenty years with an early promotion to DCI for nothing!

The meeting continued through until just before one o'clock when a knock on the door indicated that one of Charlton's admin staff had brought a selection of boxed pizzas including a Four - Cheese, Meat Feast and an Hawaiian. Jugs of orange juice and water were placed on the table along with two towers of plastic tumblers; a twenty minutes break given. Every member of the investigating team had made a contribution during the lively morning session, with Jim Adamson taking copious notes.

'So, were the victims connected other than by the Expo convention?'

'Any idea as to where their possessions are now?'

'Do we need a better psychological profile on the perp or perps?'

'So, do we have any idea why the killer or killers used these methods?'

'Who were the men seen at the Cleveland Bay restaurant?'

'Why haven't we spoken to Maria Dawson, yet?'

'What do we know about her husband?'

'Are we 100% sure about all of our witness statements?'

'Do we need to talk to Karl Lamb and Andy Young again?'

'Should we . . . shall we . . . when . . . why . . . . . . '

"All right, everybody, let's call it a day." Harry Charlton had stood up and stretched. "Jim, have you enough to formulate the next stages?" The DCI rubbed his eyes.

"We don't need to meet tomorrow. I'll arrange a media briefing for Wednesday – 3.00 pm here. From our meeting today, I think you all know your next moves. Keep Kev Straker in any communication loop. We'll call this exercise *Operation Domino* and all information must remain within this group. Understood?" Everyone replied in the affirmative. The wall clock showed 4.20 pm as the officers left IR4. Kev Straker was the last one out of the room having tidied up, put some crockery on a tray and dumped cardboard plates and tumblers into a black bin liner. These were left outside the door where the contract cleaners would attend to them. DS Straker locked the door. Nothing would be touched in there.

At almost 4.30 pm Straker was feeling weary, the tension of the day having seeped into his bones and muscles, but the DS went back to his desk and made a phone call. He'd told his boss that he was planning to ring GoWorldTravel to try to talk to Maria Dawson. He had found out that Dawson and Karl Lamb were on the *same* Jet2 aircraft to St. Petersburg for the Expoforum, a fact he'd shared in the meeting that day. Not only that, but they had sat next to each other on *both* outward *and* return flights. Now was that a coincidence? It could have been, but unlikely. Evidence was piling up against Maria Dawson and Kev Straker desperately wanted to talk to her.

"Hello, GoWorld Travel, Julie speaking. How may I help?"

"Oh, hi. Detective Sergeant Kevin Straker here. May I have a quick word with Mrs. Maria Dawson, please?"

"Maria? No, she's left. Handed her notice in. She came back into the office on, let me see, yes, I think it was the day after the Bank Holiday Monday, so that was the thirtieth of August. She collected a few personal things and waltzed out as cool as a cucumber."

"Do you know where she's gone? I mean to another job?"

"No idea, sorry," replied Julie. Straker ended the call. 'Sod it,' he thought. Why hadn't he pushed to interview Dawson sooner? Adamson wanted to do it . . . Straker himself was going to do it . . . and now she'd resigned from her role at the travel agency. Would the Managing Director know where she'd gone? Never mind, Kev Straker was going to visit 89, St. Roseberry Close and talk to Maria Dawson there.

***

DC Dave Hodgson had been doing some investigating. After the meeting in IR4 he'd gone back to his desk following a conversation with Kev Straker. There were two matters he was to pursue immediately. Had someone in the Teesside area bought a set of kitchen knives from Smart-Cut Blades, and who did the 01642 telephone number belong to?

It didn't take Hodgson long to contact the knife company. The web site gave details on their Home page. Based in Norwich, Smart-Cut Blades were situated on an industrial estate on the outskirts of the city. The telephone number was shown below the address.

He briefly explained the situation but gave nothing away. Within a few minutes a helpful Customer Services employee gave DC Hodgson the names of two people on Teesside who'd bought a set of 'Belle Cuisine' knives since the start of 2016. They offered to go back further but the detective constable was happy with that for now.

Checks with British Telecom established that the 01642 telephone number belonged to a public phone box situated on the Guisborough road. So, DS Straker was going to be disappointed! He'd told the DC that he felt certain it was a private phone number. It wasn't - anyone could use it. The caller who'd contacted *Pistils and Roses* had made several calls from this box. Putting a surveillance on this telephone kiosk simply wasn't going to be cost effective, and even Hodgson knew Harry Charlton wouldn't sanction it.

Hodgson looked at the names of the Smart-Cut Blades customers. Mr. Charles Langtry from Redcar and a Miss Rebecca Robinson in Norton. He had their full addresses and contact details and decided to make a telephone call straight-away. Charles Langtry confirmed he'd bought the 'Belle Cuisine' set in January of 2016 after a friend had recommended the knives during a Christmas party. One had carved the turkey a real treat. All knives were still in Langtry's possession, and available for inspection if necessary. Hodgson declined the offer and thanked Langtry before ending the call. The DC dialled the phone number for the Norton address. The call was answered by a woman with a soft, but hesitant voice.

"Hello?" DC Hodgson introduced himself and gave the reason for the call. "How do I know you're the police? Is this a scam call? The number is shown as withheld! If it is, you'll be reported." Hodgson reassured Miss Robinson that it was genuine but invited her to call him back if needed. He heard her sigh. "OK, but I'm not giving out any confidential information over the phone." Hodgson was dealing with a woman who may have been conned before. He continued.

"Miss Robinson, can you say whether you purchased the set of knives I've mentioned? That's all I need to know right now." Rebecca Robinson told the DC that she'd bought the set, plus wooden block, on-line in February. She'd seen a small advert in a Sunday colour supplement and decided they'd complement her kitchen, most of her other knives were either blunt or the handles were loose. "And do you still have all the knives in the set?" Miss Robinson hesitated. Why on earth was a detective asking her about her bloody cutlery?

"Yes, but one is missing. I can't think for the life of me

where it's gone."

"And the set, there are five in total, each with a good, strong wooden handle and three brass rivets?"

"Yes, that's correct. What's this about, detective?" Robinson was sounding anxious.

"Which knife is missing, Miss Robinson?"

"The largest one. The one with a ten - inch blade."

"Miss Robinson, I'm going to have to take a statement from you in the morning. Is there a convenient time?" Hodgson heard pages flicking. Confident that this was a genuine call, she replied.

"How about 8.30 am? You can see me at my home address. Do you have it?" The DC said that he did. "I work from home and my first appointment is at nine o'clock." Hodgson asked what her occupation was. "I'm a hairdresser. And please call me Becky."

***

Tommy looked at his watch and began to wonder if Gordon Ashby would turn up. He'd been parked behind the Links View hotel for almost half an hour. As he reached for some gum to freshen his breath, a black SUV slowly drove close to Tommy's car. It was Gordon Ashby; Tommy gave him a wave. The vehicle parked two spaces away, then Ashby got out and came towards Tommy's car. Ashby opened the passenger door and got in. He looked ashen.

"Morning, Gordon. You OK? You look a bit, well, not too good to be honest." Ashby stared through the windscreen. His eyes wide. It was several seconds before the estate agent spoke.

"So, what news on Dick? Don't mince your words, Tommy. Get to the point." Tommy swallowed, the mint flavoured saliva easing down his throat.

"Well, Gordon, it's bad news, I'm afraid. Dick is dead." Ashby took in a sharp intake of breath, coupled with a slight wince as if he'd been poked with a sharp needle. "I had my suspicions that Dick was either being helped by one of his mates, perhaps Dave Teague or Steve Attridge that you'd mentioned before, or that he was being held against his will somewhere. I thought about anybody who may have tried to hide him, or where he could have gone after the car accident on the Whitby road. You'd mentioned his coin collection and I knew Roger Grimes, the landlord at the Frog and Ferret in Pomfreton was interested in coins. I began to wonder if he might have gone back to the pub that night and asked Grimes for a place to lay his head, so to speak. I'd also asked some questions about the landlord of a couple of people in the village that I could trust. Did you know that Dick and Roger Grimes' son, Ian, were at the same school?"

"No. Dick rarely spoke about any of the others at Yarm School. But what of it?" Tommy quietly moved the gum around his mouth. Left to right and back again.

"Well, I believe that Dick was bullying Grimes' son at school. Taking the mickey about his disabled mother, too. Ian committed suicide." Tommy paused to let that last sentence sink in. "You'd said that Dick sometimes had a non-alcoholic drink in the bar and so perhaps he established a friendship with the landlord, chatting about coins and not really thinking about Ian that much. My guess is that Grimes *groomed* Dick, if that's the way to put it, with a view to getting rid of him. I don't think it was sexual." Ashby moved uneasily, his hands clasped, thumbs twiddling.

"What have you seen, Tommy? Have you seen Dick?" Tommy turned further toward Gordon Ashby, keeping his right hand on the steering wheel which he gripped tightly.

Tommy went on to explain what he'd done that night in the Frog and Ferret, and as he told Ashby it felt, in a surreal manner, as if he was recounting a scene in a James Bond film. He decided to tell all – the toilet vigil, creeping down the cellar steps, going into the damp cellar and seeing Dick sat upright on the dirty bedclothes. Except no mention was made of glass eyes, and certainly not the one still on his floor at home under his cap. Ashby was appearing sickly and Tommy didn't want to have to clean the VW Golf if Ashby puked up in the floor well. Ashby put his head back and ran his fingers through his hair before thumping the dashboard with his left fist.

"Bloody hell, Tommy! So, Roger Grimes murdered my son!" Tommy jumped. He prayed that Ashby wasn't going to turn green and have his shirt splitting like the 'Incredible Hulk.' He interjected quickly.

"Roger, we don't know if Roger Grimes killed Dick. It would seem that Dick may have been held there since some time after the car accident, assuming that my theory is correct. A form of torture . . . retribution for his bullying of Ian Grimes. Knowing the landlord as I do, I'd say it wasn't Roger Grimes. I'd say he had someone do it. Perhaps a regular at the pub, someone that Grimes trusted implicitly?" Gordon Ashby opened the car door, but it was only for fresh air. The car park was quiet, lunchtime customers yet to arrive.

"Got any water?" asked Ashby. Tommy passed him a bottle of still water from the car door recess. Ashby took two white tablets from a small, matchbox size, plastic container and popped them into his mouth. A good swig of water followed as Ashby gulped them down. Neither spoke for a while.

"Tommy, there's something I need to tell you . . . something I have to get off my chest. It's been building up inside me for a long time. I think you're the guy to tell." Suddenly Gordon Ashby burst into tears and cried the cry of a man sounding as if a valve on a pressure cooker had been released a bit too quickly.

***

DC Hodgson had phoned Kev Straker at a little before 8.00 am to tell the DS that he was on his way to see a Miss Rebecca Robinson regarding the 'Belle Cuisine' knives. Straker had taken the call after filling up the Vauxhall at a Shell fuel station near Billingham. The detective sergeant was on his way to see Maria Dawson and hoped that at about half past eight she'd be up and ready to talk to him. Kev Straker had also spoken to Jim Adamson that morning giving him an update on his movements.

"Once I've seen Dawson, sir, I'm going to the travel agent to talk with Clarke again. He hasn't told us everything he knows. There are some loose ends that need tying up. And, now that we know Dawson and Karl Lamb travelled together to the Russian meeting, I want to see Lamb again. He's already told us that he didn't know Maria Dawson. Has he spun a web of lies?" Kev Straker parked a few car lengths away from Dawson's home in St. Roseberry Close. A black Ford Fiesta was parked on the drive. He rang the bell. Seconds later a woman answered the door. Straker was already holding his police ID in his right palm by his side.

"Yes?" said the woman, her short, dark brown hair in need of brushing.

"Mrs. Maria Dawson?" Maria nodded. "I'm Detective Sergeant Kevin Straker." He showed Maria his Cleveland Police badge. "I have a few questions in connection with events that have taken place in this area recently. May I come in?"

"Events? What kind of events?" Maria appeared guarded in her response . . . often a sign that a person just might have something to hide.

"I think it would be best if I came in, Mrs. Dawson." Straker smiled to reduce the slight tension. "Unless you want the neighbours wondering what's going on?" Maria looked across the road and spotted Joan Smith peeking out of her front room window, lace curtains fluttering. Standing back, she opened the door wider and the DS went in. He followed Maria into the lounge where she pointed to an armchair. Straker sat down.

The detective and Maria talked for 45 minutes. He took notes, his mouth feeling dry, but no offer of tea or coffee was made. Maria was dressed in a loose Regatta top and a pair of grey jogging bottoms and probably had already breakfasted. Her pink socks contrasted with the black pumps she was wearing on her feet. She seemed calm and answered questions succinctly, with little or no extra information. Straker had interviewed many times and in most cases, he got more facts thrown at him than he wanted – it was a psychological defence mechanism for the majority of interviewees. Not so with Maria Dawson. She was cool, precise and to the point.

Had she met with Stavinsky, Kodric, Dalopov and Bukelis? 'Yes,' she admitted she had seen them and briefly gave an explanation.

Why had she met with them? *'I got on well with them at the Expoforum and they told me they planned to visit England sometime. I gave them my details and suggested they get in touch if they wanted to meet up. The meeting with Ned Kodric was at the invitation of my boss, Alan Clarke.'*

Did your husband know you were meeting these men? *'Yes, of course, but he didn't mind.'*

Did she know that some of their belongings had gone missing just prior to, or just after, their deaths? *'No, I didn't know that. Why would I? It hasn't been on the news has it?'*

Was there anything she could tell the police about their deaths? *'No. When I heard about each one, I'd been surprised and saddened. I had no idea why the men had been murdered. I wondered if I was putting a jinx on things.'*

And your husband's employment? *'He works at the central library.'*

Have you any brothers or sisters? *'Yes, I have a sister who lives in Lincoln. No brothers.'*

When did you last see your sister? *'A couple of weeks ago or so. She hadn't been feeling well so I paid her a visit.'*

Do you know Andy Young and Karl Lamb? *'Yes, they were at the convention in St. Petersburg.'*

Did you travel to the venue with either of them? *'Yes, I*

travelled with Karl from Leeds Bradford airport.'

Did you know him before you went to the convention? *'No.'*

You've recently resigned from your job at GoWorldTravel? *'Yes. I was getting bored with the job.'*

How did you get on with your boss, Alan Clarke? *'OK. He was fair but tough at times.'*

Do you have any hobbies, Mrs. Dawson, any interests? *'I collect dolls.'*

Do you have many? *'21 in total, and a few odd Russian dolls.'*

Do you work out, I mean keep yourself fit? *'I go to a gym when I can. Yes.'*

Kev Straker stood up and slipped his notebook into his inside jacket pocket with his ball-point pen.

"Well thank you for your time, Mrs. Dawson." Straker made his way to the front door as he handed her his contact card. "Before I go, do you know Rebecca Robinson?"

"Why, yes. Any reason for asking?"

"It's a name that's cropped up amongst lots of others in our enquiries. Is she a friend?" Maria nodded. "When did you last see Rebecca?" Maria explained that she met with Rebecca, whom she called Becky, now and again. Becky was like a sister to her. She and her husband Paul had been to her home a couple of times. The DS stepped outside. "Thank you again, Mrs. Dawson. If there is anything else you remember that may help us in our enquiries, please give me a call." Maria didn't reply as she watched the detective walk down the drive.

Kev Straker had concerns about Maria Dawson's story. How much was truth – how much lies? He'd held back on the questioning, didn't want to frighten her off. It was looking more and more likely that he'd ask Maria to go down to the nearest police station very soon and get her fingerprinted. Maria Dawson closed her front door and locked it. She had a lot to think about. Maria pulled the counterbalanced wooden ladder down and slowly climbed up to the loft.

As Kev Straker started the car engine there was one thing that slightly bugged him. He hadn't seen a single photograph in Maria Dawson's home. No husband, no parents, no friends. Not one. Driving back to the police HQ he also reflected on comments made by Adam Harper on the profile of the perpetrator of the crimes.

'Male, but possibly female. Physically and mentally strong. An unhappy childhood. Probably a loner. Doesn't pay much attention to family relationships. May have killed animals as a child . . .'

***

Jim Adamson was sitting in his office thinking about the missing items from the four murder victims. The luggage they were seen carrying - the suitcase of Ivo Stavinsky, light blue rucksack of Nejc Kodric, the light - brown, wheeled case belonging to Sergio Dalopov, and the red and black case of Marin Bukelis. Their wallets and phones had still not been recovered apart from Bukelis', nor passports apart from that of Stavinsky found in his Skoda. He had to assume the killer (or killers) was holding the missing items, Dr Adam Harper having told DS Straker that the perpetrator (or perpetrators) was likely to get a thrill from touching the items and the power buzz of being in possession of them. If only he could get a lead on any of these – a member of the public finding a discarded wallet or passport perhaps, or one of the phones being used to make a call. So far nothing, apart from the Samsung phone, had been forthcoming. Fingerprints had only been found on the knife used to murder Bukelis, but no other items – neither the domino nor the marble octagon.

Kev Straker had briefed Adamson on Maria Dawson's visit to Lincoln, but something didn't quite sit right with that. Nobody had actually seen her sister, and who was the man wearing a New York Yankees baseball cap that had visited the property in Tower Street when Lincolnshire

Police were keeping it under surveillance?

***

"Becky, this receipt shows that you bought the 'Belle Cuisine' set of knives on the fourth of February this year. What made you buy them?" DC Hodgson was looking at the receipt that Becky Robinson had printed off at home after her internet purchase. She nodded.

"Yes, there was a promotional DVD being shown in a garden centre near Thirsk that I visited with a friend at the back end of last year. I've got a few knives, but the set looked smart and *very sharp*. I thought the five knives would cover all my needs – I'm not a good cook – but when I use a knife it like it to slice like a razor blade!" Hodgson moved slightly uncomfortably as he imagined Robinson using a knife on a tender part of his anatomy.

"And then you noticed that one of the knives, the longest one with, a ten - inch blade, was missing?"

"Yes, come through here and I'll show you the set." They both stood and Becky led the way into the small kitchen. At the end of the worktop next to an espresso coffee machine was the polished wooden block, minus one knife. "I don't remember when it went missing, I mean there were some days when I wouldn't use a knife, you know, have a take-away or something. Once I did notice it, I tried to think where it might have gone. Had I taken it out of the block and used it elsewhere in the house . . . but no, I'm certain I hadn't done that. Oh, wait a second." She hesitated. "I did use the ten - inch knife on the seventh of August. A girlfriend came around and I used that knife to slice some Yorkshire ham. It was her birthday. That's how I remember." They returned to the lounge and sat down. Hodgson opened his notebook again.

"Do you have friends that visit you, apart from the girlfriend you've mentioned?" A silly question, Hodgson thought to himself, but it needed to be asked.

"Yes, a few. Let me think. I've probably had about eight

or nine in the last few months." Robinson took her time as she tapped, and counted, the tips of her right fingers and thumb twice with her left index finger.

"Would any of those might have taken the knife?" Becky looked out of the window, clearly thinking about the visitors to her home. After a few seconds she spoke.

"Not really. Why would anyone want to steal a knife from my kitchen?" She hesitated. "I did have the plumber in about a fortnight ago . . . he was in here on his own for half an hour. Could it have been him?" Hodgson asked for the name of the plumber.

"Do you have any concerns for any of your friends, anyone who might have taken it to spite you, for example?" The DC knew it was a long shot but hoped it may have jogged her memory – some subconscious link, a so-called friend who had a gripe about something? Becky glanced at her wristwatch, aware that her first client would be arriving soon.

"No, there isn't anyone that I'd invite here that would pinch a knife from me, especially from a set!" Becky stood up. "I'm sorry but I'm expecting Mrs. Pender in a few minutes – she wants a perm. Hodgson knew it was time to wrap up. He slipped his note-book into his pocket.

"Here's a card, Becky. If you do think of anybody who just might have taken the knife, even perhaps as a prank, could you let us know?' Minutes after the DC had left, Mrs. Pender rang the doorbell. Becky let her in and showed her to the chair for her perm.

"Hello, Becky, hope you are OK today. I could murder a cup of tea." Becky put the kettle on.

DC Hodgson had checked on the plumber's visit to Becky's house. He'd mended a leaking joint under the kitchen sink at around 10.00 am, swore he hadn't taken the knife, but had noticed it was still in the beech block when he left half an hour later. Hodgson believed him.

The plumber had done the job on the ninth of August. Hodgson looked at the information loaded on his ipad.

Marin Bukelis had been neatly disembowelled two days later.

***

Gordon Ashby had composed himself. A small pack of tissues had been half emptied from blowing his nose and wiping his eyes and face; his cheeks had a reddish tinge. Tommy decided to remain silent, let Ashby speak in his own good time. The car park was getting busier, but nobody was taking much notice of 'two businessman' having a discussion in a car. Ashby blew his nose one last time, scrunched up the tissue into a wad and slipped it into his jacket pocket. He smoothed his eyebrows with both hands as he took a deep breath followed by a long, slow exhalation.

"I've always had problems with my son. From an early age he was a handful. I don't know how his mother coped. His school reports were bad in terms of his behaviour, but he was a bright boy. Getting him into Yarm School, which has a good reputation and a brilliant Ofsted review, wasn't difficult. He excelled in most subjects, but then fell in with a bad crowd. He lied a lot, first saying he was having a sleepover with a good friend in Middlesbrough or Stockton or wherever, then he wanted to spend a week-end with another school chum somewhere. We believed him! Too naïve not to realise what he might be up to. There'd been a couple of visits from the police. One regarding him being picked up in a club that was well known for drug pushing, then another when he was found in possession of cannabis that one of his mates had been growing in his loft!

One day in the office I had a visit from a guy saying he was looking to buy a place. He'd just moved up from Birmingham and landed a job on Teesside. He was single, well educated, and seemed positive about things. He ended up with a two bedroomed apartment in a smart area of Middlesbrough, not far from Ormesby Hall. After we'd sorted the place out for him, he phoned me one day and said he'd heard stories about the drug scene on Teesside and mentioned Dick. I thought that was strange, but I guessed someone may have mentioned it to him if he'd said he had bought his apartment from Ashby Estate Agents. Anyway, we got talking and he very casually he asked me if I was interested in making a bit of cash 'on the side.' There'd been a downturn in the property market and I was starting to struggle, even thinking of closing the agency. He was very calm about the whole matter and over a period of a few weeks, when we'd met several times, I was helping him with his interest in drugs.

In my youth I hadn't been a saint, and my mother sometimes used to call me a 'little brat.' It's probably my fault that Dick turned out like he did. If I wanted anything from a shop it was a pleasure to steal it rather than pay for it. Recently, Alan Clarke invited me to dinner saying he was meeting with a friend from Lithuania. I refused, saying I couldn't make it, always thought Clarke was a bit, you know." Ashby flipped his limp wrist forwards. "I didn't know who this friend, Ned, was, but when I heard the news about the murder in the hotel, I realised how close I'd been to getting into shit street. Bloody hell. Talk about playing with fire! I've always considered myself a respectable estate agent, but am I? I dress the part, or try to – suit, waistcoat, clean shirt every day, smart tie, polished shoes . . . And now my son is dead! Down in a pub cellar! What the hell am I going to do, Tommy?" Tommy Archer had never heard an outpouring like this before. He felt like a Catholic priest on the other side of the confessional box. Ashby blew his nose again and pocketed the tissue.

"Gordon, can I ask you a question? Have *you* yourself been involved with drugs?" He had, Ashby going on to explain, and admit, that he'd been a provider in the Teesside underworld a while back but wanted to wash his hands of the whole affair. Tommy guessed that the bleach-type smell in Ashby's office was probably the remnants of cannabis. That was a key reason, too, why he wanted

Tommy to find Dick. His son had threatened Gordon that he would inform the police about everything his father had been doing after a massive family bust up. Again, the interior of the VW Golf fell silent.

"Do you know what I'm going to do about Dick, Tommy?" The PI looked at him and braced himself for the answer.

"Absolutely nothing!"

***

Kodric's green holdall found at Darlington station was re-examined at police HQ. Included with a few personal items, they had found a digital camera wrapped in a waterproof pouch, secreted in a washbag, alongside shampoo and toothpaste. Adamson called Straker who was out in his unmarked car. The DS picked up on the hands-free unit.

"Hi, boss."

"Kev, we've seen about thirty images from Kodric's digital camera that's been found after another search of the holdall. They're dated over the four days he was in Gateshead. You need to see them. Basically, they show some lewd images taken inside a room somewhere. I asked one of the DC's to email two images that had been cropped, but which show the furnishings, a tall vase and a bookcase, to the letting agency. They've just come back – it's the apartment that Kodric used before he arrived in Yarm. The letting agency also told us that they'd had complaints about noise from the apartment. Partying, I would assume. There's no doubt that Kodric was gay. That begs the question – is Clarke gay, and did something happen that might have been a motive for Clarke to murder him? Have you seen Alan Clarke, yet? You said you were going over to the travel agent's sometime today."

"Funny you should call now but I've *just* left GoWorldTravel." Before Straker could say much more, his DCI continued quickly.

"Kev, it's important that we see Clarke again. He could well be linked to the murder of Nedj Kodric. We know he collected Kodric from the Yarm hotel and later took him back there. Said he'd stayed for an hour for an orange juice but we do not have any witnesses that saw him leave the hotel.

***

DS Straker was meeting with DC Hodgson over a coffee to catch up on Hodgson's meeting with Becky Robinson. The DC went through his notes, then got to the point. Whoever took the knife from her kitchen did so between the plumber's visit on the morning of 9 August and the death of Marin Bukelis on the evening of 11 August. The DS asked the obvious question. 'Did Becky have any visitors between those times? Particularly on the evening of 10 August?' Hodgson was heading for Norton to see the hairdresser, his coffee now drunk. Straker was now on his way to see Karl Lamb in Whickham to ask a few more questions. He knew Lamb wasn't telling the truth – he'd denied knowing Maria Dawson. What other lies had he told? The DS had the flight and seat numbers for Lamb's trip to the Expoforum, his room number at the Corinthia Hotel and a copy of his hotel receipt that showed a large bar bill. Before the close of play that day *four* key facts had emerged.

One: DC Hodgson had found that Becky Robinson recalled that she'd had only one visit to her home between 9 and 11 August. Paul and Maria Dawson had dropped by on the evening of Wednesday the tenth to check on the catering arrangements for an upcoming party and to drop off a shopping catalogue. They stayed an hour or so, but Becky could not be certain if either Paul or Maria had been in the kitchen on their own. It was possible, she'd said. Maybe to get some ice for their drinks?

Two: Hodgson had asked if Becky knew whether Paul or Maria were left - handed. Yes, she knew . . . they were both left - handed.

Three: Straker had spoken to Karl Lamb who had confessed to knowing Maria Dawson and to travelling with her to St. Petersburg, but they'd booked the outbound flight separately and it was a coincidence that they were sat together. On the return they had managed to re-book their seats to enable them to sit in adjacent seats. He apologised to the DS for being economical with the truth on his previous visit, but he was 'out of sorts' as he put it. A bad day in the funeral parlour.

Four: When asked about his relations, Lamb told Straker that he had no immediate family – only an uncle in North Yorkshire and a cousin, Stuart Ladd, who resided in Lincoln.

But before DCI Adamson or any of his staff working on the case of the murders of the East Europeans had finally gone to bed that night, breaking news was hitting the media.

***

"Good morning. Here is the news. The body of a man has been found by police divers in the River Tees. It is believed to be that of Harry Nevin, a window cleaner from Redcar. Mr. Nevin had been to the James Cook hospital for his regular renal dialysis but never arrived home. Police are following up on several witness statements, but at this stage, foul play is not suspected. Now to other news . . ."

***

Tommy had gone back home after his talk with Gordon Ashby. He needed time to consider things. Ashby had said he was going back to his office, but Tommy couldn't understand how he'd be able to get much done after he'd delivered the news on his son.

Tommy eased open his front door, avoiding his flat cap and the eye ball laying underneath. He headed for the kitchen and put the kettle on – a saviour under these conditions. Tommy flipped a saccharin into his black coffee, and walked into the lounge. It was a little after 12.30 pm but he wasn't feeling hungry. Gordon Ashby had asked Tommy to email him his last invoice and payment would be prompt. It was a 'cleansing of hands' time for Ashby . . . pay Tommy off and that would close the file on his tear-away son. Sort of. Except that there was a body lying on a rusty bed frame in a pub cellar not three hundred yards from where Tommy was now sitting.

Tommy got up and opened the sideboard cupboard. He took out a whisky bottle. Pouring himself half a glassful, he sipped at the amber liquid. It was burning his throat, but he closed his eyes and put his head back on the comfortable armchair. 'I can't believe this' he thought to himself. 'If it's not enough to have been involved with Maria Dawson, I'm now witness to a corpse in a cellar.'

A month back he'd debated long and hard about informing Jim Adamson via an anonymous phone call or letter about what he knew. The murders of the four East Europeans – how close he'd been to those. Hell, he'd taken photographs; had evidence of Dawson with each of the four men, seen Clarke with Nejc Kodric. Witnessed some of what had happened at the scenes of crime, watched Stavinsky carry the brown suitcase into the Seaview Hotel, followed Dalopov in Middlesbrough when the Ukrainian had met with Dawson, watched Bukelis and Dawson have dinner in the Leven restaurant at the Crathorne Park hotel. He knew such a lot, and yet he knew nothing.

Who were these four men? Why had Maria Dawson met them? Tommy's involvement in all of this stemmed from Paul Dawson asking him to follow his wife since she was going out now and again and he wanted to know where. That was all. But over the weeks and months he'd been sucked into the drama, unfolding like a six - part television crime series every Tuesday night at nine o'clock. Tommy sipped his whisky.

He wasn't aware of all police developments other than

what he'd heard or seen on the news at media conferences, or snippets of updates from Joe Blackwell. He knew well enough that Adamson and his team would be careful in what they let the public know. Just sufficient for 'anyone with any information to contact' . . . the usual stuff. But Tommy had a stack of information that was in his head, in a folder in a bureau, and what had been sealed in brown envelopes and sent to Paul Dawson. Was it time to shred the evidence he had at home? But what about that held by Paul? Tommy wondered where Paul Dawson kept the photos and reports? It could only be one of two places – at home or in the library. What if the police searched the Dawson residence? Found everything Tommy had passed onto Dawson. Would he be an 'accessory after the fact?'

Tommy finished the whisky and put the glass into the washing up bowl. The remains of the coffee stung his throat as he swallowed the dregs. He hadn't seen Maria since the Bukelis incident and wondered what she was up to now. He'd heard that she'd left the travel agency. Perhaps he could contact her. Stalk her, maybe sidle up next to her in a supermarket and make out he remembered her from school as he bumped into her shopping trolley? He'd need to shave his beard off or she might recognise him from any of the venues where he'd followed her . . .

But more important than all this, Tommy thought as he rinsed the glass and mug, was the question 'Who murdered the four men?' Was there a serial killer on the loose on Teesside? When he considered who knew something about these guys, there were a few names that went 'into the hat.' Maria and Paul Dawson, Joe Stockwell, possibly Alan Clarke and Gordon Ashby (but they were only linked to Kodric), and some hotel staff. Becky and Rachel probably didn't, and it was doubtful if anyone in Pomfreton would know. He discounted Dave Teague and Steve Attridge. The only other person was Tommy himself. How would it look in a court of law?

'Mr. Archer, from the evidence before this court, I put it to you that you were able to murder all four men and your

motivation was greed. You saw an opportunity to retrace your steps on the dates in question, commit the heinous crimes presented to the jury, and make financial gain from your actions. The jury has heard that you enjoy gardening, flowers in particular, and pastimes such as scrabble and dominoes. You have tried to hide your guilt by portraying yourself as innocent of all four counts of murder but you do not fool me, Mr. Archer! What do you have to say to that?'

Tommy was convincing himself of committing the murders! And, add to all that the finding of the body of Dick Ashby in a cellar . . . Tommy was going down for thirty years minimum. After drying the cut glass tumbler, Tommy opened the sideboard door and poured himself three fingers of whisky. Just enough to calm him. He wasn't planning on going far today.

***

"Good afternoon, Mr. Clarke. Thank you for seeing us." DCI Adamson and DS Straker were sat in his office, coffee and biscuits on the table. It was a few minutes after three o'clock. "We're here to ask a few more questions with regard to recent events that have occurred in the area." Adamson took charge of the discussion and asked Clarke about his background, Maria Dawson, and the recent visit of Nejc Kodric. He left time between questions and answers, often doing that in interviews, seeing what information might be volunteered, sometimes a route to a degree of guilt on behalf of the interviewee. If he sensed that Clarke was lying, he'd be straight back down to Middlesbrough police station for a taped interview.

Alan Clarke appeared somewhat nervous, but without the sense of unease or perspiring. No rapid eye movements from the DCI to Straker, no scratching of the nose. His hands were clasped on the desk in front of him throughout. Clarke reaffirmed that he'd set up the dinner meeting with Kodric after collecting him from his hotel. He'd invited

Maria Dawson along because she could speak Lithuanian. Adamson had pressed Clarke on any possible motive for the murder of the Lithuanian, but he was at a loss to explain it. He could not think of anyone who had anything bad to say about Kodric.

"Do you think Nejc Kodric was gay?" asked Straker directly.

"I've absolutely no idea! Why do you ask?" Adamson told Clarke about the images on the camera, but only in outline.

"It seems he had seen a number of gay men on Tyneside before arriving in Yarm. Then he met with you. We found an open rail ticket for King's Cross in his luggage." Clarke fidgeted slightly, then shrugged. Adamson moved on, asking Clarke about Maria Dawson. He explained that she had made a contribution to the travel agency and he was sorry to see her leave. Her numeracy skills and attention to detail had been an asset. Asked whether Clarke thought she might be involved with drugs in any way, he replied 'definitely not.' He wished her success in whatever she had decided to do. And finally, had Clarke heard of a town-twinning convention held in September 2015 in St. Petersburg? No, not at all. Why would he?

"Well, Mr. Clarke, thank you for your time." The two detectives moved to the door. "If you remember anything else that you feel may be useful in our enquiries, please don't hesitate to call us." Clarke smiled as Adamson handed him a card. Out in the unmarked car Straker fired up the engine and reversed out of the parking space, avoiding a group of nuns walking past.

"What do you think, boss?"

"I don't think we need to bother him again," remarked the DCI. "It's not a crime being gay these days. And we have a witness statement regarding Clarke parking the Audi on his drive at about 11.00 pm next to his own BMW on the night of the murder. Neither car moved after that. The autopsy report put Kodric's death at between 1.00 and

2.00 am." Adamson paused, as Straker braked hard to avoid a pedestrian crossing the road using his mobile phone. He tutted loudly. "Interesting to hear Clarke say that Maria had been an asset, though – numeracy skills and attention to detail. The numbers cut into the arm of Stavinsky, zero, one, one, two, three. A domino with a two and a three on it, flower stems neatly tied and cut to exactly the same length, a straight median incision into the abdomen of Bukelis . . . hmm. Dr Adam Harper's profile report mentioned 'a person of precision." Seconds passed, fine - grain sand dropping through Adamson's brain like an egg-timer.

"Bugger me, boss, I'm on your wavelength. You could be right. Do you believe we've enough to bring Maria Dawson in?" Adamson nodded, and proposed they do it tomorrow. They'd ask Dawson to come to the station in the afternoon – exact time to be agreed. When Straker got back to his desk around 5.30 pm there was a message for him from DS Robin Green of Lincolnshire Police.

'Kev. Not sure if it's of interest but the landlord of 1, Tower Street is a Mr. Stuart Ladd. He owns a few properties in the city. He has a cousin that lives in Whickham called Karl Lamb. The woman who lives at number 3 says she knows Lamb and saw him at the house on the week-end you asked us to watch it. She saw the woman we observed pick up the front door key from under a plant pot at the back door around tea-time on the Friday. Cheers, Rob.'

Things were getting a whole lot worse for Mrs. Dawson.

***

The plan was for Adamson and Straker to bring Maria Dawson in for questioning at 2.30 pm. Both wanted time to collect as much information on her as possible, and to make sure they had all the facts. She'd be photographed and have fingerprints taken. Straker worked into the night.

He planned to visit Karl Lamb first thing in the morning. He'd either catch him at home or at the funeral parlour. Lamb had not told the DS that he was in Lincoln visiting Dawson on the week-end of 20 and 21 August. Why not? Because he had something to hide? Straker didn't trust Lamb the first time he saw him. Shifty eyes – that's what did it. Maria Dawson had used the property in Tower Street to meet Lamb, or vice versa. Either way there was something going on there.

Straker had found Lamb just about to leave home. It took ten minutes for Lamb to come clean. He seemed relieved, like a man given a reprieve from hanging when the noose is round his neck. With little prompting, Lamb spoke as the DS made notes . . . the trip to Expoforum, what went on there, Dawson's involvement in drugs, the contacts she'd made at the convention which included Stavinsky, Dalopov and Bukelis, how she'd drawn him into meeting him in Lincoln to pass on drugs which he reluctantly handled and sold for Dawson . . . Lincoln offered a high degree of anonymity . . . and the house did belong to his cousin, Stuart Ladd. It had been unoccupied for three months. Lamb had pre-arranged to leave the backdoor key under a plant pot. Lamb was aware of the Teesside murders but didn't think Maria had been involved. He did not know who Nejc Kodric was, and didn't recall him being at the town twinning convention. Lamb had met Maria only once before they flew to St. Petersburg . . . at a party in June, 2015. She was there with a couple of girlfriends but he couldn't recall their names. They'd exchanged phone numbers and both were slightly tipsy most of the evening.

Straker told Lamb that he now had to pass the information regarding the drugs onto Durham Police and he'd be hearing from them in due course. Lamb, looking drained, accepted that. By the time the DS was back at Middlesbrough police station he had more information on Dawson than he had expected. Briefing Adamson on his trip to Whickham in under five minutes, they prepared their compiled notes and grabbed a coffee. Maria Dawson was due to arrive soon.

Ten minutes later Adamson and Straker were sitting opposite Maria Dawson in a small interview room lit by two double neon strips. Dawson had dressed soberly in a dark two-piece suit, white silk blouse and black leather shoes with a medium heel, coffee in a cardboard cup to her left. Her dark hair was neatly trimmed in a bob cut. As the DCI was about to start there was a loud knock at the door. A PC standing inside the room opened it to reveal a uniformed sergeant.

"Sorry, to bother you sir, but there is a telephone call for Detective Sergeant Straker. The caller says it is very important." Adamson, glancing at his wristwatch, nodded for Straker to take the call. The DCI apologised to Mrs. Dawson, using her surname for the time being. Straker was back inside four minutes with a look that his superior found difficulty in comprehending; a satisfied grin, but not a smile, eyes with an eagerness about them.

"An update from Adam Harper," whispered Straker. Adamson turned on the CD twin recording machine and pointed to the camera up in the corner of the room.

***

Tommy Archer had woken up with a thumping headache. Two paracetamol tablets might begin to ease the throb but he doubted it. As Tommy had put the kettle on, he reflected on his chat with Gordon Ashby, his words 'absolutely nothing' with regard to taking any action on Dick still ringing clear. How could a father not wish to do something about his son, last seen by Tommy in a pub cellar? Stiff as a board. If the police were to be informed, they'd find Dick Ashby down in that damp place. Then an enquiry would begin, lots of questions asked, Gordon being implicated with the Teesside drug scene, his reputation smeared. His wife, Joan, had left him a year ago. 'Irreconcilable differences' her solicitor had said. She was now living in Canada and there'd been no contact with

Gordon at all. As far as he knew, she too, had washed her hands of her wayward son.

But didn't Gordon want closure on Dick's life? His own flesh and blood in a cellar! But was it for Tommy to voice an opinion? It was Gordon's decision, wasn't it? And the estate agent was the *only one* who knew that Tommy Archer had seen the corpse under the Frog and Ferret. If all this came out where would it leave Tommy if Ashby blabbed? Words like 'creek' and 'paddle' came to mind. No, Tommy had to let it lie. He'd fulfilled his obligation – found Dick Ashby – and reported back to Gordon. End of assignment. Payment made. There was no point in trying to be a saint.

Tommy also wondered what Roger Grimes was doing now? He'd have been down the concrete steps, found Dick slumped across the bed, and if he looked closely, with only one eye! Would the landlord get rid of the body? Lock the cellar door and throw away the key? Destroy the evidence? And Tommy had wondered if he'd ever go into the pub again? Could he look Grimes 'in the eye' without giving something away?

Finishing his black coffee, Tommy's thoughts turned to Maria again. His childhood sweetheart, Looby Loo. What was she doing right now? He could phone Paul and ask. Was she relaxing at home in Eston, feet up watching afternoon television, perhaps a good film or somebody wanting to buy a place in the sun? After everything that had gone on, Tommy's common sense told him to leave it. But what if Maria was in trouble with the police? He could help her, couldn't he? As far as Tommy was aware the police had nothing on Maria. They didn't know what Tommy knew. OK, she was around when the four East Europeans met their grizzly end, but there was nothing more than circumstantial evidence to link her with the murders. The media had still been conservative with news reports but Joe had shared with Tommy what *he* knew.

Police asking Joe's wife, Chloe, about her florist business was odd, too. There'd been some comments made on local television and radio news about flowers, inserted into the bodies of Dalopov and Bukelis. Tommy always connected flowers with love, not death. Well apart from funerals, he supposed. Either way, given as a sign of adoration and respect.

***

Adamson and Straker were nearing the end of their interview with Maria Dawson. She had provided the two detectives with enough information for now. Dawson seemed to have been honest, and didn't feel the need to ask for her solicitor. Neither did she say 'no comment' to any of the questions – always a sure sign of probable guilt. She'd corroborated Karl Lamb's story about travel to St. Petersburg for the convention, her movements whilst there and the connection she had with Stavinsky, Dalopov and Bukelis. She'd only met Nejc Kodric when Clarke invited her to dinner in Kirklevington. Maria knew nothing about Kodric, except he was a Lithuanian who'd met her manager when he'd spent a fortnight in Vilnius on holiday.

Maria admitted that she'd had contact with each of the three murdered men who wanted to visit her after they'd struck up a friendship in St. Petersburg. She'd met Ivo Stavinsky at a hotel in Marske, had dinner, then drove home, and it was pretty much the same with Marin Bukelis at the Crathorne Park hotel. As regards Dalopov, he was in town when Maria had planned the week-end with her two friends, Becky and Rachel. She was going to the theatre to see a show, but Dalopov had been in touch two days before, and she'd told him she was staying at the Travelodge in Newport Road. She decided to meet him for a drink at Chambers bar in Middlesbrough. At about a quarter to eleven on that evening she felt very tired, left the bar alone and walked back to the Travelodge where she was staying.

Straker asked Maria about any luggage that the men were carrying. No, she hadn't seen any. Why should she?

There was no sexual chemistry between her and any of the three East Europeans, they were simply friends. Wallets? Maria thought about the times when drinks or food were bought and paid for . . . yes, she recalled that when that happened each of the men pulled out a wallet and paid cash or used a credit card. 'Nothing strange in that,' she remarked to Straker. Had she seen either their passports or mobile phones at all? 'No,' she replied. Had she any idea where they might be, as none had been recovered? 'No, none at all . . . why would I?'

Maria was asked if she'd had a happy childhood. Smiling, she recalled that she'd enjoyed her youth, summer holidays with her parents to the Baltic states, had kept some pets – her favourite was a guinea pig named Lenin – and liked school where she always got top marks in mathematics. She had collected dolls since she was very young and had a varied collection. As they were valuable, she kept them in the loft at home. Asked if she had any idea why the four men were so brutally killed, Maria simply shook her head and began to weep. She took out a handkerchief and wiped her nose.

Adamson raised the matter of Tower Street in Lincoln. It was the only time during the interview Maria changed her demeanour. She sat upright as if pricked from behind with a sharp pin. After a few seconds silence, presumably for her to gather her thoughts, Maria glanced first at the recording machine, then back to Adamson.

"I'd been having an affair with Karl Lamb for a few months, meeting when we could somewhere between here and Whickham. I don't know why I was so silly, but he was dealing in drugs and asked if I wanted to reap the benefits of an easy way to make money. I told my husband, Paul, that I had a sick sister in Lincoln and needed to see her. He believed me. I met Karl there at an empty house owned by a cousin. He left a key for me to get in. We talked about a possible future together . . . exchanged texts and emails. I liked him from the very first time I saw him – that lovely smile." Maria wiped her nose and brushed back a few strands of hair from her face, eyes now becoming slightly red and puffy. "God! How could I have been so stupid!" Adamson waited.

"Do you have a sister?" Maria wiped her nose again as she looked away towards the high window.

"No. But I always wanted one. I was an only child. She was a figment of my imagination. Becky was almost like a sister to me." Her eyes seemed to glaze over. Adamson paused as Maria composed herself. 'Figment of my imagination' gave the DCI the shivers. Was Maria Dawson a psycho?

"Well, Maria, thank you for being so frank and honest with us. Interview with Maria Dawson concluded at 15.33 pm." Adamson switched off the recorder. He explained that, as a matter of routine in such cases, he'd have DS Straker take her fingerprints and several head and shoulder photos before she left the station. Twenty minutes later Maria Dawson left the building feeling very pleased with herself. She'd answered all of the questions, so why not stop off at Hobsons Garden Centre, the restaurant renowned for its tasty dishes, and treat herself to high tea? She felt she deserved it. And maybe a glass of Prosecco?

***

"Good evening. Here is the news. The post mortem on Harry Nevin, whose body was found in the River Tees two days ago, showed no signs of a struggle. Mr. Nevin couldn't swim, and police have stated that he very probably took his own life. He was living with a married woman in Redcar and it is believed she had been receiving treatment for mental problems. She is being cared for by Support Officers. Now other news . . ."

***

"And so, what news from Dr Harper, Kev? Something useful, I hope." Adamson fixed his stare on his DS in the police canteen over a coffee.

"Well, I think so . . . he'd had a chat with a university colleague – a guy from the mathematics department – over lunch yesterday. He'd told him about our case in confidence and the maths lecturer came out with a surprising comment!" Straker sipped from his cardboard cup as if building up to a climactic remark. His DCI tapped his fingers on the table. "The number cruncher mentioned the Fibonacci sequence to Dr Harper."

"The what!"

"The Fibonacci sequence . . . F-I-B-O-N-A-C-C-I. It's a mathematical series of numbers devised by an Italian mathematician from the thirteenth century called Leonardo Fibonacci. Basically, it adds numbers beginning with zero, followed by one, then you continue to add the numbers ad infinitum. So, you've got nought, one, one, two, three, five, eight, thirteen, twenty-one, and so forth." Adamson's neural cogs were engaged.

"The next would be thirteen plus twenty-one, er . . . thirty-four. Yes?" Straker smiled approvingly at the light bulb moment. "Bloody hell, Kev, do you realise what you've just said? Nought, one, one, two and three were the numbers cut into the arm of Ivo Stavinsky! Not a bloody telephone dialling code! Then with Nejc Kodric, the domino . . . a two and a three . . . that makes five . . . and the octagon with eight faces!" Hang on, where do we go with Sergio Dalopov? Flowers down his throat and up his backside? And then Marin Bukelis – more bloody flowers!" Straker emptied his cup.

"Good point, sir. We're then looking at thirteen, twenty-one, thirty-four, fifty-five . . . I don't get it. Flowers and numbers?" Straker recalled the contact with the department of botany at Durham University by one of the forensics team. "I'll make a call to the botany guy that we spoke to before – there has to be a link with the Fibonacci sequence."

"OK, I'll leave it with you, Kev. Dawson told us she enjoyed maths! Fibonacci, eh? I wonder if the fingerprint boys have checked Dawson's prints with those on the kitchen knife? I suppose it's too much to think they are hers?" The two detectives returned to their desks. Straker made a call to the lab where the knife was being kept.

"Hi Alec, any news on the prints – is there a match?"

"Yes, Kev. A perfect match."

***

Twenty minutes later Straker had some vital information from the botany department. Corn marigolds have thirteen petals and asters have twenty-one – both found on the body of Sergio Dalopov. Marin Bukelis, sliced open with a kitchen knife at Crathorne Park, had two types of large-petal daisies in his abdomen. One had thirty-four petals, the other fifty-five. The botanist had also told Straker that Fibonacci numbers apply to seed heads and the spiral pattern of many larger flowers. So that was it! A killer with perverted sense of humour? And wanting to prove that he or she knew about the Fibonacci series. As soon as Straker told his DCI, the plan was put in place to pay a visit to 89, St. Roseberry Close. The two detectives with two PC's would arrive unannounced at 7.00 am with a search warrant. The whole place would be turned upside down. Maria Dawson would be arrested on suspicion of the murder of Stavinsky, Kodric, Dalopov and Bukelis. With fingerprints on the murder weapon used on Marin Bukelis, Dawson had a lot of explaining to do.

There was one thing puzzling Jim Adamson, though. Chloe Stockwell, who ran *Pistils 'n Roses*, said that a man had ordered the flowers, not a woman, the calls being made from a public telephone box. Was Maria Dawson working with somebody else?

***

Two unmarked police cars stopped outside of 89, St. Roseberry Close. It was 6.53 am on a cool, cloudy morning. The two detectives went to the front door whilst two uniformed constables walked around the back. Adamson rang the bell. After half a minute he rang it again. Noises came from inside as the front door eased open, a security chain stretched across it.

"Mr. Dawson? DCI Adamson from Cleveland C.I.D." He showed his ID. "We have a warrant to search your property. May we come in?" The door closed slightly as Dawson took the chain off, and then opened it fully. They went in.

"If this is about Maria not being here, I can explain. She sometimes stays away and there was no point in reporting it yet." Straker had let the two officers in via the back door. Adamson hadn't expected Maria to be out.

"Your wife is away? What do you mean 'away'?" Dawson tightened his dressing gown cord and took a seat. "Has she gone to see another relation?" asked Straker with a hint of sarcasm.

"Well, she's been acting strange lately, seemed distant, in her own world somehow. She wasn't here when I arrived home yesterday . . . around six o'clock. A neighbour may have seen her leave. I don't know." The DCI wasn't going into that right now. The search warrant needed to be executed.

"As I say, we're here to search your premises Mr. Dawson so if you just sit there, we'll take a look around. We shall be removing some items such as computers, i-pads and so forth. We'll need your mobile phone . . . and you will get an inventory of what we remove." Dawson moved uneasily.

"What are you looking for? I mean, what is this all about?" Adamson explained that they wanted to talk to Maria in relation to the four murders that took place on Teesside between 12 July and 11 August, more than that he was unwilling to discuss. Paul Dawson was staggered to think that his wife was implicated in these crimes. "I know she came to the station to answer some questions recently but you don't honestly believe that she's connected with any of them, do you?" The policemen went about their business, bagging and labelling a laptop, an i-pad, Paul Dawson's smartphone, a diary, and a notebook from next to the telephone in the hallway. A pair of Ray-Ban's weren't touched. The two constables had been through drawers and cupboards, entered the loft, and were satisfied that they had the relevant items they'd come for. Everything was plastic-bagged and labelled.

"We'll let you have a list shortly, and you'll get things returned as soon as we've had a chance to look at them. I'm afraid I can't discuss any more with you, Mr. Dawson. We need to talk to Maria. If you do contact her, or vice versa, can you ask her to phone me on this number." The DCI handed him a card. It was 7.34 am when the two unmarked cars left the Close.

'Damn it,' thought Paul Dawson as he watched the vehicles drive away. He was feeling uneasy, trying to recall where he'd left his thin gold bracelet, the one with the small charm showing the letters PFD. OK, Maria was with the four dead men, he knew that. He'd left Tommy Archer's photos and reports at the library – in the small room for which only he had a key. The pay-as-you-go mobile phone was in the locked draw of his desk there, too . . . the one he'd always used to contact Tommy. It was only last evening he'd deleted a number of emails and history of google searches from his laptop.

But where was Maria? She hadn't said she was going anywhere. The police didn't have her computer or phone, and it appeared that a small travel bag was missing, as well as her passport.

***

A black Ford Fiesta, registration number AZ 13 WFT, had been parked behind The Seaview Hotel for about two weeks. It had eventually attracted the attention of Joe Blackwell on one of his routine security visits. Joe had mistakenly thought that it belonged to a temporary member of staff. He'd tried the car doors and boot before he'd telephoned the police to report the vehicle. It wasn't long before it came to the attention of DCI Adamson. He recognised the vehicle as belonging to Maria Dawson. When Adamson and Straker arrived at the hotel they noticed the car was parked in a corner farthest from the rear hotel entrance. Looking through a side window, Straker could only see a soft, medium sized bag on the back seat. Within an hour the Fiesta had been taken to the police pound on the back of a low-loader. Access to the vehicle took minutes and Straker removed the bag from the inside. The boot was slowly opened, and Adamson gasped as he stared at a corpse, curled up in the foetal position, wrapped in a heavy gauge polythene bag.

The police soon identified the body as that of Maria Dawson who'd been missing for three weeks. Dusted for fingerprints, the only ones found on the car bodywork belonged to Joe Stockwell. The pathologist listed the cause of death as a broken neck, two cervical vertebrae being snapped in half. They had to break the news to her husband, who had twice appeared on local television in a tearful plea to the general public in an attempt to find her. This news was going to hit him like a sledgehammer.

DCI Jim Adamson and DS Kev Straker were on their way to Middlesbrough Central Library on a mild, sunny afternoon to talk to Mr. Dawson, who was now Head Librarian. What was the motive behind the murder of Maria Dawson? Adamson was not a man to jump to conclusions quickly and he hoped Paul Dawson would be able to throw some light on matters. Paul Dawson had not heard from his wife since the day he'd come home to find her gone. There wasn't sufficient reason for him to kill her that Adamson knew. Could someone else have arranged to meet Maria at The Seaview Hotel, suggesting she park round the back? Maybe a plan that went wrong? Joe Stockwell could add little to what he'd already told them about the Fiesta parked at The Seaview, and there was no sign of the i-phone or laptop that belonged to Maria.

The two detectives asked Paul Dawson if they could find somewhere quiet and secluded. Paul took them to the room to which only he had a key. There were three office chairs in there as well as a small desk, a safe with a combination lock, and a tall bookshelf. Adamson had composed himself as he'd sat down and delivered the news. Dawson held his head in his hands as he wept, Straker's eyes scanning the room as Paul cried. The DCI went on to explain that he was going to arrest Maria in connection with the deaths of the four East Europeans, her fingerprints on the knife used to kill Marin Bukelis being the key proof they needed. Having found nothing on the phone or computer of Paul Dawson that gave him any concerns, Adamson placed Paul in the clear. Having blown his nose and wiped his eyes, Paul Dawson again totally refused to accept that his beloved wife had any connection to these heinous crimes.

As the unmarked car returned to police HQ, Adamson wondered if they should talk again to Karl Lamb, Andy Young or Joe Blackwell. Before they'd stopped at the first set of traffic lights Straker spoke.

"We need to go back and talk to Dawson. I noticed something in the room that's of interest." The DCI gave him an enquiring glance. "There were some numbers on the underside of a shelf on the bookcase. I noticed them from where I was sitting as I bent to tie a shoelace . . . and I have a nagging feeling about that safe. And did you notice the long scratches on his neck?"

***

The following morning at a few minutes before the library opened, the two detectives and a uniformed officer made their way to Central Square. As Paul Dawson opened the glass doors the three policemen entered. Two other members of staff took over as Adamson asked Dawson to take them into the room, the one they had used the day before. Straker looked under the shelf and saw six numbers – 3,5,8,13,21 and 34. Dawson looked surprised and was unable to explain the reason for them being there.

"Can you open the safe for us, Mr. Dawson?" asked Jim Adamson. The Head Librarian said he didn't know the combination, never had done. Straker moved forward.

"Perhaps the numbers under your shelf might help?" The DS knelt down in front of the metal safe. He'd done this before . . . entering the six digits, listening to a tiny click between each number, and as he did so Straker knew that he was putting in figures from the Fibonacci sequence. The door squeaked open and both detectives stared at the contents.

***

Paul Dawson was arrested for the murder of Ivo Stavinsky, Nedj Kodric, Sergio Dalopov and Marin Bukelis. The safe contained the personal belongings of the dead men – four wallets, a set of car keys, three passports and three i-phones, all covered in the fingerprints of Dawson. A Pay-As-You-Go phone lay near the back. It had the fingerprints of Maria Dawson on it, and the number that had been called by the purple Samsung iPhone belonging to Bukelis. A locked cupboard in the same room held a blue rucksack belonging to Kodric, and two small cases that had been seen with Dalopov and Bukelis. All of these pieces of luggage had traces of drugs found on them, but no actual drug content.

Paul Dawson was also arrested for the murder of his wife, his gold bracelet found inside the thick polythene sheet in which her body was wrapped, dislodged from his wrist during the struggle to kill her. There was evidence that Paul had strangled his wife in the kitchen of their home. Fresh traces of her blood were found in between the floor tiles and on the edge of the worktop from a wound on her head. Tiny fragments of skin from Paul Dawson were found under the nails of her right – hand as she'd clawed at her husband's neck in self - defence. It most probably occurred the day before Adamson and Straker paid their visit. A domino set found in the sideboard had the 2 and 3 dot domino missing, and a set of marble shapes on an oak plinth, with shallow recesses for each, was without one of them – an octagon. In Dawson's garage was a blood - stained Stanley knife, the blood, group O, matching Ivo Stavinsky. A drum of white, 5 mm cord was on a low shelf, identical to that used to strangle the Estonian.

Paul Dawson appeared at Teesside Crown Court in December, 2016, and was charged on all five counts of murder. The jury found him guilty. Judge Samuel Becket-Risbridger sentenced Paul Dawson to 30 years imprisonment. He was taken to Durham gaol. When Judge Becket-Risbridger asked Dawson for his views on matters he had declined to comment. However, the counsel for the prosecution had stated that Paul Dawson had undergone a troubled childhood with family abuse and a record of killing several pet animals at his primary school. His favourite subject was maths. Before being taken to Durham, Dawson had undergone a psychiatric assessment. He had severe mental issues that allowed the word 'psychopath' to be added to his clinical notes along with the phrase 'high jealousy factor.' He admitted that he felt revulsion at the thought of his beautiful wife seeing other men. It was stated that Paul Dawson had the wherewithal to place his wife's fingerprints on the kitchen knife that he stole from Becky Robinson and which he used to murder Marin Bukelis wearing powdered latex gloves, a box of which were found in his garage.

There was a high degree of certainty that Dawson had followed his wife when she had left their home, hidden somewhere near the scene of each crime, and murdered each of the East Europeans shortly afterwards. On the night that Kodric was murdered, Maria stayed with Becky and Paul Dawson had been alone all night. He had the opportunity to go to the Yarm hotel and commit murder. The phone box with the 01642 number on the Guisborough road had been checked and several hairs had been found, the DNA of three hairs matching that of Dawson. He'd always worn Ray-Ban sunglasses when he collected the flowers, and Chloe Blackwell admitted in court that she had not recognised him even though they'd briefly met at a wedding reception a year previously.

It transpired that Maria Dawson had been engaged in handling high quality heroin smuggled into the UK by the East Europeans, hidden in their luggage, undetected by any regulatory authorities. That was, apart from Ivo Stavinsky, who'd handed over a suitcase at The Seaview Hotel containing Russian dolls whose contents were double-wrapped in aluminium foil and not detected by the sniffer dog that had checked his Skoda, nor by Port of Tyne on arrival in the UK. That suitcase was found in the loft at 89, St. Roseberry Close.

Northumbria Police had been put on a covert operation in connection with Karl Lamb. Following on from what Maria had told the two detectives in an interview, Lamb was heavily involved with the business of selling drugs, including the heroin sold to him by Maria. The property in Lincoln, 'a smack house,' was under surveillance again, and Adamson believed it was only a matter of time before they'd have enough evidence to convict Lamb.

The Expoforum convention had been the kernel of the whole drugs affair, it was where much of the planning had taken place for the transit of drugs into the UK. No one could be sure how much Andy Young knew of the arrangements between Maria and the four dead men. Young had been interviewed again, and although Adamson and Straker were unsure about his motives for attending the convention, the two detectives had nothing definite to go on. He continued teaching geography at Durham School, but six months later, he left his wife after an amicable separation agreement, and took up a teaching post at the International School in Tallinn.

He changed his name on his application form – he decided it was time for a new identity. Nobody queried it.

It wasn't long before he met a woman at the school

who taught mathematics. Her name was Helga Stavinsky. She was coming to terms with losing her partner a year ago, but found solace in the arms of the charming man called Terence Hetherington. She had banked the substantial life insurance payment following Ivo's death. To his surprise, she was agreeable to opening a joint bank account with him. And it wasn't long before he asked her if she'd be interested in attending a town-twinning convention due to be held in Poland.

"I would love that, Terence," she replied.

Epilogue

Tommy Archer never told the police what he knew. It was all too late, too far past the events that started in the summer of 2016. He'd have a whole lot of very difficult explaining to do. Thankful that he was never identified on any CCTV footage, and having made a pact with Joe Stockwell that neither would discuss the matter ever again, Tommy gave up being a private investigator and moved away from Pomfreton. He had a cousin that lived in Melbourne, Australia, on the Yarra river, and he was planning to turn over a new leaf 'down under.' The pen microphone and lapel camera were crushed with a hammer and went into the appropriate dump bin at the local civic amenity tip. Tommy kept the glass eye as a souvenir.

Gordon Ashby had thought about his son, Dick, not long after his talk with Tommy in the Links View hotel car park. If his son was dead in that pub cellar, he thought it right to give him a proper send off. He'd told Cleveland Police about his suspicions a short time later - about the coin collection, and his apparent friendliness with Roger Grimes. Police inspected the Frog and Ferret, searched it thoroughly, but no sign of a body was ever found. An installed camera with a 'HighVisibility' company label, placed by a Mr. Dave Teague, had been removed from the cellar.

And one bright, sunny day not long after Paul Dawson had been sentenced, a funeral service at Gateshead crematorium was in progress. There were no mourners at the service to say 'good-bye' to the four-ply coffin with bamboo handles that slowly moved through the velvet curtains on the narrow conveyor belt. Only the four miserable looking coffin bearers in their creased, cheap black suits stood as the wooden container moved toward the burners. The thin, brass replica plate on the lid read:

James Anthony Rogers 21-04-71 to 29-12-16 R.I.P.

Only it wasn't James Anthony Rogers . . . it was a body with a single glass eye that had been moved from a pub cellar a while ago, embalmed by Karl Lamb for his Uncle Roger.

And he never did get paid for doing it.

Eighteen months later a woman called Helga Stavinsky went missing in Tallinn.

She still hasn't been found.

Acknowledgements

I'd like to thank my wife, Nora, for her comments, suggestions and patience as I wrote this novel. She was often an alternative to my trusted Thesaurus. Retired police sergeant, Chris Wayman, added his views on some of the characters, especially DS Kev Straker. Published crime author K. A. Richardson also helped with advice on crime scenes and procedures. I'd also like to thank readers who have made remarks about my previous novels, all of which were logged in my memory and have flowed onto these pages. A new, young author, C. J. Grayson, also inspired me to continue my writing with his recent comments. 'Thank you' must go to an old friend and avid reader, Ian Pomfret, after whom Pomfreton was created. Thank you, Ian. And lastly, to all the readers who beg, borrow or steal what I have managed to get published!

Any mistakes and errors are entirely down to me. I've used some real place names mixed with fictional locations and the characters and plot are created entirely from my own imagination.

Novels by A. K. Adams

AN UNKNOWN PARADISE

David and Hazel Tate live in a leafy Surrey suburb. They chose Chile for a holiday and fly to Santiago for the warmer weather, good wine and the local culture. By chance they visit a nunnery on the edge of the Andes. Little did they know then what an impact that was to have on them. They could not have predicted how life changing it was to be. Reaching emotional highs and lows, they also plunge the depths of despair – but they had faith. Without that they had nothing…

SEARCHING FOR JULIETTE

A note had been stuck on the touring caravan window making a cash offer to buy it. Harry and Anthea soon began to wish they'd never followed it up as a Chinese guy, Hokun Tu Ying, started to make life difficult for them. A murder and a cash deal that went wrong landed Harry in trouble. Years earlier, Anthea's daughter from her first marriage, Juliette, had gone missing on a school exchange visit to Denmark – simply vanishing from a café on a busy Saturday morning. Despite some early leads, the trail went cold. And if only people could be trusted. . . sometimes those who you think are closest to you can spring a surprise – and some surprises are much worse than others.

SHOULDN'T HAVE DONE THAT

Evil may always be around the next corner. And so, it came to pass as Giles Chambers got a divorce from his wife, Prunella, and moved in with a work colleague, Olivia Patterson. But as time went by, he discovered dark secrets about her, things that ought to be forgotten, left alone. When Olivia realised this, she knew she had to get rid of him, and there was somebody who could help her to achieve it. Giles became the hunted, became the prey. He had to get away, to run, but who could he trust? Time was running out. Fast. Then he had an idea...

THEY FADE AND DIE

Jane Lester from Yorkshire takes up a job as a nanny with the Gardner family in San Francisco. Howard is a hospital surgeon and his wife, Amanda, is a psychiatrist with her own practice. Jane begins to wonder about their marriage relationship as she cares for the children, Teresa and Ryan. A newspaper headline mentions a headless torso found in the woods, and on the other side of the city, Jack Bauer hasn't been seen for four months. The previous nanny, Caroline, had left the Gardner family under a cloud, but what went wrong? Jane began to ask questions, but how do you tell lies from the truth – fact from fiction? It's easy…you don't.

THE LOCKED ROOM

Charles Watson is offered a job at the Royal Navy dockyard stores in Plymouth in 1849. He leaves his parents and travels from Chatham and down to Devon by railway and mail coach. His new landlady, Martha, has one of her rooms burgled and something valuable is stolen. When one of her lodgers mysteriously disappears, local tongues begin to wag. A local cholera outbreak kills 25 people. A body is found in a barn, and Charles' landlady is threatened by a strange caller. But one day Charles receives a letter that will change his life forever. And then there came a knock on the front door, but who was it?